CALICO MOUNTAINS

447

Gerlach

PYRAMID
LAKE

NORTH

NEVADA

CLAN ALPINE MOUNTAINS

Nixon

Wadsworth

ernley

Fallon

50

Middle Gate

Austin

Eureka

REESE
RIVER
VALLEY

GREAT

BASIN

TOIYABE RANGE

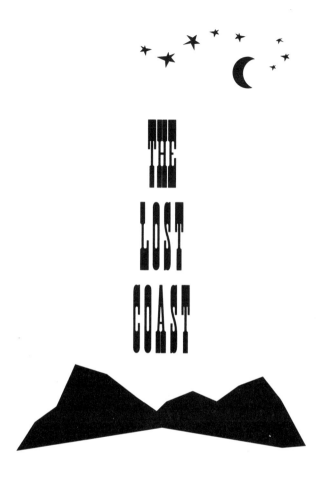

THE LOST COAST

STEVEN NIGHTINGALE

ST. MARTIN'S PRESS ⚜ NEW YORK

A Thomas Dunne Book
An imprint of St. Martin's Press

Design by Pei Koay
Endpaper map illustration by Ellisa Mitchell

Library of Congress Cataloging-in-Publication Data

Nightingale, Steven.
    The Lost coast / by Steven Nightingale.
        p.   cm.
    "A Thomas Dunne book."
    ISBN 0-312-14007-X
        1. Travelers—California—Fiction.   2. Travelers—
Nevada—Fiction.   3. Wilderness areas—Nevada—
Fiction.   4. Storytelling—California—Fiction.
5. Storytelling—Nevada—Fiction.   I. Title.
    PS3564.I3637L67   1996   95-45093
    813'.54—dc20   CIP

First Edition: March 1996

10 9 8 7 6 5 4 3 2 1

FOR ANDREA

ACKNOWLEDGMENTS

My thanks to Tom Dunne, an editor with guts and savvy, the best of men to find in a publishing house—dedicated to writers and to literature.

My agent, Robert Stricker, is a pro, just the man to bear a manuscript to New York City. He does the one thing that counts: he fights for books, because he loves them.

Neal Bascomb at St. Martin's Press worked on this book with alacrity and intelligence.

It was my friend Tom Gregory who, years ago, first introduced me to the backcountry of the Sierra and the Great Basin. Nothing can repay such a favor. May his days be full of dependable splendors.

I thank Rachel Jacoff, so extraordinary a friend, so conversant with good books and the beauties of language. At her dinner table, young men think about becoming novelists.

Tom Radko, Director of the University of Nevada Press, has been generous with his time and literary counsel. Many writers in Nevada and the West have reason to be grateful to this man.

Lexine Alpert took the beautiful photographs of the Black Rock Desert and of Gerlach that adorn the jacket of this book. May her work with her camera win the wide audience it so much merits.

Elizabeth Dilly, that far-traveling, gifted woman, made a midnight phone call from Paris to give me valuable advice on the page proofs.

And I thank Ian Chisholm, that little blessing, for being dear, and for being the future.

And most of all: to my beloved wife, Andrea, so lucid and splendid: If this book is alive, it is because of you, and all you have brought me—the jokes and wild times, the metaphysics and delectations.

THE
LOST
COAST

PART 1

EUREKA
TO
DOWNIEVILLE

COOKIE—COWGIRL, line cook, wife—strode into her kitchen and, standing straight and happy, strung a beautiful arrow in her hunting bow. She aimed it at all the world. It made her grin. Her husband, Kenny, though, thought she was going to shoot him. He was feeding on thick strips of bacon that Cookie had fried in her demure and obliging manner; and his cowboy's appetite, which had roared like a lion, now mewed like a kitten.

He had to admit she was *smooth* when she drew an arrow.

"Honey," she said, "I've never felt so good."

"You want to let that arrow down?"

"Sure!" she said, and—shining in the morning light, with a zip and release that matched the incorrigible velocity of her soul— the arrow sang from the bowstring and passed lovingly just to the right side of his head; the feathers on the shaft kissed his cheek, leaving a fire-mark that would make him a rakish figure in the barrooms—a mark whose heat he felt all the rest of his life.

Kenny sighed. It looked like Cookie was in a mood.

She strung another arrow.

"As I was sayin', Kenny my boy, I have made me a discovery. Lemme tell you about it."

"I ain't never been one to shut you up, sweetheart."

She relaxed the bow, but kept it at the ready.

"Well, this is it: number one—we're through! Now you got some flame-throwin' ways in bed, and that soft wind-chimin' way of makin' love-talk, but . . . Kenny, we're like most married folks: gone from party-and-slambang springtime, to steady sweaty summer, and on to look-back-what-the-hell-happened-anyway autumn, to winter cold that froze my goddam eyes solid. It's springtime again, Kenny."

Cookie loosed the second arrow, which picked up a loaf of bread and fixed it to the wall in a place convenient to the toaster.

"But let me get to number two, which you have got figured by now. Kenny, I'm takin' my ass on the road—"

"It's just the goddam full moon again, Cookie," argued her good husband.

"You know how I love cookin'," she went on. "I am the best fry cook ever was in all of Nevada, but this little town, this little town . . ."—she strung another arrow—"now we got a nice hundred acres, but it's land."

"Land?" said Kenny, not understanding. He thought of her outside in the middle of winter, digging postholes and spitting tobacco, grunting and smiling.

"It's just too solid," mused Cookie.

Kenny crinkled up his brow at that one.

"Well, I can't just stick around here, all solid, you and me one more solid bumpety-bump man and wife, damn it all!"

"Bumpety-bump?" he inquired.

She brandished her bow alarmingly.

"And so I'm just going to cook and buck my way west, from right here in Eureka all the way to the coast. A girl can go far on chicken-fried steak. And there I'll be, no land, no husband, light off the sea like wind in my face. Kenny, I want to *get* there, stand and praise—all that crap, you know?"

She gave him a long look: "You know you cain't win, you men—if you're lousy, we leave for something better; if you're good, we leave 'cause we feel so fine."

"You are one strong pretty bitch," he said.

"You bet I am," she said.

"And number three?"

"Three is: I love you, Kenny!" she said, as she loosed the third arrow.

And it was as the arrow left the bow that Chiara drove into Eureka. At her side, her sixteen-year-old daughter, Isabella Boccaccio Acappella Mandragora Palmieri, known to all as Izzy. And Izzy, with hair like obsidian and eyes like opals, had her demands.

"Mom, stop the car so I can get out and dance!"

"You danced in the last town," replied her Mediterranean mother, who insisted on recounting how in Ely, Nevada, her daughter, satisfied and lickerish, breaking all laws regarding the comportment of young women, had danced in the whiskey-scented rambunctious bars of the little town until three in the morning.

"I wanted to give you your chance with that blue-eyed cowboy," said Izzy primly, taking the high ground, though even she regarded the night as a kind of splendid disgrace.

"Oh, I need *your* help to take home anyone I please?" gibed her mother with delicious good reason.

"OK, maybe I'm a little cocky."

"An excellent thing in a woman," said Chiara, smiling.

"So how long are we going to be on the run?" asked Izzy as with languor she stretched her lanky young body and pulled behind her ears her glossy hair.

"Well, it's not exactly on the run, it's just that after ten years teaching in New York, I felt like the two of us should roam around for a while. Do you feel pursued?"

Izzy thought for a while.

"Yes. But who cares?"

As a matter of fact, they *were* being pursued. Chiara was a one-time mathematician with a love of physics and a passion for exploring the hinterlands of general relativity; then, at the university, because of her firm grounding in classical studies, and her fluency in Italian, French, and Spanish, she had switched into literature, which she studied with a rare sumptuous rigor, a supple passionate exactitude.

And why on earth were she and Izzy being pursued? Chiara had during the amorous months of Izzy's conception taken as lovers the leading men of her university, with some savory amendments—for example, a gentleman who overhauled diesel engines, and a piano tuner of many a playful note; a potter with hands of such strength he could glaze her in her own sweat; and a vintner who licked his wine off her breasts. At the close of this happy period, pregnant, she had informed her lovers that, though anything was possible, none of them need feel responsible—the arithmetic was just too confusing.

For if there was anything Chiara rejected, it was paternity. All the ridiculous fixity of the world could be attributed to this absurd institution, in which the transient donor of seed took on airs, huzzahed right and left, went round to be congratulated, and swaggered like a giant all the years of his child's life. Chiara wanted a child of her own.

Among the gaggle of potential fathers, however, the university men never forgot the slight, and coveted Izzy. Besides, none of them especially liked being cast as the hoodwinked, the educated chuckheads, the lustful dupes of the wily Chiara. They of course were none of these things: but as usual, not all the answers in good books, not any number of heart-polishing sonatas and star-making sonnets—none of this mattered a fig compared with one hard thing: their very own offended selves.

Upon this rock, wondered Chiara, how many would break the world?

They were not so bad as they thought: Chiara had loved them, one and all. But could they not see? What would they have her do? Keep them? And so she had approached them, she met with them every one, and in order to explain her departure had issued a list of queries:

1. Does a shooting star linger in the sky?
2. Would we stop the day in its tracks, pin the sun at its zenith?

3. The garlic, onions, butter, and spices in the pan, whose aromas make us sit up with excitement—do we let them simmer forever?
4. If we love wine, does this mean we should put nothing else in our mouths for all time, in all places, with every company?
5. Soil may have our praise, for it grows roses; but will that good soil grow nothing else, forever?
6. We stand before a painting, our souls acrobatic with its beauties; but do we honor the work by standing there, dumb as a post, all the day?

Her lovers had listened to this hot-blooded rhetoric, and in fact many of them had come round already to the idea that if a man would truly love a woman he must love her leave-taking. And so Chiara's piano was always tuned, her diesels ran superbly, and she had a cellarful of wines at the ready.

Others of her beaux, after having attended to her with loving patience, dewy-eyed attentiveness, and erudite confidence, had proceeded naturally to old-fashioned homicidal vengeance. So had commenced sixteen years of threats, teeth-gnashing midnight phone calls, legal skulduggery, and custody battles.

At present, two of these men, acting in a rational way to influence the upbringing of the girl—that is, not content to be fools, they resolved to become meddling fools—had hired private detectives to trail Izzy and Chiara through the West. They were to report on their activity, so as to build a case against the mother for not providing the proper moral environment for the incontrovertible child.

In other words, they were afraid she would turn out like Chiara.

—As though providing *any* environment for Izzy would make a difference: a mother might as well try to put a dress on a lioness.

Each of the detectives had instructions to kidnap the girl, if it seemed as though she was endangered—whatever that meant—by her caterwauling brilliant mother.

Chiara, though, knew all this, and thought the whole plan was just too crude to consider.

All the same, she was startled to see, as she went to park near the beautiful old courthouse in Eureka, an arrow whiz diagonally over the hood of the car and head up the street.

Muscovado Taine was surprised, too. He was there on the sidewalk and had just taken out a match to light a cigarette, when the steel arrow came winging toward him; he did a twist-and-slide dance step to rescue his stomach from ruin.

Dance has its uses.

He went ahead and lit up, thinking with satisfaction that he was reversing usual practice, and having good tobacco just *after* his attempted execution. And, sitting on a street bench, he asked himself what on earth he was doing in Eureka, Nevada.

He thought through his thirty years: upbringing in Kingston, Jamaica, many years of dreadlocks, his studies with his strict grandfather, a wrathful minister; his dancing (the grandfather was also a lead guitar), his lovers like waves falling on a hidden Caribbean beach—women, he thought, are the constant wilderness of the world; a surprise scholarship to a university in Boston, where he was treated as the Hope of the Useless Malodorous Third World; gigs working as a journalist on big newspapers in Miami, New York, and Philadelphia, where he wrote with a lilt overlying a solid prose rhythm—a reggae prose.

He missed the Caribbean, its islands like a bracelet of jewels, like the curving line of a song sung to the woman in whose pleasure you live; like the spirit-curve of the woman you love as she comes round in bed to the irreproachable honey of her own soul.

Kingston to Boston to the big cities—he knew what he was up to: go where you shouldn't, do what you can. He had picked Eureka off the map: central Nevada, not next to anything, set there within a land inhabited only by sage, light, animals, and a laudable incivility to all of us.

It was a land whose welcome was surly, secretive, promising, difficult.

It looked good to him, just because it didn't look like Jamaica, or any other place he loved. In fact, there was nothing here he recognized. He liked it, this crash landing—he liked the wreckage of himself. It made him want to sing. But he thought that might be unwise.

He began to sing immediately.

He was, officially, on leave: he could send in a thoughtful dispatch now and then, and get a check back in the mail. In the meantime, he wanted to see the big dry valleys—after a few shots of white rum. And, cigarette lit, he was headed his melodious way for a bar when in front of him there emerged from a dusty car two lustrous dark-haired women who looked almost as if they could be mother and daughter.

But that, like the world, would be too good to be true.

Izzy and Chiara looked at him: swarthy, singing—like a night sky full of music. He had soft heat in his hands and salt waves in his step. The two women looked and smiled.

There is a choreography working deep in the days—at all times, in all places: a bright pattern within events.

So, in Eureka, we have: Cookie coming forth from her house into the somersaulting light of the morning, and thinking she would like to hear a jukebox jam some music; Muscovado moving in his own memory, feeling trade winds bearing jasmine and pepper as he faced Chiara and Izzy on the street; and, sitting in the bar toward which the gravity of the day was calling all things—a bar famous among mustangs and cowboys, the Owl Club—we have our friend Juha of Juha General Contractor, Inc. Juha built houses; not surprisingly, he was himself built like a house—a man so burly that giant sequoias wanted mistakenly to pollinate him. His voice was so deep he was sometimes called upon to stand in as a bass fiddle.

It was Juha's secret that, even though he was built for amorous undertakings (according to the ancient formula *mas oso, mas hermoso*), he was exceptionally shy with women, and so he was not himself able to pollinate nearly as often as he wanted.

With him was the couple whose ranch house he had just finished building. Juha, in his businesslike way, was presenting the final contract for payment.

Hansel and Gertie, the two ranchers in from the country, were mad.

"In the first place, you're a prick," said Hansel, as he worked over his gums with a juniper twig. "And in the second place, we ain't payin' shit to a half-breed newfangled rusharound scumbag like you."

"You screwed up the porch, and how am I going to do any shootin'?" added Gertie. "All this hammering and fuckin' around, and now if I sit myself on the porch and lay my rifle on your goddam railing the barrel points too damn high for me to shoot anything out front! What if there's a cougar out there? What if there's one of them big ugly badgers diggin' holes so as my horses will break their stupid legs, you know there's badgers out there who eat horses *alive*, they jes' lie in wait picking dirt out of their claws, in the meantimes coyotes are comin' for us in the night to eat us, you know some coyotes will ambush a house and if they can't get live flesh they'll go for the closet and eat up your *clothes*, tha's right, your clothes so they got your smell and the rest of their lives they hunt for you and for you alone and if they have pups the pups have your smell too till there's whole families of coyotes thinking of nothing but chowin' down and on who? On who? On *me*, that's who, and you are telling me you do all that work to our goddam ranch"—Gertie pounded her big fist on the table—"and we can't even shoot straight off the fuckin' porch and if we do shoot we shoot high—what are we goin' to shoot, the stars?—are we going to shoot the goddam *stars* whiles coyotes eat the hem off my goddam dress and the owls fly straight into the house hootin' back and forth and kill us and carry us out the window off into the night, the big-horned owls will jes' eat us out and use our goddam hollow bodies for *nests*, hear that? *Nests!*"

But Hansel and Gertie had underestimated Juha; he loved ranchers, and knew what to do.

Juha stood up, enormous. He was silent. He looked Hansel

in the eye, he looked Gertie in the eye. He winked aggressively. And then, standing very still, he began to make the little snorkeling noises of a piglet; next, the chortling of a foal; he passed brusquely on then, his lips drawn back from his teeth, to the foam-fed breathing of a stallion approaching the back of a mare in heat—this breathiness Juha mimicked with excellent fidelity; then he baaed like a sheep and lowed like a mother cow after her calf. And was Juha to be stilled? No. Head thrown back, he turned loose the throaty yowl of the white wolf; and very irresponsibly roaming farther afield he sang like a cheetah, gabbled like a turkey, clanged like a bell-bird, cheecheed like a cheechee bird; finally then he stood close to Hansel and Gertie and, as he howled, walloped himself repeatedly on the chest like a great ape.

Juha sat himself down. "I'll lower the railing on the porch," he said.

"I'll have the check ready in the morning," said Hansel.

"Could you do the cheechee bird again?" asked Gertie.

Muscovado, Izzy, Chiara, and Cookie swept into the bar—it was a foursome that could, just by standing there, run amuck. The bartender, who was entranced with Izzy and had concerns about the progress of the girl's soul, demanded she step outside away from the plenteous enticements of alcohol. He wanted to explain privately to her the dangers to physiology and mentation; in other words, the bartender lusted after our Iz.

The girl, however, had her strategy all worked out. "I can't be in here? Well, I don't want a drink anyways, I'm not here as a customer—I'm here to take your job."

Izzy muscled her way behind the bar and stood there expectantly, waiting for orders.

The bartender, who had never seen a sixteen-year-old girl muscle her way anywhere, retreated to the corner and stood there like a broom.

Muscovado sauntered up to the bar. "A shot of white rum, please, ma'am."

Cookie stepped up to the bar. "A shot of Jose Cuervo, some salt and lime," she snapped out.

Juha piped up from his table. "A margarita for me, beer for Gertie, whiskey for Hansel."

The bartender, whose motor skills had an automatic response to such utterances, tried to move. But an arrow (the citizens of Eureka were afterwards to swear that the projectile had made a right-angled turn in front of the bar) flew in the door, thudding into the wall beside him.

Izzy proceeded with great suavity to serve up the drinks.

"It just goes to show!" philosophized Cookie.

"Show what?" asked Izzy.

"That when the time is right, put your arrow in the air, go find the party: you'll get your OK sign, a double thumbs-up, the whole world comes to tickle things up a little."

"Tickle?" asked the terrified bartender.

"Could I get you a drink?" asked Izzy of the displaced fellow.

"A glass of soda water," he said.

"Soda water!" cried everyone in the bar at once.

"With a side of pretzels," said the bartender with dignity. And he took in hand the insipid combination duly served him by Izzy, and stalked out the door, warily, in case any more arrows should come his way. Sipping his contemptible water, he leaves our story here.

And yet, as he leaves, who should be passing him on the way into the bar? Who on earth? Renato, that's who: a local painter of landscapes, portraits, still lifes, miniatures—and, in a pinch, a house painter. He was here to meet with Juha and get paid for painting the ranch house whose construction the contractor had finished with such resounding success.

And why would so skilled an artist set his canvases aside for the coarse plebeian work of house painting? Easily answered: Renato loved coarse plebeian work. And in addition, he held the view that the world portrayed in the paintings of our heritage— that is, taking all the Duccios, the Vuillards, the Kandinskys and Rousseaus, the Picassos, Fra Angelicos and so on, together—the world there was not just a matter of imagination. Of course not. Rather, these paintings depicted a real omnipresent restorative ecstatic available world, which any of us could visit; it was the world within this one, the place we find when our minutes flower within our vision, and we can see where we are, how to live, what to do—in other words, see how to quit being such bimbos.

And so, why paint houses? Given his theory, he could not help but expect it to be amusing to paint entire houses: for he was painting on the canvas of the world. In fact, here in Eureka, he had gone to the mayor and offered to paint the whole town. He wanted to paint it as it really was. He figured he could bring the appearance of Eureka into alignment with its real metaphysical station in the world. The mayor had listened; and he had risen from his chair and thumped Renato on the side of the head.

Gertie, discomfited because she had not done any pounding for so long, glared at Renato and Juha and slammed the table five big resounding wallops. "This *wimp!* And you asked this wimp to paint our house? Huh? Why didn't you just come by the ranch and ask a sack of pigshit to stand up and take the brush! Huh?"

Both Renato and Juha thought how much they liked Gertie.

Cookie, taking Muscovado roughly by the arm, sounded off at the bar:

"I'm going on the road. Mebbe I don't even need to take my bow and arrow. Don't need any weapons. I'll be my own weapon."

"You don't think you'd need protection from me, I hope," responded Muscovado.

"Are you kidding?" Cookie laughed. "A boy like you, I'd fry you like a handful of hashed potatoes."

"What exactly do you mean by that?" asked Izzy, and they both swiveled around, happy to give Izzy an introduction to the art of the aggressive sexual innuendo.

Renato, too, swiveled, to gaze at Izzy and remember the origins of his love of painting: he was sixteen, in bed with his first lover, after a romp that left both quiet because of the tornadoes in their souls—and it was just then he had reached over to a table, taken up his softest brush, and in bed, using only the colors of love, began painting the inner thigh of his girl. In that soft passage he found his work; while she found as he extended his brushwork that tornadoes can travel more widely than she had theretofore considered.

Ananda, her name was. She was blond: she had hair the color of pale honey; she had hair whose gold drifted down like autumn cottonwood leaves; she had hair like light—on moonless evenings they had made love in her plain female radiance.

That was twenty-five years ago.

And we have to ask (who could hold back?): What on earth happened to the generous Ananda? Well, it had been a while since her inner thighs had been painted with the colors of love. After a stint as a jazz trumpeter, she had cruised into law school. And then spent the last fifteen years as a Los Angeles securities attorney, taking companies public, advising on mergers and acquisitions, being responsible for the minutiae of the law that governed the florid unanswerable desires of commerce. For years there had been nothing that made Ananda happier than working eighteen hours a day, reading boxes of documents with enthused exactitude, so that on the trapeze of language, she was the linking intelligence whose midair spins, backflips weightless under the lights, and one-handed landings after unbelievable soaring brought the show to a climax and a closing.

And after a closing, she would go off to a little bar with blue lights and play the trumpet a few nights.

After such labors, she was, by a course of nature, rich. But unlike so many of the newly wealthy, she had decided, against the advice of all her colleagues who sounded the klaxon of disbelief, that she should absent herself for a couple of years—to take stock. Why? and Why? they had all asked her, honking and sniggering.

To see if the work was killing her, she had replied.

People examine their sentences to see if their grammar is correct. Should we not stop to see if our lives make any sense?

Her plan had an amusing beginning: in an amorous coda to her life in Los Angeles, she had been taken by her lover, a young director of films, to dinner and then to bed, where they had played parts in a long adventure of devil-may-care stunts, dramatic turns of phrase, surprises having both languor and pepper; and so to an inclusive finale that resolved the baroque plot of the evening.

In other words, they were both too tired the next morning to lift even a single little spoon. Just the same: she wanted a change of story, some new story—something, to see if love would come and listen.

She had left the next day, with her cat, Tupelo. With a cat like that, purring on her lap through the long drive, Ananda had decided to navigate by whimsy. In fact, loving language as she did, she made her decisions for travel based solely on which names on the map she found most seductive. Given such an eccentricity, it was a cinch she would head straight for the town—you guessed it—of Eureka, Nevada.

It had taken her three days to get there; she stopped in Death Valley, she stopped in Big Smokey Valley, and all through the Great Basin, in the barely—and then, curiously—inhabited parts of North America. And driving along, she more than once had occasion to ask herself, My, oh my, what is that soft brushing?

So it was that the unforgettable Ananda came to walk though the door of the Owl Club.

"One thing I know for sure," said Renato, "there's no way you could be Ananda. Not a chance in the world, nothing so good could ever happen, no man could be so lucky as I would be if standing right there before me was Ananda my sometime lover who just this moment in my memory I was holding."

"Hello Renato," she said.

"For heaven's sake!" he exclaimed. "What in all the world?" And he jumped up, wanting to embrace her, wild with the strange momentum of the day, and shy as he had ever felt in his life.

"Ya come into town to do some business, and the place fills up with bitches!" said Gertie.

"Speak for yourself, you old battle-ax!" cried Izzy from behind the bar.

Huge, Gertie towered out of her chair, stamped over to the bar, slammed her way behind the counter; and enclosed the petrified Izzy in an embrace of remarkable gentleness and affection.

"My kind of girl!" said Gertie, and she went over to Chiara and gave her a few explosive pops on the back.

"Did a good job with the wild thing!" she cried.

Hansel looked admiringly at his wife. Then he looked skeptically at Juha, whom he had come to like; more, even, than a hog he was sending to slaughter. Not as much as his old saddle, his three-year-old palomino mare, Hallelujah, or his bullwhip, with which he could pick horseflies off a pad of butter, leaving no mark; at the same time, though, he liked Juha more than the ranch's billy goat, who smelled like week-old haddock in hot sun; and more even than his own brother, who was no more articulate than a cow's udder.

Ananda and Renato stood out by the door of the bar, looking at each other with astonishment. Their teenage love affair each of them had carried within, like a peach always ripe that they could at any time reach for and take a taste of sweet juices—to remind themselves that happiness is not trivial, just because it is easy.

Ananda and Renato stood, wild with stories.

Chiara and Gertie fell to chattering about pigs and calculus.

Hansel decided on the spot that Juha was screwing up his life; he was sure that Juha, like everyone, needed some advice from him.

"You know, Juha," he said, chewing his cud, "I blundered around, taking my own sweet time, I done me my share of wrongs, but now everything is jes' dandy. Most days I feel pretty chipper, know what I mean?" Hansel looked appraisingly at Juha. "I feel like a helluva lot better man than you, fer instance." Hansel slugged down some Wild Turkey. "Juha, you're startin' to get that musty smell of thems that work too much, it's the grave-smell, a lot of folks is buried alive. Dead from workin'. You want to see it—go to a city, it's weird: you ring a bell and presto! all these zombies come out and dither around. Amazin'!"

Hansel hacked and spit and swung back around, bellicose and happy.

"Let me give you a tip, Juha: take the money from this job, and get the fuck out."

Juha looked over this fifty-year-old rancher with a body tough as the wood of an old bristlecone pine. He could hear Gertie talking to Chiara.

"I can see it, I can see what you mean," Gertie was saying, "it sounds like all them numbers an' words is jes' like living out here in Eureka. I live out here so's what I have is my own, nobody can jes' barge in, they got to follow old country roads to come to me." Gertie, brightening, paused to spike home her logical conclusion. "Now with you, to come near, they got to go 'cross a field of numbers an' words, they have to see what you love, to get to you. You're protected, jes' like I am. Goddam! It's good! It's always good to meet another smart-ass bitch!" she thundered, shaking the glasses and ashtrays. She looked at Chiara with big fiery appreciative eyes.

Chiara saw she was right, and she felt like kissing Gertie on her frizzy bull's head.

Izzy, from her post behind the bar, looked upon the two: Gertie, she of the calluses, the gristle, the capacious voice that in its volume could gather entire rooms, there in company with her willowy mother, she of the sharp dark graces, sassy, quick-firing, mercury-minded. Gertie stomped her feet, stroked Chiara's hair with her hamlike hands and gave her big winks that sounded like windowshades being lowered and snapped back into place; the two women went on talking like some strange female equation of mass and energy.

Izzy settled into the noon: Renato and Ananda strolled over to the bar, and their talk swept like currents, spilling over the banks of the years.

Ananda told of her journeys to madcap harlequin cities; he of his journeys inside his own vehement canvases. She described her midnight work sessions, high in a skyscraper over the home-grounds of her city, setting paragraphs spinning; he recounted his beloved habit of going to the desert with palette and brush to work in the mint of the dawn.

"Let's do some shooting!" suggested Cookie.

"Another round!" cried Juha.

"It's a bar, ain't it? Why shouldn't we all pick each other up!" Cookie went on.

"Feelin' cantankerous is a good thing. Has to be. Ain't God cantankerous? You bet he is. Should we stay in here all day? You bet we should," mused Hansel, who had always liked answering his own questions.

"This is a good-lookin' pack of animals," commented Gertie.

"I've got to bring Tupelo in to see this," said Ananda.

"I'd like to do a little shooting myself," said Juha, looking around.

"You talkin' to me?" asked Cookie, who could not help but wonder, given his mastery of animal calls, what hooting she might do with him.

With all this, Izzy was hardly surprised when Muscovado Taine leaned over the bar and asked for her hand in marriage.

AND SO in Eureka, Nevada, in the dusk of a spring day early in April, inside a bar that sounded even when empty with the trickery of romance and the clangor of celebration, our friends made their rendezvous. It was a little-planned and long-sought meeting, undertaken, unbeknownst to them, with the assistance of angels who will in the coming travels visit them. It was a meeting compelled by shared speculations on the nature of the soul and by the ocean-going delights of hard liquor; by an intimation that the secrets of life would be revealed in gritty detail; by a love of the desert, a hope for the sea, an expectation of jokes; and by immodest sexual longings that made their blood run like warm nectar.

So delicious was the rendezvous, none of them could have conceived of Tabby, the seventeen-year-old boy who before long was going to shoot one of them.

Just then, not even Tabby was thinking about shooting anybody. In San Jose, California, he was sitting in the gun shop owned by the parents of his friend Grimes. The shop was closed. He and Grimes were reading comics, one after another; there were comics strewn all over the floor. They read and listened to classical cello blasting out of speakers that the two friends rigged up after hours. Tabby loved the cello; his father always played it in his church—the great solos, Mendelssohn, Saint-Saëns, Bach.

Both of them were sore: they had pushed hard at the weight room. They always worked out together with the free weights, in their muscle shirts and headbands, down at the gym with the ex-fighters, and the ex-cons who wanted to fuck them, both their young pretty asses. But Tabby and Grimes had plans for the ex-cons.

The two of them loved heroes. They had seen enough, both of them, of the world. How did it all go so wrong? No one expected them to sign up, did they? To beg for a place in this shithouse, please please please let me let me— What for? To join the cowards and fools? To walk down the street and step over the drunks and have to deal with gibbering freaks as the limousines went by with people bloated from lunch? No one was doing anything about it.

But they could do something.

Key to the plan was knowing who was out there. Tabby and Grimes had it figured: one night after lifting, bulked out, floating along on malt beer, they divided up the world:

1) The Suits—a lot of them were fat, all of them were rich. They could talk better than anybody, and their houses were like huge plastic cathedrals full of crap. They ate fancy lettuce. They hated hard, quiet, and deep. They were all buried together, to make a kind of toxic waste dump.

2) The Chumps—worked for the suits. Lots of scar tissue, like all the losers. Got patted on the back, just before they got shit on. Grateful like dogs. Decent and solid, like a brick, but squishy inside. Spent seventy years getting their guts unraveled. Took everything seriously.

3) The Freaks—never did make it. Rings in their noses or

their tits. Loved being punished, it meant they were su-
perior. Leather jackets, always wanted to look as good
as morons can look. Lived off the scraps of the culture,
like pigs. Would be fun to kill, because they were all so
scared.

4) The Maggots—no house, no money, no clean clothes,
walked around just like the Muselmen of Auschwitz.
Good with cardboard. If you looked hard, you could see
them festering. Track them by listening for the dry
heaves.

5) The Bone People—the sick and the old, there were so
many. Why did people keep getting sick? It was too bad,
one long sickness could make a Suit, presto! into a
Maggot, which was always funny. And the old! Everywhere! That sweet-and-sour trying-to-die smell! Filling
whole rooms, like bagfuls of rotten teeth.

6) The Monsters—they were out there, the fast-talkers,
perverts, thieves, big-dealers, hotheads, nitpickers, chis-
elers; they hid themselves—could be Freaks, Chumps,
Suits, any of the rest. Hidden, but you could find them,
always, always. They hurt your feelings. They were in
your way. They made you mad. The world was turning
to shit and pus because no one could deal with the
Monsters. And no one would, except for

7) The Heroes, who had to protect

8) The Innocent.

Tabby and Grimes loved being bulked out. They always lifted
before coming to the shop with the comics. Both of them were
big for their age. They were excited.

We cannot assume that it was warm nectar that moved in Cookie
and Juha, as they sat at a table in the Owl Club, and Cookie
downed with gusto a number of Jose Cuervos; though such was

the shining of her eyes, and the free play of her hands, that we might assume Juha was rather more than a friend. In fact, she was kissing Juha's neck in such a way to make it unlikely that Juha would return immediately to work.

"I hope you don't think, by my kissing your neck, that I like you," said Cookie.

Juha had not only assumed; his flesh was blossoming in those transports of anticipation so familiar to young men. It was hard to be shy, even for him. He thought how he might entice her further, which was amusing to Cookie, since he had done nothing to entice her in the first place. She had felt the warm winds blow through her soul, even though he had just been sitting there like a stump.

"I've got more animal noises," he said. "You should hear me in private, that's when I can really let my pipes out, Cookie—"

"Lemme tell you something, you dumb thing," she said sweetly. "I'm a cook, and I know that there ain't nothing so good as a long simmer, followed by a red rippin' steam-makin' hold-it-forever-on-high heat. You know what I mean?"

Juha looked at her wide-eyed.

"I mean a heat that melts down the goddam stove, that's what I mean," continued Cookie in her expository way.

Juha, decisive and idiotic, rose from his chair and held out his hand to her. He meant it to be brusque, strong. Some men, he thought, can make unabashed promises of pleasure. He looked at her in what he meant to be a tried-and-true manner: this was the time to yield to manly certainty. In other words, he looked with spaniel-eyed pleading: were they going to get it on? Or not?

Cookie yanked him back down to his chair.

"And lemme tell you this: I mean heat that burns down the whole blessed kitchen, and burns the house down with it—but after the fire, all you want to do is cook again. And you do, too."

"It's lucky I'm a contractor," sighed Juha.

"Excuse me," threw in Chiara from the next table, "but are you two discussing the relation between sex and the traditional three meals?" Chiara liked her analogies clean, logical, self-evident.

"You're right about that!" exclaimed Cookie. "And Juha here seems to have a real interest—yesiree, Juha!" She reached over and passed her hand through his hair. "Now, if you and Gertie would care to join us here, I'll go into more detail on this subject."

"I s'pose it might jes' turn out he's good fer somethin'," said Gertie skeptically, as she swung her great buffalo's physique over to his side. Chiara came round, and they all looked at Juha with amusement.

At the bar, Muscovado peppered the nubile Izzy with his provocations.

"What's wrong with marriage? Especially a sudden, foolish marriage to a stranger? Where's your sense of adventure?" he asked calmly, with his happy lilt. He floated in the bar, as a tropical island floats in the sea: with the momentum of paradise.

Izzy looked at Muscovado, who had more allspice in his voice than even he knew. She found him completely convincing. And, having both her fancy and fantasy tickled, she decided to accept—though not for several years.

Or maybe even several hundred.

"What makes you think," she said warmly, "that you could handle a sixteen-year-old girl, innocent, homely. I am not used to the devilish press of you men." (Izzy was trying to remember phrases from pulp novels, and, putting a prissy quaver in her voice, managed to come up with a set.) "I don't know what to do, I—I'm all confused, what if I make a big mistake? A girl's whole life might be undone! Wronged by her first love! Oh, the devastation! What to do, what to do? . . . I've never been with a man."

"She's not just a bitch. She a *lying* bitch," said Gertie, elbowing Chiara and grinning.

Muscovado pretended to think it over. Izzy, though, could not be reluctant more than a few seconds, and was looking at him as though this was not a game—staring at him with a hereditary brazenness. More than brazen: he could smell smoke. And so he really did think it over.

"I'll braid your hair in the mornings, and sing to you at night," he promised.

"And what will you sing?" she asked.

"I'll sing of nights in Jamaica in meadows by the sea, where we used to go and make big fires, and when the moon was high we would go catch crabs and bring them back and there in the grasses eat them with hot butter and drink white rum all night. The moon was so bright we could see the mist on the Blue Mountains; and as the mist turned around the peaks we would sing ballads; in them were legends of pleasure: those are the songs I would sing to you."

Izzy thought, Hmm!—doesn't really sound that bad so far!

"And what would you say, in the morning, as you braided my hair?" she asked.

Muscovado looked at her shining young jet-black hair; he leaned over the bar and spoke in a low voice, so that she had to bend toward him to hear.

"First, as I brushed your hair, I would whisper to you. I would say, Your hair shines, because the morning light is calling you to the world. I know you will go—but I want you always to come home to me."

"Well, you're right—I would go," said Izzy delightedly.

"Are you sure you're sixteen?" asked Muscovado suspiciously.

"Don't break the mood, dummy!" she retorted.

"Since you're goin' on together so, why don't you come over here, you two, and sit with us," sang out Cookie, who wanted her table, right there in a bar in the middle of Eureka, to be the very spicery of romance for all the world.

"But who will tend bar?" asked Izzy, who, for all her attraction to spiceries, wanted to make sure her vocational responsibilities were addressed with honor. In other words, she wanted to be alone with Muscovado.

"I'll tend bar!" cried out Ananda. And so it was that the Owl Club obtained as a bartender, for the first time, a distinguished Los Angeles securities attorney. Joining her was Renato, who at that moment would have followed her to the far ends of the cosmos. It was his turn to lean over the bar.

"I have now a much wider selection of brushes than I did when I was sixteen," he suggested innocently.

"Is there any chance that you now have those brushes a skilled painter would use to brush long, brush slow, brush with a sense of the colors changing under his strokes?" asked Ananda, in her legalistic way.

"I think we're all going to get along just fine!" shot out Juha.

"If you were any more brawny, I wouldn't come near you except with a whip and a chair," commented Cookie to the general contractor.

"Pff!" countered Gertie. "He's a pollywog of a man."

"Izzy, no more romance until you finish the Rilke I gave you, and do your partial differentials," remonstrated her mother.

"I've finished the poems. I've finished the equations. Three days ago," riposted Iz.

"Well, could I buy you a drink, then?" asked her mother.

Hansel was thinking that this was probably better than the zoo.

Tabby and Grimes were waiting in the gun shop for their whore, Angelica. She hated the comics—but it wasn't much for a trick to ask. And they had a good time reading them together—all the important ones, the Avengers, the Punishers. It was a world full of heroes. They read them aloud. Things counted for something.

The two adolescents posed in the mirrors of the gun shop between comics. Tabby had won some bodybuilding contests; he had the energy, the cock-of-the-walk step on the stage; there were trophies lined up at the back of the room.

It was in the gun shop they practiced, wearing nothing but the shorts required for the competitions. They had mirrors everywhere. They posed, they strutted, they critiqued each other. Sometimes to help their concentration they would take fingerpaint and outline individual muscles on each other's chests. It took a long time.

Tabby had stolen Angelica from his father, Ben, who preached at the pentecostal church that he had founded after he got out of prison. He had seen that he had to reform, rescue his soul, and help other people. He was thought of as a convict who had come back and made a man of himself.

Ben was a big man with a big voice. He looked like a prophet. He had a radio show. There were big donations. Ben took plenty of bills for himself every week; he needed the money, and no one worked harder than this grizzled and distinguished pastor. He never missed a sermon, he had always a gentle word, he tended the sick, he was there for every death in his congregation. He married, blessed, gave advice, he figured he earned the fucking money tending to this cringing bunch of suckers. And of course there was his scam with the mortuaries and the teaching hospitals—a thing of beauty, the best thing he had pulled.

He cut Tabby in on the take, though when he found out about Angelica he was sorry he did.

Ben was proud of Tabby. He had taught him all about the cello, which he had learned to play in prison. Ben loved the cello. He had gotten his lessons after they had put the plate in his head. He thought the plate made him more sensitive to certain kinds of music, it was some kind of acoustical thing.

He read Tabby Revelation, which his son loved—it was so much like the comic books, all that power and dressing up and punishment. It scared people.

The Bible was never far from Ben's hand. After a sermon or even a speech to a civic group he would come home and put on the cello recordings loud and read Revelation in his deep voice, pausing to watch as two or three of his whores undressed for him.

Ben had taught his son about salvation. He never thought his son would get those kind of muscles.

But Tabby needed the muscles.

Speaking of zoos: After another few hours, the cages of daily life—whose fastenings are not in any case, for any of us, secure—had fallen away; and, at their liberty, after these zephyrs of affection and rolling laughter, trustworthy seduction, brouhaha, singsong and derision: after such hours, what had our friends?

"OK, this is our strategy," summarized Cookie: "Touch and go."

"You ain't goin' nowhere before supper, ya pack of fools," said Hansel amiably.

And with that suave injunction, Hansel and Gertie, who had experience with stock animals, rounded up the whole group: the golden Ananda and her Renato, the shy Juha, the bellicose ecstatic Cookie, fragrant Muscovado Taine and Izzy, the shining Chiara: the seven blasted their way out into the dusk of the Eureka street. Yet before they were loaded unceremoniously into a pickup truck for the ride to the ranch, before they were commanded by a ranch marriage that worked because Hansel and Gertie walked on the bedrock of the world, before one more thing could happen, they had to brace themselves just to hold their footing. It was not easy because on this earth there is no force that can match the cyclonic stillness of a desert twilight.

When air and light are left alone to work rough delicate stratagems; when sagebrush with its scent passes on its metaphysical intimations; when the desert carries irresponsibly, irresistibly, the whole velocity of its silence into a clear, still, dusky hour; when the peace that is at midheart of this world and the next, makes itself material and comes for us as a gift at the end of the day—when these things occur, well, it makes us think that hard liquor has its uses. And that the world, which usually just goes its own way, sometimes stops so we can have a look.

Anyway, the dogs in the back of Hansel and Gertie's pickup started to yap.

Everybody piled in.

"Hold on tight, suckers!" boomed Gertie as she slammed shut the tailgate of the pickup.

"I'll build us a little house right here on the bed of this truck," promised Juha.

"And so, tell me—what exactly is this 'touch and go' policy?

I mean, is this something we're deciding for all time?" Izzy wanted to know.

Hansel, behind the wheel, gunned them all out of town.

At the ranch they found Hansel's stew: big chunks of ranch beef simmered in an oven for hours with onions, bacon, tomatoes, carrots, stock, and excellent cheap red wine, with potatoes and more wine and seasoning added at the end, all to be consumed with fresh bread that was placed steaming on the table. They found ranch hands, men and women so rough that as they grew old their skin was replaced with juniper bark; ravens that flew into the kitchen and perched with maniacal glossiness on Gertie's huge hand; stallions who had fucked themselves cross-eyed; little foals, each one a crescendo of quicksilver.

They found, as well, the ranch house constructed by Juha, whose design was so subtle that it seemed, among the big poplars, to be in motion like an animal, a sentence; like a planet.

And they found that—if they had ever had any chance at all— it was becoming rather less likely all the time that any of them would be returning to the world.

Such was their conclusion, as they sat around the hearth at the ranch, that very night. The fire, banked high in the big stones, unfolded bright chapters they wanted to read; and the country, which is resident in every house set in these distant valleys, came for them like an old friend, so that our seven cohorts had for company not only Hansel, Gertie, and the ranch hands; they had the whole Nevada high desert, right there by the side of the hearth.

"They'll never find us here," said Chiara, with her arm around her daughter. Izzy grinned, and the two gave each other, close by the fire, a look of delicious complicity.

The next morning, Renato was up early, out by the corrals sketching the foals, the stables, the mountains with their stands of piñon pine and juniper. Ananda was inside at the breakfast table, letting the motion of the morning substitute for the welter of responsibilities she had for so many years faced first in the day. Even with the banter and rustle of everyone at the ranch going to work, the morning, absent the clamor of her own labors, seemed velvety, promising. When someone, having so much to do, finishes decisively her agreed work and puts aside her life, then it is she recalls how many heavens an early hour can hold.

Besides all that, she wanted to see how Renato would study her, before painting her. She knew, just now, that Renato was outside painting—just because she could feel his thoughts inside, with her. Yet even Ananda, sitting there just then, had no idea of the high jinks she had in store for him.

Izzy and Chiara got Muscovado Taine to croon an early-hour rendition of a song he knew as a child, which celebrated each one of the tiniest birds in Jamaica, and included their all calling to one another. It was the first time so many little tropical birds had visited Nevada.

Muscovado looked at the two women who listened to him—their dark features, sanctified recklessness, savvy undeceivable working knowledge of the love of men. Muscovado wanted, even though it was too early, to regale them. And why? Because he loved them. Tropical moonlight blew though his body.

Cookie had been up early and rolled some dough and baked three kinds of bread; and then commandeered the ranch stove and cooked everybody up a gargantuan breakfast. Fragrant with wheat and rye and honey and molasses, she teased the hungry Juha.

"What exactly is the breakfast fuck?" she asked in her meditative and scholarly way, there over the sizzling eggs.

Juha drew near her, as she worked tumultuously at the stove.

"Do you think you can just take me over with suggestive talk?" he asked indignantly.

"You betcha," said Cookie.

"Well, you're goddam right you can!" said Juha, abandoning his few ideas about the etiquette of seduction.

Cookie looked at him through the early morning light, through the bright lens of her desire, through the aromatic clouds rising from the grill.

"Let me tell ya why we should hit the road together, and why I'm going to take you to bed and ring you like a bell," she said calmly, as she tended to the crackling eggs, hash browns, cakes, sausages, bacon, a few steaks—

"And let me tell ya one thing more," she said, deftly moving things around on the grill, "I like you not jes' 'cause you're burly as a big oak; it's mostly 'cause of that crazy streak. So don't go flat on me." She slipped some eggs onto their plates, she flipped some pancakes and poured more out, with a sidearm twist she zipped a cake right through the window to the hungry dogs outside. "Most men have the craziness pounded right out of 'em, so that when you look in their eyes after a whiles you see there's nothin' there but little plugs of dried scum. Don't let it happen to you." Cookie finished dishing up twenty-four steaming plates of breakfast, and, wiping her hands on a towel, with a little sweat shining on her face from the heat of the stove and of her thoughts, she turned to face Juha.

Juha looked back at the stocky Cookie; he was in love, too. It was an epidemic.

Hansel, having eaten like a wild dog his own breakfast, walked up with a coffee mug, irritated at having to fight his way though the meteorological din. "Juha, you want to come away from yer ladyfriend there, jes' mosey right on over here, we got to settle up."

Cookie smiled at him. "You got to finish with the world," she said.

Ananda, who had gone out to watch Renato work, now returned inside with him. They were comparing the morning light with the twilight that had arrested them all in town the night before.

Renato was all wound up. "Just before the sun rises," he was saying, "the valley here—I didn't get it for a long time."

Cookie, who had overheard, cried out, "It's jes' what I was sayin': plugs! You got to take the plugs out, doofus!"

"I want to paint the corral and the foal," continued Renato, "the light in the valleys, just so, just so . . . we can take up our oldest promise—"

"Promise?" asked Ananda.

"A promise to come home to a heaven here before us," he said.

"You mean heaven metaphorically?"

"No," he said, "I mean heaven in the flesh."

Ananda thought this over. "It's adolescent romanticism."

"It worked for us once," he pointed out.

And, arm in arm, they walked up to the brawling breakfast table; they saw Hansel sitting down with Cookie and Juha, and near them, with storytelling expressions, Muscovado with Chiara and Izzy.

Hansel looked at Juha with hostility, because he loved hostility. Cookie laughed at him, and Juha did, too. Our contractor had learned something, at least, in his labors.

"Juha," said Hansel as he rolled a cigarette, "I understand that you and this bunch of fast-talkin' misfits is all goin' on the road together."

"We are?" asked Juha.

"You betcha," said Cookie.

"So I'm goin' to make you a deal. Instead of me payin' you in cold cash for the work here on the house, I'm goin' to offer you a couple o' cars that you all could pile in and do some tourin'. I mean road cars. Beat to smithereens and glad of it. Kinda like me." Hansel glinted at Juha and Cookie.

"I want the money," said Juha.

"But we're out here to roam around!" cried Izzy from the other side of the table. "I love old cars!"

Ananda saw a use for her riches. "You get the cars, Juha, and I'll throw in the gas money. We go where we want to go."

"I will contribute a fresh paint job for these automobiles," offered Renato, "so that when we hit the road, we may move with a style and coloration derived from mural painting."

"What a lot of crap! Can't anybody stop this guy paintin'? But there should be one crazy on every trip—jes' like one drunk in every town," said Cookie.

"*One* crazy!" snorted Hansel.

Ananda looked over. "Juha, let me give you the impartial analysis of an attorney as to your chances in this negotiation with Hansel. If you try to go for all cash, or get going into an argument about various values and payment schedules, you will lose. I'm talking vital organs."

"If only one of the cars was a station wagon," lamented Izzy, who could get enthusiastic only about cars of real dilapidation.

"Now, it jes' so happens that I have an old station wagon on the property that I could throw into the deal," said Hansel.

"Amazin'!"

"Were you ever a securities trader?" asked Ananda.

"Now, the old flatbed I brought you out here in, now you could throw up a little wood house on the back of it, put two or three of you back there, plenty of room. Fact is now, Juha, I seem to 'member you already promisin' to do some hammering on the back of that truck. Hell, it jes' may be that we've already made a deal."

Hansel looked at Juha as, in other circumstances, someone walking into a restaurant might look at a lobster in a tank.

Gertie looked Juha over, and felt she should encourage him.

"I'm kinda gettin' used to havin' you around," she said. "I could almost see you hanging from a hook in our big walk-in freezer. I'd like that."

"You know," said Juha, "I really do love you two old bullriders, but if there's no cash to go along with the cars, I'll dynamite this ranch house, and it'll take the barn down with it. It might even take the mountain down with it." He felt very cheerful.

"I'd be proud to have a son like you," said Gertie.

"What about the cars and thirty thousand in cash?" suggested Hansel.

It did not take the contractor long to build a little house on the back of the flatbed truck. But what a house it was: with its swooping lines, tiny gables, minuscule turrets; its shingled exterior, small-pane windows, little peepholes, and here and there the flaring ornament—what kind of aerodynamic performance could they really expect on the road? And why on earth did Juha get so carried away?

He got carried away because every morning Cookie came to his bed and fucked him loco; and then leaped up and dressed and went into the ranch house to cook another breakfast for thousands.

This tradition had begun when, rumpled from her own slumbers, she had walked in at dawn to his little room in an outbuilding on the ranch property and taken off her clothes, while presenting her views on the sleepy rollicking to come.

"The breakfast fuck," she explained as she stretched out full length upon his astonished form, "is the strangest fuck, 'cause it's always rough and ready, nobody's had time to get riled up thinking ahead on it, it's got that am-I-awake? or am-I-dreamin'? and is-this-who-I-think-it-is? kinda kick to it. I mean," she said, as she kissed his neck slowly and settled onto him like a warm gold oil; as she kissed him with the certainty of a woman who knew that some men's souls learn to move in the world only because women's pleasure is a world. "I mean that if you know that when you wake up you may jes' wake up inside me, why, I betcha it's goin' to change your whole way of layin' down, your whole way of gettin' up, now you're goin' to wake up inside me every mornin', sweet man," she said as she sat up on him, with her hands on his chest, "every mornin'. Until you don't have a mornin', except me." She smiled at him.

Juha, we may say, was no longer sleepy. He raised his big hands to her face, and cradled her in the unbelieving touch of a man all of whose veins held a syrup he wanted to pour into her.

"And that sweet syrup—" she said jauntily. "Fill me up. What's breakfast for?"

So it was Juha learned to cook.

It was near midnight.

"Heroes, where do they come from?" asked Tabby, in motion,

always in motion, and looking in the mirror. "They are men who decide. They're not meat. They don't argue. They decide."

"We're not good enough with the guns yet," said Grimes.

"The scum. What's on the streets. You're not going to back out, are you? Are you? We have to do it. Are you with me? Are you with me?" asked Tabby.

Tabby slapped Grimes, who slapped him back, hard. They both started laughing.

Tabby put on the music; sonorous pieces, Bach's Arioso and Fauré's Elégie, rolled through the shop. He started one of his muscle-show routines, stalking across the room.

The gun shop sat just down the block from the church and right next to a liquor store and a row of little businesses—cleaners, a hairdresser, a pizzeria; then there were a couple of vacant lots with some big sewer pipes where three people lived. You could hear the gunfire at night, and the sirens; Grimes loved that, he was in the middle of everything here. He liked the store just like this, with the lights out, nothing but the glow from the neon of the liquor store.

Justice always comes out of the dark.

Sometimes he would go out late and drag some Maggot off the street and pound the shit out of him, goddam sick petty thieves.

Every siren made Grimes feel stronger. If only the police were given a free hand, they could clean it up; some of them had the guts to clean out all the shit. People cleaned guns, they cleaned engines, pipes, houses. But the world? Who cleaned the fucking world?

He knew all the cops. Sometimes they let him ride around in the patrol cars—he loved that. Where there's a cop, there's action. Someone to help, or someone to pound on, to slam against the car, all sloppy, bags of sleaze.

Some of the cops liked him. They worked closely, Grimes and his family, with the police. It was not just tracing guns that were used in killings; the shop referred its customers, the ones who wanted to protect themselves, to the police academy for training in the use of firearms. Grimes loved the cops, he loved the uniforms. So proper. That was what he wanted. To always be proper. To be the man that people could count on.

Tabby didn't always understand, but Grimes was trying to teach him some manners. He had taught him so much about guns, he thought by now his friend would see you had to be responsible. You had to carry yourself right. Square and strong, wherever you were, whatever you were doing, even if you were stepping over puke.

There were some bars around the corner, it meant more puke on the sidewalks of their block. But there was more everywhere.

The shop did well. It did so well that Grimes's parents left every spring for a two-month vacation, and Grimes had the run of the store. He knew how to run it, and the family had fixed everything with the police. The cops would look in on him, stop to talk over the day, make sure everything was going OK. Grimes loved their uniforms, that deep blue like the sky. Justice has to be everywhere, like the sky.

They were good days, the best of days. Grimes always thought, They will all be so proud of me.

Tabby looked at him in the mirror. They had been friends for years. "You're a brave one. You'll stand up." He kicked at Grimes, stood up, threw a few jabs and crosses, kicked again.

"When do we start? Really start? This taking down a Maggot now and then, it don't mean nothing. Nobody really does anything. I'm ready to move on. You are the one that put together the plan. But you're so calm. Don't you want to yell about it? C'mon!"

Tabby walked back to the mirror in his white briefs, rubbed some oil into his chest so the skin would shine under the lights; they had rigged the lights just like in the shows. The light showed off Tabby's big shoulders. He was tall and graceful with a small waist and long legs spindled with muscles.

"I want Monsters. What do you want?"

Tabby did a few turns in the mirror, he struck a pose, he pirouetted, he worked his physique. He popped a quad, showed the delts and abs, did some marching and scowling.

"They've fucked it up. What do you smell? In the lot. On the street. Maggot shit, that's what you smell. It's time to fix it, just like you said."

Grimes watched Tabby's moves critically; he walked over to join him in front of the mirror. Grimes was shorter, with a crew-cut and the body of a bulldog. A solid, cabled neck, thick torso, heavy legs.

"It has to be right. Lawful. That's why we have a plan. We'll go when I say we're ready."

Tabby turned around and reached over and slapped Grimes across the face again.

"Maybe you don't have the heart for it. The feelings. No heart. You just got a cockroach in your chest."

Grimes dived for him, the two of them wrestled on the floor of the shop, rolling over and over; they sprang to their feet and locked up, flaring, then took each other down again; they cracked a gun case, the cello roaring. Grimes pinned Tabby down hard, but slowly Tabby arched his body away and spun round and threw himself on Grimes; he took one of Grimes's arms and forced it behind his back and ground his friend's face into the floor. They were both sweating. Grimes lifted himself with one arm, enough to twist around and knee Tabby, and as the boy fell back holding himself, Grimes took a Mauser from the counter display and shoved it hard between his friend's teeth.

"Lemme see—is this a Monster? A Monster?"

Grimes looked him over.

"I think it is! It is! Can Monsters feel pain? I wonder? I really wonder!"

He looked real close.

"Oh shit! It's my buddy Tabby! It's only Tabby. He's OK!"

And laughing, he yanked Tabby to his feet. They were both laughing when Angelica knocked at the back door.

Grimes went to let her in.

"We're goin' to be a legend. A goddam legend," he said.

* * *

It was morning in the Great Basin. Our Izzy, awake early, walked out behind the ranch house, and in the dawn hour of the desert clarions, a glittering passed around the big valley; and she was quiet, and listened to the musicks of her own heart.

Music she knew; and, like every teenager, she thought that right then and there she would take stock of her life and plan in detail her whole future.

To start with: she inhabited her body with unreserved, transcendent satisfaction. This, because she had a body, one of her own: because from her body—its growth, its softness, its extravagant skybound hopefulness—she had excluded the thoughts of everyone else in the world. And it's no small thing, she thought, at sixteen, to have gotten the world to stop yammering at her.

She did not see herself from outside. She did not have in her head voices of those who, in looking at her, would have her recite to herself what they thought about what they saw. She did not linger before mirrors, which she saw as places where people rushed helplessly to submit themselves to the miserable gossip of all the world. She had, in other words, a body formed of an old-fashioned, solemnly pledged, easy bemused ecstatic marriage of earth and soul; rather than a composite, tinsel body contaminated by other people's ideas, breeding like bacteria.

Izzy stood in the desert dawn gawky, wide-eyed, cooled by the mint light on her skin; with longings that made her thoughts pitch and sparkle, with a recondite delicious innocence, with all the velocities of love loosed in her flesh, she stood: just one more teenage girl.

And what of Chiara that morning? She had tucked herself into an old flannel sleeping bag and lay out atop a little hill that overlooked the ranch house. She gazed down at the outbuildings, the corral with its horses like visitors strong and curious from some better world; the barn, Hansel and Gertie's shocking ramshackle array of trucks, farm machinery, and sundry mechanical contraptions that had no conceivable use, unless they were used, in passage through the Milky Way, to harvest the stars.

She saw her daughter out by the corrals; and the light, like a protectress of silk, wrapped her Izzy in its folds. Chiara looked down at her, and thought how it was impossible to have children without wanting to make the world over again: to make a world plentiful and amorous in its promised deliverance.

The sun was rising to the harmonies of the meadowlarks. She nestled down in the bag for a last sweet morning sleep.

Muscovado Taine sat at the breakfast table with Hansel and Gertie.

"Now where is this Jamaica again? Somewhere near Philadelphia?" asked Hansel. He had never seen the ocean, so the notion of an island was obscure to him.

"Out in the Caribbean sea," explained Musco.

"Bullshit! In a sea! Bullshit!" Hansel cried, with a big smile. "You know, Mucus, or whatever the hell yer name is, you might as well know I don't believe in the ocean. I've heard of it. But I haven't seen it."

"Prove it!" demanded Gertie. "We want proof!"

Renato walked in to rescue the beleaguered Muscovado. "I figure this group of misfits may just have to drive together all the way to the ocean. And when we get there, I'll paint you a canvas of the water, and send it back. That be good enough?"

Hansel and Gertie, who knew Renato as the weirdo painter of the town, thought it over.

"Hell, no," said Hansel, "not unless you send a bottle of so-called ocean water. Don't believe in nothin' I cain't taste."

Gertie stomped over to a drawer and pulled out a map of the West. "I want to see where you're headed, and as soon as Juha is finished banging on the goddam truck, I want you to get the hell out. All of you together. Don't be leaving no stragglers."

She pummeled the map a few times, and Muscovado and Renato leaned over to see.

There in the middle of the still-visible impressions of her fist was a section of northern California littoral: LOST COAST, said the map.

"Huh! Looky that. Now, if that ain't the place you lot of fatheads are all bound for, I'll eat my own beard," said Hansel.

Later, after Cookie had slung together another breakfast, she stood by the map with the haggard and smiling Juha; Chiara and Izzy, arm in arm and looking dangerous, leaned against the table; Ananda, swaying between Muscovado and Renato, as a beautiful cottonwood will sway before winds that blow from the future, looked at the unknown country between Eureka, Nevada, and the Lost Coast; and she said to everyone with relief:

"If we have to be lost, it's good to know where we're going."

3

THE MORNING OF the departure, Hansel and Gertie stood before the scene: there were the seven voyagers, their station
wagon, and the outlandishly rebuilt truck. Everyone had stashed
their things in the little house on the flatbed, or in the back of
the wagon. Chiara signed her car over to Hansel for some money
for the trip.

All in all, they looked like a group of refugees.

"I feel like a slumlord," said Hansel.

Ananda stood cradling like a baby in her arms the enthusiastic Tupelo, whose gray fur was soft—theologically soft—against
her bare arms.

"So, what's the name of the truck?" asked Gertie. She knew
that names were important, to focus people's minds at the beginning of foolish journeys.

Everyone looked at Juha.

"What? Me? I have to say?" he asked.

"You did it, Juha, and I like it," said Izzy, who walked up to
the massive contractor and kissed both his cheeks. Juha blushed.
The crowd gave some approving oohs and aahs. Chiara and
Ananda glided up and added their kisses. And with all this,

following upon Cookie's just completed morning visit, Juha felt faint. He felt wobbly.

"O fer Christ's sake, someone else name the damn things," demanded Gertie.

"We'll name these two magnificent vehicles when we get to the ocean," said Chiara. "By then, we'll know what we're doing."

"I want to ride in the truck," demanded Izzy.

"Done!" chimed in one and all.

"I want to drive the truck." Izzy upped the ante.

"Granted!" everyone said, demonstrating that a girl should be thoughtful about her antes.

"A young girl driving such a vehicle? Without a responsible adult near to help in taking this tonnage down the lonely highways? I volunteer to ride up front with this brave young woman!" So expatiated the gallant Muscovado.

"Just keep your hands off me," advised Izzy.

"I think I'll just take this dizzy guy into the back of the truck, and give him some medical attention," offered Cookie, who was sure that Juha would feel much better if he was able to sweat as he blushed.

"C'mon, big fella, lay down in your own house."

"To the Lost Coast!" cried Gertie, who wanted them to get the hell out.

Ananda, Chiara, and Renato headed for the wagon; Muscovado and Izzy for the cab of the truck; Cookie and Juha to the newly painted house perched on the truck's flatbed.

The station wagon pulled out.

"This is a doomed expedition if I ever seen one," said Hansel, smiling.

Izzy backed the truck into a fence, lurched into the pigpen, spun the wheels, got free, and with an imperious sweetness in her bones went careening down the road.

"One by one, I'd say maybe. But you put the seven of 'em together, and you got *no* chance. None. Finito. It's like sending a ton of sludge into the world." So continued Hansel with his analysis.

*   *   *

Renato, in the front seat between the dark Chiara and the blond Ananda, as though headed down the road between Night and Day, had a question. "What is it we expect, anyway?"

Ananda and Chiara looked at each other.

"Who knows?" replied Chiara quickly. "The thing is to get started."

"But why?" he followed up.

"Everybody goes on the road somehow. Mostly, they just throw a bag of pretzels in the car, and go."

"Everybody? After all, nobody *has* to do anything."

"They have to die—pretzels or no pretzels," observed Ananda, very cheerily and prettily.

How, we may ask, could the painter understand a crack like that? Yet Renato—because he lived in a world where light moved not just by physical law, but for amusement; where light came not just to shine, it came to play; because in light, as a painter, he lived—Renato could see vaguely what these women meant.

Ananda and Chiara sat quietly, listening to Renato think; until they both started laughing at once.

"Attaboy, Renato!" said Chiara.

In the cab of the truck, Muscovado decided to make a last try at teasing Izzy into matrimony.

"Izzy," he said, "when I lived in Jamaica I knew a Carib Indian, a healer—for a thousand years they had all the islands to themselves—and he taught me a magic word: and with this magic word, I can ask birds down out of the sky—they perch on my shoulder, they talk to me, and, over the years, they are teaching me how to fly."

"That's the most harebrained thing I ever heard," said Izzy, who, behind the wheel of the big truck, felt even more confident than usual; that is, she felt like all the world belonged to her.

"I want to teach you this magic word," continued Muscovado, in his voice of salt and allspice.

Tangled up and straightened out, lost and found deep inside Cookie, Juha felt considerably revived.

Though Juha, too, had his questions. "What about my construction company? My plans, my work, my job?"

Cookie kissed him. She smelled like bread.

"Wherever we go, you build a kitchen, I'll cook some meals for everybody, and then we can be on our way. This trip will be a sort of Kitchen's Progress."

Juha thought about this—to no avail.

"But what are we up to, for heaven's sake?" Juha was not used to talking about life-changing propositions while flat on his back, in the arms of a woman who found his muscles, like rebar, to be a ground for such slow wayfaring—especially now that they had advanced from the breakfast fuck to the easygoing midmorning fuck.

Cookie, in sex, liked to pause, to make experimental mixes of spice, to tease, to stop and talk; she liked to season on the fly, to taste along a whole way of preparations, to use both salt and sweet, to introduce an impulsive variation in the driving flames, so as to provoke a streaming of flavors.

In other words, Juha's whole life had gone up in smoke. Such are the hazards of culinary training. He sighed.

"I love you so much I've gone wacky. I'm just a man that won't stop going off. In a few days, I've blown everything up."

Cookie rolled over on top of him again.

"Now, I figure when somebody blows it all sky-high, at least you got something left: you got yourself a fire. Now, this teaching you to cook, why, all you *need* is a fire."

Juha, for some reason, felt comforted by this cowgirl logic.

"Why go anywhere?" asked Renato, since it seemed to be his role to ask the humdrum questions.

"Good question," said Chiara. "Let's ask somebody in the next town."

The Great Basin, which takes its humans with a low and constant laugh, spread around, hidden in iridescent green haze.

The next town could be reached only by driving through Big Smokey Valley, and in the two cars all seven of them felt deranged. But there is no derangement like having a real chance.

They drove into Austin, with the truck in the lead: Izzy, grinning, had passed the wagon halfway through Big Smokey, and once in town had pulled into a mechanic's yard, where she leaped out and swaggered around. She felt a need, though, for some chewing tobacco, so that climbing down from the cab she might turn loose some noisy, manly, comely spits.

The lone mechanic in the yard watched her, and what with Izzy's lustrous black hair, proud carriage, and fantastical adolescent grace, he thought she looked like a woman who might have visions that would scare the bejesus out of people. The mechanic, a Shoshone medicine man wearing a bear claw necklace, knew a spirit-traveler when he saw one. It made him want to party.

Drawn by the wilderness in the man, the whole party of them followed Izzy over to the mechanic, whose name was Antelope on the Moon.

Antelope was a good mechanic; in fact, he loved machines. At least the Anglos had brought the pickup truck into the world. Problem was, figured Antelope, the pickup was about all they brought that counted. Besides that, all they had done was slobber together a culture that worked like a kind of animated dog vomit.

Just at the moment, however, he found himself surrounded by a group who looked crazed by the story they were making—and this, even though they were just getting started.

They all looked at him.

"We've decided!" said Izzy with intemperate finality.

"Let me draw out the meaning of my daughter's statement," offered Chiara.

"Let's go inside," said Antelope, gesturing to the big cool tin shed, clamorous with shadows, that stood in his yard. The Antelope thought they should talk in the shade, lounging around, rather than melting under the sun like so many dumplings.

Once inside, Chiara sat down by the side of the Shoshone, and the whole company paused to watch them there: Night by the side of Antelope. All the shadows in the room rushed to them and pooled around, strange and soothing. Antelope looked around at all of them: at Chiara, at Muscovado, at the lot. All of a sudden he felt acutely how long he had gone without a good tirade.

"So what is this," he asked, "the odyssey of the racially mixed Americanos? Are we all posing for some goddam soap advertisement in Happy-Go-Lucky America? Are you going to bring out a gun, tote it around, and kill something in a let-'er-rip, feel-good frenzy? Are you come to explain the 'snuff the world for God' routine?" Antelope smiled. He felt in an exceptionally good mood.

Somebody had to reply, and so Juha stood up and made some earthquake noises. Cookie smiled. She loved the baritone. For all her escapades, Juha was her first real baritone. It changed everything, and very amusingly. Juha's pleasure seemed to come from deep in the earth. It was not just ejaculation—it was more like some sulfurous fumarole going off.

Muscovado was thinking maybe he would fly around the room, and show this haughty Indian a thing or two.

"One of us is learning to fly," said Antelope on the Moon, "that's the reason I let you in here."

Ananda looked around at the greasy shop.

"I don't think you're ready for a public offering," she said briskly. "But if you're ever seeking representation, I'll be happy to take you on as a client. You don't even have to go on the waiting list. You're one lucky Indian," she said, smiling.

"Could you come sit over here?" asked Antelope, and Ananda did, throwing from the motions of her hair a lazy lightning across the room.

And so Antelope, surrounded by Day and Night, found himself in storytelling country: in dusk.

Seeing him there, Renato understood why all day he had felt so dreamy—it was that, sitting between those two women, a man's thoughts moved full of the lavender proclamations of twilight.

Muscovado and Izzy sat arm in arm, her black hair spilling over his black skin. Cookie leaned back in the gigantic arms of Juha. And Antelope lit a cigarette and began to tell

THE STORY OF COYOTE FINDING HIS WAY INSIDE THE WORLD

"Once there was a coyote who could not find his way in the world, even though coyotes are full of spirits. Now, this animal lived the life of the desert, killin' rabbits, stalkin' mice and downin' 'em at a single gulp, and racin' around like a sidekick of the wind. But he didn't want to be just a sidekick—he wanted to marry the wind, to be like her—to *be* her."

Antelope paused to take a few drags, and he reached below the workbench and brought out a flask of whiskey, from which he took a generous swig. Chiara and Ananda both reached for the flask at once, but Antelope, grinning, capped it and slipped it into his pants.

"And so Coyote spoke to the wind. He said, 'Wind, sister that you are, help me, do not leave me on the ground my whole life.' And the wind whistled around Coyote, and in it he thought he heard instructions, he thought he heard about a future.

"And so Coyote started to run with the wind, changin' his pace, slowin' down in the dawn for the slightest of breezes out of the east, burstin' through little canyons in the heat of the afternoon to the beat of the zephyrs in the big cottonwoods. All over the desert he ran, he ran wild, charged up with midnight storms; he ran light, so that up on the buttes he didn't put any more pressure on the ground than would footprints of air."

Antelope paused again for swigs and a long drag; his smoke

drifted, a slick blue in the slanting light from the window. He looked around. The heat of the sun, showing on the tin roof, made madcap little waves in the air. Juha had folded up Cookie in his massive frame. But the rest of them were watching Antelope so closely that he knew they really did want a story to eat.

"But still Coyote was sad—he could run with the wind, but he was still on the ground. And so he went to listen again for messages in the air; he thought he heard something, and sure enough he started to learn words from the wind: down in the draws where he had his den, he hummed like air comin' over the playas; up in the foothills of the Basin ranges he called with a rough-brushy sound the wind has when it moves in aspen; and up top, on the rimrock he turned loose a howl like a racin' of wind over bare rock.

"But though he could move like the wind, and talk in the voice of the wind, still: Coyote was himself."

Antelope stopped; Muscovado and Izzy moved their bench nearer to him, and Izzy had her arm around the wiry Jamaican. The shadows in the room swirled around them. Juha carried Cookie over in front of Antelope, sat down on the floor, leaned against a bench, and enfolded the cowgirl once again in his arms like oak branches. Our storyteller could feel the pressure of Ananda and Chiara on either side of him.

All things taken together, in fact, it seemed to Antelope on the Moon that this squad of crazy Americans were gathering round to devour him.

"What a bunch!" he said.

"Your whiskey or your story—what'll it be?" inquired Chiara in a sugary menacing way.

Antelope thought it over.

"And so Coyote went for a third time to listen under the stars for what the wind would tell him, and what he heard made him sad; the wind told him that to go any farther he would have to stop being a coyote at all. Now, this was news to him. After all, he was damn good at being a coyote. Otherwise, why in tarnation would people be telling stories about him all over the West? Why else would he have such a reputation as a wily character, who knew what to do about anything? And so Coyote went to kill a rabbit and then on to his den to have a long dinner and to think it all over.

"He thought and thought—but anybody knows that thinking is not enough. Chew all you want, your cud is still your cud. So Coyote did the obvious thing: he decided to go visit the wind in her own house. Question was, how to find the house; answer is, everybody, even the wind, has to go home sooner or later.

"And so the next morning Coyote set out, followin' the dawn breeze, for the House of the Winds. He padded after the air that moved down the sides of canyon walls. He loped after the noon gusts sweepin' up whirligigs from the alkali of the Basin; bounded after the currents that flowed out of the centers of storms, shot down from the high ranges with winds that carry the evenin' away. Day after day he traveled, night after night, through badlands and forest, through open plains and over the glitterin' mountains, until by stark wild wanderin' up a valley and then to the top of an unmapped side canyon, back in his own territory by a little stand of cottonwood he came to the House of the Winds."

Izzy, taking her hands off Muscovado, leaned forward and broke in on Antelope's story: "What did he see? Tell us, what did he see?"

Antelope didn't say anything, he just reached in his pants to get his flask, and glugged a few shots. He looked around in a satisfied way.

"It's hard to finish this story; now I guess I just can't quite remember what it was that happened next. Why, I'll just have to have me a think. Why, I jes' may be sitting here for a spell. A long spell," he said, grinning.

Ananda, who had seen it all before, reached into her pocket and took out a crisp twenty-dollar bill. Folding it into a paper airplane, she let it fly out in mad loop-the-loops around the room, until it fluttered down in Antelope's lap.

Antelope looked at the bill. "What is this, a rummage sale? Are we talkin' a going-out-of-business sale of the animal gods? Are you nuts?"

Ananda, who was treasurer, was able with different aerodynamic designs to launch and land two more bills, and so Antelope on the Moon was able to recover his memory. Financiers should take note: such are the uses of investment banking, once self-interest is really paramount.

Antelope sighed at the perversity of the world, and was happy.

"The House of the Winds was titanic; all the winds of the world, all the winds of the past and future, lived there in a little room, sometimes with a deep whisper like velvet, sometimes with a noise like a tearin' of the sky to pieces. And Coyote stopped short. Maybe he shouldn't go in without knocking, he thought—even though it seemed that somehow he knew the place.

"And so he knocked, and said, " 'It's Coyote, and I want to be one of you!'

" 'Go away and don't come back!' said the Winds.

" 'I have come all this way,' complained the Coyote.

" 'You coyotes are too tricky for your own good,' said the voice of the House of the Winds.

" 'I know for sure I'm trickier than the wind!' said Coyote in his smart-alecky way.

" 'You think that after you come in and we make you Wind, that you will still be Coyote and do what you want, and keep your coyote tricks.'

" 'You bet I will!' said Coyote.

"The House of the Winds spun in the brightness of its powers, and it said, 'Once you visit us, and become a coyote with a will of wind, then you must go on, you have no choice, to visit the House of Great Waters, and then the House of Light. And then what will you do, poor wily Coyote?'

"And the House shut its door tight.

"Coyote thought this over. This was getting complicated. Great Waters and Light? He called out, 'Winds, hear me! I give up! I'm going now! Who needs a blowhard like you anyway!' And Coyote ambled off down the canyon."

Antelope stood up.

"He did not amble for long, however. For when he was just far enough away—just at sprintin' distance—he turned and took off as fast as he could for the door of the House of the Winds, and with all the speed he had from his wandering, with all the speed of his wily coyote soul he burst through the door—burst through into the regions of wild air—"

Antelope took one more swig. Renato was staring at him wide-eyed. No one said a word. In the garage the shadows and the sunshine mixed strangely, as though the one had broken through to the other, and there was a mingling of waves.

"—So Coyote was going as fast as he could into the heart of the house. And now you are gonna ask, did Coyote learn the secrets of air? If he did, was he still a coyote? Did he come back to fly over the earth like the wind? And if he could fly, is he here to teach us all his secrets? Or did he pass on over the planet to the House of Great Waters, did he travel over the world asking his way to the House of Light? And what would he find in these places? Can we follow him?"

There was a scratching outside the door of the garage. Muscovado stood up, Ananda looked around, Renato drew closer in.

"Was Coyote torn apart by the winds? Or is he even now among us?"

There was a rustling and then a growling all along the tin walls of the garage.

Juha stood up, his fists clenched.

"And if he is back, is he hungry? What is the hunger that will take you to the House of the Winds? What is the hunger that will take you to the House of Great Waters?"

The walls of the building shook with the force outside, there was a slamming against the tin. Renato rose and went to the side of Ananda.

"What is the hunger that will take you to the House of Light?"

The garage swirled with darkness.

They could all hear the howling.

"He did come back! He did come back! And now you can all just get the hell out of my garage. Out! Now! Get out!"

Antelope stood up. Everyone was on their feet. Juha stalked around, he picked up a crowbar and hefted it in his big hands.

Muscovado was staring at the Indian, and looking around wildly. The tin walls of the garage were buckling, there was a roaring in the air. Chiara and Ananda looked at each other, they stepped close together for a whispered consultation, Renato all at once was by their side—

The door of the garage was thrown violently open.

AND THROUGH the door shuffled Slim Blackburn, from the Bar-S-Triple Looper Ranch.

"Antelope," he said, "I reckon you've 'bout got the transmission done in my pickup. Where is the damn thing?"

"I've got it round back," said Antelope amiably.

Slim glanced around at the company. "Who's the big gorilla with the crowbar?" he asked, looking dubiously at Juha.

"Now these is jes' some folks that stopped by for a little chat," said Antelope, smiling.

"A chat? With you?" Slim laughed. "You poor bastards, the last one to try that was my little old grandmother from the Triple Looper, and she went out of here cackling like a chicken. Even laid eggs for three weeks. Big ones, too." Slim hacked and spit and grinned himself.

"Poor bastards," he said, shaking his head. "Course then there's you ladies. Would you like a ride in the pickup of a lonesome cowboy?"

"Only," replied the recovered Chiara, "if we can drag you behind, like a sack of manure."

Angelica didn't mind Tabby and Grimes. They paid her triple, sometimes more. They showered for her at the weight room. They told her she was beautiful, that they were going to protect her. They told her they loved her, that was the funniest part. But at least they were young, not like those rich fat ones with the pig snouts.

Besides, she knew the money came from the church—this was not just a job, this was religious, like prayer or something.

Tabby and Grimes were three days a week. Ben was still three times a week. A couple more weeklies like them, she'd have a schedule. Regular hours and everything.

She looked at the boys. She liked the way they waited for her, how they thought they were on her side, that they were rescuing her. It was cute. Hating them was different from hating her other johns; these kids charmed her. She never fantasized about killing them. She wanted to see what they were going to do.

It was a cinch, with all their bullshit, that someone was going to make a mess of them.

"We're heroes, aren't we?" asked Tabby, who, red in the face and sweating, was doing a post-fuck turn in the mirror, studying his profile in pink and blue flarings of the neon lights from the street.

Angelica looked at the two of them, bulked out more every month. She looked around at the walls hung with rifles, the cases full of pistols and scopes and knives and ammunition, at the stacks of comic books with their flaming covers—death-rays streaming, whole planets brushed out of existence; she watched Grimes doing tricks with a long-barreled revolver, just for her, spinning it round his waist, through his legs. He struck poses with shotguns and automatic rifles; then he brought big polished knives over to her, and held them up so she could see her face reflected. He wiped the gun barrels along her leg, high up—

"These guns will never be cleaned so good," exclaimed Grimes. The twenty-dollar bills were fanned on the counter.

"You're heroes," she said. "Superheroes."

Our pilgrims drove west out of town, and then went up a dirt road toward the headwaters of the Reese River.

"Remember," Antelope had said when they were leaving, "the coyote went one house at a time. Take it easy. Don't get impulsive."

Now the lot of them sat lounging in the shade of the Toiyabe Mountains.

"Well, it's working so far," said Izzy in her daft sure young naiveté.

Ananda and Chiara had been talking all the way out of town. The women found that ideas moved very tastily between them, as though they were handing back and forth ripe, full-to-bursting grapes.

More than that: they were used to being in command, Ananda from her running the high-pressure day-after-day drafting of thousands of pages of arcane details, her ballistic symphony of money and power. And Chiara, she of the astounding legion of inamorati: in the academy she had taught everyone. It was not just the sibylline stars left in the heads of some of her students; it was the bedazzlement of her colleagues, who followed where in her savory indisputable workings she led them.

Ananda and Chiara called the group together, there in the folds of the Toiyabes, by the headwaters of a desert river, in view of conifers soft with dustings of pollen. They were in a little valley, a pocket formed by a branching of the big range, so that mountains held them close, and the pine and rock handed them down a protected hour.

The other five of our bedraggled party assembled in front of the outlandish truck, and attended to the striding, thoughtful women.

"First of all," led off Ananda, "you pack of coyotes—"

"Wait a minute, whoa, hold on just a second, you lost me already," said Muscovado, who had fully expected they were going to be eaten alive.

"Coyote took a chance, went on a hunt, which led on to another hunt. We took a chance, and got from Antelope a story. And now we know what to do—"

"OK, what?" asked Izzy in a rush.

"Keep on driving, and everywhere we go, find ourselves another story," said Chiara, her black hair incandescent in the light.

Renato was laughing. "So I guess now we really *have* to stay on the road," he said, "unless this is getting too weird already for us, and we should just forget it—"

"No chance," said Muscovado, who still had the opalescent Izzy by his side. Such was his desire, that it felt almost like courage. He went on: "You can't take an island out of the sea. You can't take this group out of their truck and wagon."

They all looked dubiously at the truck with its tiny perched Victorian house, its bright hues and gingerbread ornament, its peephole windows, stubby chimney. To everyone's surprise, this truck-bed demesne had survived its initial foray down the highway; it did not, however, look any more likely.

And they all looked suspiciously at the station wagon, its back crammed full of clothes. The old car listed to one side. The side panels were uneven. The headlights were cracked. The back windshield had a bullet hole, with the usual sidereal radiations. Even with Renato's last minute paint job, the car looked like it had been bombed and strafed.

"It's like the beauty and the beast," said Izzy.

Everyone looked at Cookie and Juha. Juha blushed.

"Well, at least we know where we're headed," said Chiara.

"Oh my yes," said Muscovado, gazing at Izzy.

Cookie was kissing Juha again. "You're no ordinary bohunk," she said, "and your syrup, I betcha, is going to get even sweeter. I'm warnin' ya, though, I'll have to resort to the old taste test to make sure."

Juha thought of their volcanic pleasures, and wondered idly whether on the way to the ocean his rocky body might, by a sort of geologic imperative, just turn to magma and ooze away.

"So we'll just keep on going to the Lost Coast, what a deal," said Izzy, who had never seen the Pacific Ocean.

"Of course we will," said Ananda, who had unbound her blond hair and so had a sunlit waterfall running down her back. "The question is, how we get there."

"OK, OK, so what do we do?" asked Juha, bulky with impatience.

"Everywhere we go, we get directions," said Chiara.

"Directions?" they all cried skeptically.

"I know it will work. There has to be somebody who knows the way. Dante had Virgil to show him around—we've got Shoshone auto mechanics."

"We're going to *need* mechanics," said Juha with another glance at the wagon.

Chiara went on. "You know, in the academy, you hear a lot about the laws of nature. The great symmetries and regularities of the world. But what if it's all hokum? What if"—she waved her hand—"it all moves, day after day, by improvisation?"

"In other words," said Ananda, "it's going to work."

"We already knew that," said Izzy.

"This is a hungry bunch!" said Chiara.

"I think I get the idea," said Cookie with satisfaction.

"We're going to have stories to eat!" Chiara was on a roll.

"I think you've cracked up," said the fragrant Izzy.

"Just you wait," said Chiara, winking at her daughter.

And, as though to confirm their improvisational strategy, a shot rang out.

Finally having caught up with errant child and mother, the long-lost private detectives hired by two self-appointed fathers of Izzy had been watching from a hilltop overlooking the valley. They hated Nevada. So dry, so inhospitable, so primitive. They were hot. They needed a shower. They were mad. And so they had aimed and fired their rifles, fitted for the occasion with tele-scopic sights. And while the bullets are on their way, let us re-view how these two pieces of good citizenry met.

—In Denver by accident: in a bowling alley, where the two of them had repaired for a little recreation, to soothe their abraded, bleeding, ordinary souls. Michelas Perkin and Jebediah Elmer were their names, and they had, like most of us, loved—but maybe not learned. This had led to lives of haughty complacent posturing, such as would make one more modern novel, chock-full of psychological rumination.

In any case, Mike and Jeb, on adjacent lanes, in the way of men fell into grunty conversation and discovered they both liked fly fishing and skeet shooting and duck hunting and power boat-ing; and, further, after throwing simultaneous strikes and down-ing a sixer together they found they had been hired to pursue the same two women, the infamous Chiara and Izzy. And, more-over, hired by jilted professors who, Mike and Jeb agreed, ranked on the evolutionary scale somewhere behind goat snot. What, being jilted was so tough? It was happening more and more often. So many sovereign women around. Everything was out of kilter. There was a general feeling of teetering to the world. His-tory was on the blink. Soon the planet would be jarred from its orbit.

But it was a living.

And then and there, Mike and Jeb resolved to join forces, run up the bill for the two stupid academics, and make those two sassy bitches rue the day they went on the road.

To get back to the bullet: they had taken it into their heads to whiz a few bullets by the shimmering Izzy, to make her real-ize that the world was keeping track, and was not about to let her go sauntering off without the traditional discouragements, punishments, and humbug. Just as they were aiming, they heard a flapping of wings, and, looking up, what should they see but an astounding brandy-and-sunset-colored eagle. Now, we all have our responsibilities; but who could resist the chance to blow an eagle out of the sky?

They both lifted their rifles and fired.

Down in the valley, the whole lot of them looked up—idiotically, as though to catch a bullet in the face. But it meant that they also saw the eagle. Only Chiara noted that there was something about the bird that reminded her of Antelope on the Moon.

Of course it *was* Antelope on the Moon: he was a shapeshifter who could take on any animal form, and had flown out from his garage to distract the dear venal detectives. Mike and Jeb, forgetting all about Izzy and her compatriots, got off a few more rounds. The bullets went right through the phantom body of the eagle, stupefying our investigators. They watched as he circled, and in the fullness of his powers, with the inevitability of a sacrament, calling coarsely, dark against the sky, the giant bird swooped low over them and plumped some shit right down on their heads.

This incident marked the first time in Great Basin history that an Indian sorcerer had made a strategic elimination in favor of such newly joined pilgrims. It must have been the charm of their bumbling metaphysical efforts.

Not long afterward, anyone who was looking in Austin, Nevada, would have seen an eagle alight near the big mechanic's shed, and then from behind the shed the old familiar mechanic walk out and set to work on a ranch pickup. Just near the truck, the required tools were laid out, since Antelope had everything arranged so that all necessary work could get done. We might speculate, then, that the whole world might be repaired by one Shoshone auto mechanic, if only the machinery of civilization would offer itself to his ministrations.

But, of course, no one was looking. And so no such speculations were heard. And no such offer has yet been made.

That night, out in the Reese River Valley, in the folds of the Toiyabe Mountains, our seven fools, our seven beauties built a campfire. The fire settled their spirits, in accordance with the ancient maxim: When things get strange, stay warm.

The whole desert held Renato's desire, as he took a cloak of firelight and drew it around Chiara and Ananda; as he took the golden cloak and passed round them a shining that he had in his hands, that held his hunger to have them in his sight.

The two women sat close, talking; the mountains glided near, to listen.

"I feel like we're being sought out," said Chiara, grinning. She had experience in this field. "Maybe we'll see our names written in air by the smoke of this fire."

"Only if we've got smoke in our eyes," said the practical Ananda.

"Don't be such a worldly bitch," said Chiara. "You can take two companies and with a thousand pages of contracts merge them together—but nothing is possible for us, no way. We cannot merge this world and the next, body and soul, what we see and how we love; no, we have to live out our stupid lives—"

But they were distracted by the fleshy splendor of Cookie and Juha on their way to the truck. They walked casually, yet like the recently enamored all over the world, sure in their sense of lucky inevitability.

"Nighty-night," said Renato.

"Renato," said Juha with a big smile, "it's a long way to the Lost Coast."

"It's not so far to the truck, though," said Renato.

But Juha could not hear him because in the shadows just outside the ring of firelight, he was kissing Cookie, running his bear's hands through her hair, and, in a baritone such as we might hear from a grizzly bear, if grizzlies could murmur, telling her that his big heart was spinning like a pinwheel firework.

Of course, Cookie had heard it all before. But who can look askance at bear's hands?

"Not me," said Cookie in Juha's ear.

Juha took this as an endearment, and, throwing off sparks, spun her over toward the truck.

"Well," said Ananda, carrying on, looking at Chiara, "I'll go this far: in Los Angeles working late some nights; on those days when your mind works with a velocity not your own—like a sailboat running before a wind from another world—I thought, If even one work is possible, then all things are possible."

"In other words, it's just like we thought: touch and go," said Renato, as he memorized for a painting the wreathing by firelight of Chiara and Ananda.

"No doubt about it," said Chiara, glancing over at Muscovado and Izzy, who sauntered in from a promenade of the little valley.

"Courtship," announced Izzy, "is *amazing*. It's like building a dam you know you're going to blow up."

"Is that so, Muscovado?" called out Chiara.

"Oh my, oh my," said our poor smoldering Jamaican.

"It's nice, walking around the desert with your very own campfire by your side," added Izzy.

And, slim, sunburnt, dark, angular, artful; with dusky finesse and her ordinary light-stepping teenage acuity, Izzy came over to the fire, pressed her mother's cheek, brought Renato close for a full-length hug, embraced Ananda.

"Good night to all," she said brightly, as she went back to Muscovado. She leaned toward him. He leaned toward her. And she gave him a kiss on the end of his nose.

"Till tomorrow, kiddo," she said, and went off to bed.

Next morning, on Highway 50, a long asphalt sentence spoken by the desert, the intrepid band headed west. Sheets of morning light streamed from the truck and wagon. They had at first fan of dawn poured down some coffee boiled in the last of the fire, and now, at their places, they moved down the road with a fanatical contentment.

Also leaving that morning was a big shiny four-wheel drive, pulling a trailer ponderous with a weight of weapons and sporting equipment. Michelas and Jebediah, washed and dried, with the determination of spiffy professionals, were right behind them.

It was when they hit the Clan Alpine Range that Renato saw the coyote.

5

WITHOUT AN animal helper, no one gets anywhere. And coyotes understand humans: getting napalmed, blown to smithereens, gutted with cyanide, continuously over a hundred years
or so, these animals have cozy relations with our dear species.
And while such treatment can build up a certain grouchiness, it
had in their case simply perfected a mercurial bemusement natural to the coyote soul.

The coyote was standing by the side of the road, and when Izzy
slowed down, and Muscovado opened the door of the cab of the
truck, the coyote leaped in and took up the space between the
two of them. Behind them in the wagon, Ananda, Chiara, and
Renato watched as the truck gathered speed again.

"Is he the wind? Is he light?" speculated Renato.

"Maybe he's just hungry," said Chiara.

Thirty miles later, they all turned off and followed a dirt road
up into a little canyon that had a hidden stream and some cottonwoods, their branches full of buds leafing out in little deto-
nations.

Renato took from the back of the wagon his easel, his palette,
and oil paints, and set up under a cottonwood. Ananda and
Chiara were by his side. Musco and Iz sat near the tree with the

coyote. The animal moved restlessly between them. She had a quickness coiled in her limbs. She was rough with the two romantics, sniffing them, pawing them, barking. She moved around them with a ferocity of attention.

Renato began to paint them.

His painting became the first in a series that he made of the journey to the Lost Coast; these canvases, over the next hundred years, were always turning up. They would hang in barrooms, in whorehouses; they would be found on the walls of little churches in unvisited mountain towns, in basements and attics across the West. Seven of them eventually would hang in the National Gallery. One of them, even today, hangs in the penthouse of an international financier in Geneva. Another hangs in the kitchen of a night janitor in Cleveland.

They will have their collectors.

In the meantime, the rest of them considered how to describe the coyote.

She was raffish honey; she was stellar, unkempt; a useless scrawny desert survivor; she was sand, water, air, light, set together in sweetness; the chrestomathy of the desert; a simple dirty curious animal; the intelligence and wanderlust of the elements; she was a hungry canine, her gut lined with parasites; the sufferance and perfection of a continent.

Her eyes were golden, radiant—

Ananda, already flecked with road dust, liked the feeling of overall grittiness.

"Was this in the brochure?" she asked primly.

Up on a hillside once again, Mike and Jeb, in spanking new outdoor apparel and classy dark glasses, surveyed their victims. From the start, Chiara and Izzy had stumped them: and so they had scarcely been prepared for the five new cohorts. Now, as they looked through their binoculars down into the canyon, looked at the vibrant Ananda, at the desirable Chiara; at the stocky confident Cookie; as they looked at the young waist of Izzy, which gave them the feeling of turning whirlwinds; as they were trying to adjust, they found themselves staring straight into two golden eyes they did not recognize.

"Jesus!" exclaimed Mike.

"What the hell is that?" whispered Jeb grittily.

"They've got some goddam animal with 'em! It's a coyote! Don't they know the danger?"

"What else is happening?" insisted Mike.

"The girl is still with the spade!"

"Maybe I should shoot the coyote?" asked Mike.

"Idiot! Look what happened last time! Nevada's too weird. We don't know what might happen. Wait till we get to California. I've done some hunting trips there—it's no problem shooting things. Everything's cool."

Down in the canyon, the coyote heard them, and not just what they said; coyotes hear what humans think. But none of it mattered to her; she had her plans, and so commenced those events they all one day would tell as

THE STORY OF COYOTE COMING TO GIVE AWAY HER VISION

The animal turned on them: turned on them all, bearing down first on Chiara, scoring her arm with a dragging bite; then, whipping around, jumped snarling at Ananda, lunging at her face, turning from there to rush at Juha, snapping at him, darting in and then dodging as Juha kicked at her.

The camp was in a turmoil. Up on the ridge, Mike and Jeb were frantic. Cookie, who had run to the truck, stepped out of the back with a pistol. Renato continued painting as if nothing had happened or ever would happen.

Muscovado had taken Izzy in his arms and now shifted her back around, keeping himself between her and the coyote, but the animal cut in and knocked him off his feet, Izzy went down with him and then rolled away, the coyote pounced on her. Izzy scrambled to her feet and the coyote, barking and lunging, started driving her up the canyon. Cookie aimed her gun, but she couldn't fire without risking a hit on Iz, Muscovado leaped up and went after the two of them, Chiara was by him but the coyote had Izzy in full flight, they were running up the streambed with the animal driving the girl, nipping and worrying her legs, moving fast up the slope of the canyon they were together now; everyone else was left behind and the coyote and Izzy were running side by side kicking up dust and as long as she was going hard the coyote did not threaten her, Izzy was breathing hard and she was going as quick as she could flying up to the head of the canyon as the coyote brushed her legs, moving in and out of her stride, she could feel the tawny fur, there was a sighing in the air, the coyote pressing against her . . . Around a bend in the streambed the two of them disappeared.

When they finally found their way up along the rocky ground, Muscovado and Chiara found Izzy at the head of the canyon, alone, on her back, an arm over her face. She looked asleep.

Now Chiara had been scared in her life, by the grotesque hatred of jilted lovers; and Muscovado had been terrorized working on a story about the drug trade in Miami, cornered there by unhappy men who made him stand against a wall for twenty minutes with a sawed-off shotgun crammed into his mouth while they talked about finger-painting with his brains—

But neither Musco nor Chiara had ever been scared as they were when Izzy, stirring in their arms, came to, sat up, and looked at them both steadily, steadily: looked with radiant golden coyote eyes. More than radiant: it was as though her eyes had so much opened, that her soul could look directly upon the world.

The gold flared for a moment; then, as they watched, her natural opals were restored.

Izzy was not scared. She glanced around, sprang onto her feet, and headed down the streambed to the rest of the group. And it was as though Musco and Chiara had been ravished by the animal—they leaned on each other, and followed Iz back to the rest of the party.

Renato, who had not moved, added to his palette some bright sharp gold.

Izzy didn't say anything, but she wouldn't be still, either. She walked around to each of the travelers, lingered, stood silently, watched the walls of the canyon; she went over to her mother and helped Cookie clean and bandage up the tear-marks left across Chiara's arm from the teeth of the coyote; and, once bound up, Chiara stood and took Izzy off to the side of the camp, where they sat down, sitting close against each other, against the trunk of a cottonwood. All of them were silent.

The only sound for hours was the gliding of brush and oil as Renato worked at his canvas.

It was as Renato was putting away his oils that Izzy walked up to him to see what he had rendered. Lighting the canvas, she looked long, and longingly, at the scene: Musco leaning toward her and whispering, herself watching him with a kind of feral detached desire, and the coyote between them arching around Izzy's waist, the animal's head above her lap, looking straight up at her.

"Well," she said musingly, "it looks like somebody's in love, all right." And she burst out laughing.

Ananda came up to see the painting, and, after several minutes of gazing, she took Renato's arm. "We can't just go to bed for old times' sake."

"Why the hell not?" asked Renato, cleaning his brushes.

"Wouldn't that be a little sentimental and rustic?"

"You? Sentimental and rustic?"

Ananda looked at the painting, and at Renato. "Do you know what's happening to us?"

Renato looked away, then back. "We're telling all our stories to the end."

Ananda leaned toward him and kissed him on the cheeks, on his brow, lightly on his mouth.

She stepped back.

"Just presume I have my brushes ready," he said.

*   *   *

Up on the hill, Mike and Jeb were feeling lonely.

Izzy had finally gone over and sat down by Muscovado Taine; Musco felt unaccountably nervous, which was natural enough: everyone wondered what Iz could see.

Coyotes, of course, can see the way home.

For the rest of Izzy's life, the gold would come into her eyes when her soul was on the move. And who would want such a thing? Amid the wind and water and light of the world—what's in it for a girl?

Izzy learned how to use what her soul could see to remake her eyes from within; just as later, our travelers learned how to use the little stories they found to remake the long story they lived.

And besides, it was easier for her to read at night.

Ananda, Chiara, and Renato were preparing to get back into the wagon and hit the road.

And, once on the road, they took the lead. Juha, Cookie, and Muscovado sat in the front of the truck and followed them down the road. Izzy was by herself in the house, listening to the wind play its earthly and unearthly music, as the diesel of the big truck marked out its bass accompaniment. Izzy felt terrific.

"Do you think that clairvoyance is natural to adolescents?" asked Chiara across the seat to Ananda, as they sped down the road.

"I think—and this is a recent opinion—that clairvoyance is natural to all of us; but that in an adolescent it would take on a raw, peculiar, ecstatic form."

"Just like everything else about Izzy," sighed Chiara. "But at the same time, Ananda, it just doesn't add up. What's going on?"

And, up ahead, Juha in the truck said, "Yeah, what *is* going on, anyway?"

"Oh c'mon, Juha, you should just ask Muscovado there," said Cookie, smiling.

Musco hadn't said a word since Izzy had gone off with the coyote. Even now, as he spoke, he did not turn to Cookie and Juha.

"Yeah, well, I thought I was coming out to Nevada to be by myself and shoot the breeze and walk around and get to know the misfits out here, and what are we doing now? What? I make a joke to a sixteen-year-old in a bar, and pretty soon I'm cooing in the girl's ear, I'm talking like a fool in love, I started to mean what I said. That's when it gets dangerous, and before I know it I'm headed down the road with a pack of lunatics. And if that weren't enough she kisses me on the goddam nose, and then throws me over for a ratty desert dog, and then she comes over to me and she's shining at me, just shining—she's quick in the way she moves, in the way she looks at me. And I'm thinking, What is this? Do I have to worry about bites? God, let me worry. Do I have to howl at night? Give me the chance. Scratch with my hind foot? What the fuck next? Pups?"

Muscovado was shaking his head, but he was radiant.

"I am telling you, one of these days we're going to go around a curve and drive dead on through the gates of paradise and all the angels will be gathered round and then what will this smart-alecky bunch do? Do I revert to form? Play rasta-man then? Do I ask the way to JaJa? On my own I've got a clue, but all together?—it's seven stooges in heaven. I'm telling you, we've got to have a gig ready. What if this is the gig that counts? Even the jokes have to be sharp! Are you ready? For all of this? And why am I scared? I got some fear building, Ja or no Ja. But all the same it's bullshit, and this is a ratty bunch, and I just wish to hell somebody would say what's what."

"And so what's what, asshole?" inquired Cookie.

"I've never had such a good time," answered Muscovado, smiling.

And so, moving through a desert that moved through them, our confident party motored west, and with no more interventions from the animals of the seething and interested invisible world they pulled into Fallon, Nevada. And what should they see on the way into town, perched on a ricky-ticky foundation, and with small-pane windows, nicked and soiled: a bar, the Double Eagle.

Cookie, driving the truck, pulled right over.

"*Another* bar?" asked Juha.

"It's twilight, it's a bar: I just want us to go in, for old times' sake. After all," she said, gesturing grandly about, "that's where it all started."

The grumbling but thirsty Juha got down from the truck, the wagon pulled in behind them, and they milled around together, swirling there as though they were meeting in the middle of the sky.

In the Double Eagle, sure enough, a mangy bartender named Stumper served up some shots, some beers, some tequila; he popped some cigarettes from his pack and offered them around; he hemmed, hawed, barked; he sized them up, clapped a few bugs out of the air and wiped them on his pants.

In other words, things were looking up.

"Are you going to tell us a story, or not?" asked the impetuous Izzy.

"You betcha," he said, and he leaned back with his arms crossed and spat a few times.

Was there some gold in his eyes? Hell, no, absolutely no gold—his eyes were brown as tobacco plugs.

"I want to tell you fools the

STORY OF PEGGY-SUE, THE LITTLE DEEF-MUTE

he said in his country drawl.

"Sounds fascinating; it's just what we need, a goddam hard-luck story," said Cookie with wholehearted contempt.

"Now this little Peggy-Sue," said Stumper, undeterred, "she was jes' a tiny girl and when she started in grade school, doing that 'rithmetic and spellin' and all the other picayune things they do there in the little schools, it jes' flabbergasted her, she jes' walked round and round in big circles, stopping every now and then sayin' *whoo-whoo* like a choo-chee train. That threw everybody into a tizzy. But she had to do it that way 'cause she didn't talk a lick. She was jes' a mumble-jumble of a kid, real irritatin'! An' so they plunked her down in the deef-n-dumb class; in there they did one thing at a time, jes' takin' it day by day, an' they was off by themselves."

Stumper paused to chew up a cigarette butt.

"Now this is a smart little girl!" exclaimed Chiara.

"You betcha," threw in Cookie. "Ya know there's a real true advantage in bein' shunted aside like a potato-shavin', and that's this: nobody pays you no attention. That Peggy-Sue, she weren't weighed down with a shitload of attentions."

"Now who is tellin' this goddam story, anyway?" broke in Stumper.

"We'll let you go on for a while," said Chiara with incivility.

"Goddam yackety-yak females," grumbled Stumper—but he took up the narrative again:

"She went about doing what she wanted to do, our little Peggy-Sue. She sat round with words and her spellin' and 'rithmetic, all until she was satisfied. The deef-mute teachers could tell she was satisfied, because she would make little gurgle-gurgle noises. She spent about ten-twelve years gurglin' an' bubblin' her way through the grades. They would shake their heads over her an' say, Oh—we're so sorry sorry, by which they meant, How did we get saddled with this little bitch? Can't we call the plumber or somethin'?"

Stumper grabbed three shot glasses and, in the tradition of bartenders everywhere, made ready to break into a mad juggling act. In his genius, though, he added a significant twist: he leaned over and tooted on a harmonica welded to the end of a length of rebar bolted to the bartop. He juggled, he tooted, he stopped, he bowed. His audience was silent as so many stones.

Stumper resumed his story. "So it was this Peggy-Sue grew the hell up—"

"That was fast," threw in Cookie sarcastically.

"Puberty gives a girl wings, I guess," added Chiara.

"Very funny," said Izzy.

"As I wuz sayin', she growed up, an' one day one of her teachers was thinking she was thirsty, an' lookin' up there was Peggy-Sue standin' there with a glass of water. Now, Peg had done jes' fine learning things, real fine, more than anybody 'spected 'cause there was no way she could say one damn thing—you jes' couldn't get a rise out of her—you jes' put her work in front of her, and that was it, it was like puttin' out food in a trough. Still, she had this curious big-eyed way o' lookin' atcha. Like a cow.

"Now it's true that she could do a few other things besides read, write, and do numbers. Everybody saw one day when she crooked her finger at a pencil and the pencil went cartwheeling 'cross the room to her hand. And then they 'membered how she cured a sick horse by jes' butting her forehead real soft up against the big critter. Mebbe the animals felt sorry for the girl, little deef-n-dumb thing.

"Now, she was gettin' to be about sixteen or so, and everybody at the school got to thinkin' that it had been a right long time since they had seen her weird family. They all lived on an alfalfa ranch outside of town, toward the east, and the girl went home every night, OK, but we was all gettin' kinda suspicious. So's we followed her. And guess what? You won't believe it!"

"She went home and played the bagpipes all night," guessed Renato.

"She had been forced to make a meatloaf of her two brothers and she never got over the shock," hypothesized Muscovado. He had reported on a similar case in Boston.

"No! No! Wrong!" gloated Stumper, who opened another bottle of whiskey. He had a unique and stylish way of doing so: instead of turning the cap, he would manfully snap off the neck of the bottle on the edge of the bar. Problem was, he could not make this move without spewing alcohol everywhere. Most of our party, however, used to adversity, ducked behind the bar-counter, and thus avoided a drenching.

"I like to put a little sparkle in my work," he explained.

"So what the hell happened to Peggy-Sue?" growled Izzy.

"Well, I am glad you asked, you brazen thing," said Stumper, and he doffed his hat at her, revealing his hair arranged in clumps around his head like a nest of mice.

"We was all looking around the road that led into the ranch house, and they weren't growin' alfalfa; all we could see were miles and miles of ding-danged flowers! Dumb! Useless! Nothin' but flowers! An' then as we came to the house we could see the deef-mute girl sitting on the porch. So's we went up to see what was what. We weren't two steps from the house when Peggy-Sue stood up an' said, 'Ladies and gentlemen, I have been expecting you,' jes' like that!

" 'We thought you wuz deef-n-dumb!' we all cried.

" 'I don't talk,' she said, 'but that doesn't mean I can't talk.'

" 'And what happened to all the goddam alfalfa?' we asked.

"*Good* question," mocked Chiara. "First things first."

"Yep, you are a smart guy," added Cookie, "smart as toast."

But Stumper didn't care a plug for all these jibes.

"But this Peggy-Sue jes' kept talkin'! Amazin'! Like listenin' to a milk-cow talk, or somethin'. An' she said, 'My story, which in the interests of hospitality, I will tell you, is this: I always knew that there was something funny about my parents. About the age of five I figured it out. They weren't just people; they were angels. It's kind of like a second job.' "

Juha groaned. "Somehow I knew this was gonna turn into some high-falutin' thing. Angels! Now let's get weird. Angels! Shit!" he complained.

But Stumper was lit up now. "Then we knew the truth about Peg: she wasn't jes' dumb, she was crazy as a june-bug! An' she went right on talkin'! A june-bug, talkin'! An' she said—

" 'I, of course, in the way of children, wanted to imitate them, and begin an angelic education. They cautioned me not to, because I was so young. But I made them promise, and so they told me what to do.' "

"Now we all jes' gathered round to hear this june-bug carry on with this crock, I mean we gathered real close, this was promisin' to be some *blather*. I mean flimflam bullshit and bunkum—good bunkum too!

" 'My parents said that every place in the world is double, it has two locations—its place on earth, and its place in paradise.' "

"*Oh c'mon!* Paradise! Who needs it! Can't we get to something familiar, like cement or something?" interjected Juha.

"It's like the coyote," observed Chiara. "He wanted to be a coyote, and at the same time a creature of air."

"I'm tellin' ya what Peggy-Sue said!" yelled Stumper. "She jes' went on an' said, 'And wherever you are you can switch back and forth between paradise and earth, just by learning an angelic word. Now, this word is what the land tells you if you do a certain kind of work on it. And so my parents showed me what the work was, here in Fallon: planting flowers, all in a certain pattern, according to how it looks to the hawks, how it looks to the clouds, if it makes sense to the moon. And now it's spring, the flowers have bloomed. I'm ready to hear the word I need.'

"Now I was sittin' right there near to Peggy-Sue, an' I jes' had to ask a question. So I did—'Peggy-Sue,' I said, 'why didn't you tell us all this cockamamie bullshit before? We been thinkin' all this time you was deef-n-dumb!' "

"Excellent comment, very logical," said Ananda.

"Way to go, Stumper, you penetrate right to the main issue," added Chiara.

Stumper glared at them. "I'm tellin' you about one tricky girl, goddammit!"

"Please go on, Stumper. Peggy-Sue was saying exactly what?" prompted Muscovado, who as a journalist helplessly wanted to get the story.

Stumper went on: "Where was I? Oh, we all said, 'We thought you was deef-n-dumb! An' we took such good care of you! Tarnation!'

" 'It was part of my task,' answered Peggy-Sue. 'You can hear the word only if you are quiet, quiet in voice—and in your own thoughts. You have to listen. I haven't spoken because I have had to practice my listening. I learned this skill of keeping quiet, by listening to all of you. You have been my world. Every one of you. You are so dear to me.'

"Well, I said to myself, Old Stumper! by Jehoshaphat! If that weren't the bee's knees! And so's we fell to yakkin' about it among ourselves there, and we talked and talked, and then we all went home to chew on this one, and we were glad to see she weren't deef-an-dumb. She was wacko. I liked that."

"And how do you know she wasn't an angel?" demanded Izzy.

"Because, she came back to school the next day and she was talkin' like normal, and so's they took her out of the deef-mute class and put her in with the rest of the kids, and we didn't have no more trouble with her. End of story."

"And what happened to the ranch of flowers?" persisted Izzy.

"Well, we didn't go out there again—why the hell should we? She was cured. She jes' wanted to jabber that shit at us. So she did. Then she was cured. End of story." Stumper was looking a little desperate.

"If there's nothing to the story, why did you tell it?" asked Ananda.

"Why don't you shut up?" suggested Stumper.

"But that's just it: she didn't shut up," noted Izzy.

"And so: can she teach us how to make our way to the paradise of where we are?" inquired Ananda in her analytic way.

Stumper tried to fend them off. "Well, however you want to put it," he insisted. "At least we didn't have to worry about the girl no more, or run round the countryside like nut-cases to find out what in the blue moon was going on, or try to figure how to look after the damn girl, or waste time feelin' sorry for the little twat. It's progress! And so I say End of Story!" finished Stumper firmly.

But it was not an end, for at that moment, out of the darkening sky, through the door into their tumbledown lives walked Peggy-Sue herself.

6

PEG STOOD IN gnarly workboots with metal toeplates (the better to protect the feet from errant chainsaws), in dusty overalls, with a straw hat on her head and a blue bandanna knotted around her neck. In her gaze upon them was a delectation of wide-open spaces. She took the time to look at each of the seven travelers at length and independently; and then she pinned Stumper to the back of the bar with a blue-eyed stare that roared like a zephyr through the Double Eagle.

No one spoke; they had to wait for her—on the chance that a celestial injunction might be served up.

"How 'bout some chew, Stumper," Peggy-Sue said in her rough and bristling voice—a voice covered with tufts of sagebrush, shadscale, thistle.

Stumper spun a tin of chewing tobacco across the room, and in a single motion she snatched it from the air, thumbed off the lid, and dug out a moist fingerful to jam into her lower lip. And, so satiated, she turned her gaze once again on the wandering seven.

Izzy, though, felt like Peg deserved some explanation, just to kick things off.

"Well, who knows what we're doing?" she said. "They're all

mad as hatters and I don't know what a nice girl like me is doing with this barful of crackpots." She glanced at Muscovado. "Except of course Muscovado, here. Sister, I know what I'm doing with him."

Peggy-Sue smiled and then walked over to Musco and gave him an oh-so-slow once-over.

"Why not? We're adolescents, ain't we?"

"Hey, wait a minute," said the protesting Muscovado, "we're talking courtship here. Justice of the Peace. Devoted love enduring through the centuries. You put on the oath and take off your clothes, forever."

Izzy and Peggy-Sue, in some unspoken teenage agreement, got on either side of the smooth delighted Musco; each took an arm, and the three of them headed for the door. On the way out, Peg turned to say to the others:

"I'm taking you to the Ranch of Flowers."

Grimes switched the lights off.

The Bach—it was the Arioso, very beautiful—blasted through the shop, comic books all over the floor with all their heroes, the Avengers, the Nighthawk, the Guardians of the Galaxy, all of them fighting. The world was easy to figure out. The sonorous music made Tabby cry, they called Angelica sweetheart, they had her take off her clothes again, there in the middle of cases of knives she was illuminated by the neon from the street and the flash of the headlights, they stretched her out on the floor, they called her sweetcakes, they called her a princess, a love, a goddess, the strobe of headlights played over row after row of pistols, holsters, rifles, submachine guns, telescopic sights, boxes of cartridges. Grimes watched it all, it was so beautiful he wished he had some shots of it, kind of like starting a family album, he thought as they dragged her over in front of the mirrors, they made her look at herself, they called her a whore. They had her say over and over how much she loved being a whore.

Tabby told her that he knew she wasn't being treated right by Ben. He was going to avenge her. He was going to fuck her in front of Ben, and then the old man was going to get punished. Angelica could watch.

And so it was that in the middle of the Nevada desert, on the veranda of a ranch house inhabited only by a seventeen-year-old girl, our travelers found themselves in the eye of a quiet storm: a tempest of petals, colors, fragrances, in a pattern swirling around them—even, and especially, when there was no wind. They all gripped the railing to keep their feet in the levitating house, whose mass was lost in the lightness of the flowers.

As they swayed, Peggy-Sue, her plug of chew firm in her lip, gave them a midnight oratory: "No one will believe it, they are too godawful proud to believe: no one believes in angels. If they'd just take it for granted that angels schmooze around on earth, stopping every now and then to put their tongues in the honeysuckle, hit the bars, cook something up in garlic and butter—if this is all on the square, then even right here in Fallon we'll be forced to look again at our chances, no?"

"What happened to the country twang you had when you were talking to Stumper?" asked the wary and close-listening Chiara.

"Been deef-n'-dumb fer so many years, I growed up to have my choice o' any kind o' voice in all creation, woman," she replied smilingly.

"Please do carry on," acknowledged Chiara.

"If we can grow alfalfa, keep our dairy herds, if we can marry, carouse, grumble—if we can do all this, well then, maybe we could keep right on going, and see what else we could do. Why, it jes' makes a girl stop and think, don't it? It makes you want to sit up and open your peepers and look around a little, don't it? Gee willikers! Good golly! Land sakes!"

"Why is every one of these teenage girls so smart-alecky?" rumbled Juha in his bovine curiosity.

Both Izzy and Peggy-Sue, as though they were ancient sisters, bowed toward Juha in so charming and dismissive a way, that he felt like a blessed man.

"And so where are your parents, anyway?" asked Iz.

"You will all meet them later, further on your way to the Lost Coast," said Peg with an uncanny grin.

It was about this time that Juha went mad. He walked up to the porch railing, and the whole order of his life—its preconceptions, its conditions, its plans—scattered away through the high-desert darkness. And he found that it is a fine thing to watch one's life disperse and disintegrate in plain sight, with a glimmer and a flutter, there in the animate silence.

Two days on the road, he thought, and they were long gone into some world that had prescient wild animals and tobacco-sucking angels-in-training.

Juha, tall, with his massive shoulders facing square onto the night, with his large rough hands on the railing, stood with an empty open heart whose beating rocked his frame. At least he had one thing to go on: the brazen arm of Cookie, which she draped around his waist as she joined him.

"Cookie!" he began.

The flowers all moved in the moonlight toward them.

Over on the other side of the porch, Peggy-Sue and the rest stood talking, and the spring fragrance of the flowers flooded into the air; across the fields it came to wrap their limbs in sweet stoles; and all this alerted Chiara to her sharply considered, lightly carried burden of maternal care. And so while Izzy was laughing and enraptured with Peggy-Sue, Chiara took Muscovado by the hand, led him off the porch, and proceeded with him along the tractor roads that set borders to the fields of flowers.

Muscovado, as the flowers swayed around them, had a heavy sense of ritual.

Renato sat with Ananda, whose hair had become the focus of all the moonlight in the world.

"I can't say it really surprises me," said Renato.

"You've been painting too long," said Ananda.

The world of the Securities and Exchange Commission, of offering prospectuses, audited financial statements, capital plans, stock purchase agreements—why, here with a budding angel at a ranch of flowers, it all seemed a trifle distant. But there was one constant, which, for Ananda, made everything simpler: at that moment, Tupelo jumped into her lap.

"The world of Peggy-Sue is the world you have when you put all the good paintings of the world together; they come together in a combustion that extends this world into the next."

"You don't talk much, Renato, but your mouth is full of sweet things."

"If I might just go nibbling?" he asked.

"All my work, just to get back to you?" she mused.

"You lawyers are always asking rhetorical questions," he sassed.

"How did you get to be so strange?" she asked.

"It started when I was a teenager. I looked around and I couldn't tell for the life of me what everybody thought they were doing. Adult life looked like hell to me. It was as though everyone had decided to spend seventy years slowly roasting themselves to death. Life as a meal for each other, a meal of the damned. This being my view, I was not eager to, say, pursue higher education and an active social life."

"Well, well, what might happen if I decided to bring my skills in mergers and acquisitions to your body?" said Ananda.

"I intend to paint your portrait, you and Tupelo, there as you sit on this veranda in a surround of flowers," he said as he took out his easel.

At the other end of the porch, Izzy and Peggy-Sue chattered on.

"But I *like* talking, it lets you get off some zingers," Iz protested.

"It's the shits," opined Peggy-Sue, "everybody barking the same thing: a frog circus."

"But you can do comebackers, you can piss them off," insisted Izzy with gusto.

"Yeah, but I got to listen to them zing themselves," replied Peg. "My biology teacher, sure I couldn't hear a thing, used to come and tell me how he and his wife make believe in bed they're different kinds of animals—you know, horses, wolves, the whole shebang. You can imagine the racket! The details! But I blew it by busting out laughing about the iguana."

"No!"

"I'm telling you, big leathery iguanas!"

"They didn't do insects, did they?"

"No kidding! They had a trapeze in their bedroom!"

As they talked, Juha, who had picked up Cookie as though she were no more than an almond, walked by in an energetic sweaty way.

"Down the hall, last room on the right," called out Peggy-Sue, and she turned back to Izzy. "How am I doing so far as a hostess?"

"You're dynamite," said Iz. "But what is an angel doing sending off people to fornicate?"

"I'm just an angel in training," she said modestly.

"It's tough being sullen teenagers, huh?" teased Izzy.

Peggy-Sue let stream over the porch railing a long arc of tobacco spittle.

All around them, the flowers drew down the moonlight.

And, out in that moonlight, Chiara and Muscovado walked the little roads left among the blooms; though Muscovado would have denied it, he harbored the fantastical hope that Chiara might be after his ass. As a matter of fact, asses were on the mind of our Mediterranean beauty with hair like midnight.

"Muscovado," she began, "my daughter has, I believe, fallen in love with you. And therefore it is natural that you and I should walk here in the wild gardens, so that I can make the usual queries, and so satisfy my maternal obligations." Chiara smiled. She loved this bullshit.

"Why don't you interview *her?*" asked Muscovado, not unreasonably. "This is just as much her idea. She is a wild, high-hearted, come-hither girl, God bless her."

"I have already spoken to my daughter on this subject,"

averred Chiara. "She is free to arrange her nights according to the heat and spice she chooses."

Muscovado felt like sprinting back to the house.

"So you walked me a mile out in this desert in the darkness to tell me that?"

"Of course not," replied Chiara, "I have taken you out here to test your knowledge of the sexual arts." And she smiled at him.

Back at the ranch, Izzy and Peggy-Sue decided to carry on their conversations over a glass of tequila on the rocks.

Legs angled up on the railing, opal eyes turning in the moonlight, body like a bank of seeds ready to flower under the touch of a lover, Izzy watched the desert night.

Peggy-Sue seemed like the perfect strange soul mate for their traveling.

"Come with us!" she said. "Come with us to the Lost Coast."

"What about if I meet you on the way?" countered Peggy-Sue.

"But you need company on the road. Think of the hazards. What if you run out of chewing tobacco?"

"Maybe that's where my parents went, Lost Coast," mused Peggy-Sue.

"No doubt about it, two angels naked on the beaches, no one there but them, nice going, out in the sun, the whole continent at their backs and the big sea making them wings," said the sweet-talking amorous Izzy.

Over on the other side of the porch, Tupelo was licking the face of Renato as Renato was kissing the neck of Ananda as Ananda leaned dreamily toward their planet of flowers as, inside, for dinner, Juha stripped Cookie.

Out along the fields, Chiara continued her investigations. "For example, are you aware of the extensive correspondences between musical expression and sexual technique?" she asked.

Muscovado didn't expect *this* jive. What did this woman want from him?

"Are you trying to educate me?" he asked carefully.

"I'm sure *you* don't need education on these fronts," she said.

"What kind of music?" he asked helplessly.

"Principally classical: You are familiar, I take it, with the range of terms for expression: telling us, for example, whether a piece should be played *appassionato* or *grazioso;* or for other pieces, *brillante, sostenuto, amabile,* and so on . . .

"Now consider a man and woman in love, say they find themselves at a ranch of flowers, the fuse of love has burned down, and by the detonation of flesh, by the heat-lightning on their skin, by their sparkling hearts—they have the feeling the night has real possibilities."

"You're crazy, woman; let-loose blood-boiling crazy!"

"Maybe you have no interest—"

"Maybe I like crazy mothers."

Chiara, with steady soul and swinging voice, walked him on. . . . "What first was a whisper of kisses takes on ripe languor, because their lips are warm as sunlight; so, they keep their clothes on; by their kisses, by embraces prolonged, by their kneading, by their coming into the perfect manias of touch, they study one another, a gift-giving of desire in their hands; summer comes then to their hands; in their hands they hold a season of lovemaking—are you with me so far?" Chiara looked at him calmly.

"I've figured it out—this is one of your old lectures on conjugation," said Muscovado with difficulty.

Chiara laughed, and went on.

"So they tease—it being summer, they bring home a harvest of caresses and suggestions; yet they keep on their clothes; desire itself is in love with them; they know the working of the hunger of the world in the hunger for a lover—and by insistence of nips, licks, nuzzle, and rub, they make a nectary of entreaties; into this nectary first one, then the other dips for the tasting of each other; for the tasting of promises—for the promises of all the world are in the promises of pleasure you make to your lover; their breaths are tense cords that bind them together, their bodies turn together; until they must go outside because no house can contain them—

"Outside in the summer air in the warm grass they come from their clothes, they glitter with sweat, the hours burn down around them; bound unto a blessing they make, she holds him in that glittering, he has her marks on his heart; and however deep into the benedictions of her pleasure he moves he will not find the end of her, not ever, not ever—this is one kind of fuck: and, old pal, you're probably curious just which one, am I right?"

Muscovado looked at her in amazement.

"You are curious!"

Muscovado stood there shining.

"It's the fuck *tumultuoso*," she said, and looked back easily at him. There was a long silence as the moon turned around the night.

"Such is the use of musical terminology. It's good to see these studies put into practice, don't you think?" she queried.

"If you think that I am going to be—" Musco began.

"You are in love with my daughter, you hopeless fool."

"Do you talk like this to your students?" he asked.

"You are my student," she pointed out calmly.

"You're putting me on," he suggested.

"Oh no, I'm riling you up, which I prefer to taking you down," she said with a smile.

"I'm trapped in a world overrun by wily females smart as coyotes," he observed.

"Celebrate while you can," she counseled.

"I hope to celebrate with music—"

"Which calls to mind another scene entirely," broke in Chiara, waving her hand. "We can see the lovers on a bed, in the twilight, the room filled with violet light, on her skin he can taste the night to come. He knows that because she is naked, the dusk loves her; because she is a woman, the dusk loves her; taking from the dusk, on his fingertips, an oil of violets, he strokes her head to toe, and he tells her, almost singing—what does he tell her, Muscovado?"

"He wants to talk about the dating of ancient papyrus," ventured Muscovado.

"Guess again, smart-aleck," she sassed back.

"He says, Hey, I thought you were inviting me for a fancy tea, you know, ruffled dresses, cold silver trays, doilies and everything," grinned our Musco.

"But we are aware that no true lovers would drink anything as insipid as tea," said Chiara, laughing, "and by music he moves to her, as he will move in her, a man who wants to know the tempo, the rhythm, and depth of her pleasure. And so to her he says that her pleasure is to him an undiscovered country, he touches the soft skin of her neck, the sides of her breasts, the curve of her hips, moving in a country of love, and he says, I live here; I will brush your skin until my hands match the motion of the light—you are the whole warm afternoon, your pleasure like light in a glade of trees: it is the midmost of your pleasure that makes the afternoon beautiful—my day and night, my love—this is the way he whispers to her, Muscovado, and when he is inside her, her moving with him makes the country they both love, because of their coming to one another, because of the homecoming of love—and what fuck is this you may ask?"

"Yep, I definitely want to know this one," said Muscovado dutifully.

"The fuck *arioso cantabile*—like a song."

Now Musco, who had no reaction to this monologue aside from falling in love with Chiara and getting hard as a crowbar, tried to retake the conversation:

"You can't do this to me!" he cried, but it is difficult to reprimand a woman there in the middle of the high desert surrounded by acres of flowers moving in the moonlight—all the more so if you are already enamored of that woman's daughter. He sighed—such are the hazards of being Muscovado.

"I can anticipate your next question," said Chiara.

"I wish you would," he said.

"You are curious about the fuck *scherzando*."

"You bet I am," he cried.

"It is in the *scherzando* that the lover's art is tested to the utmost," she said, "because in this concord of body and will the lover becomes his beloved—it is not enough that he move inside her, their souls must be at play. It is lovemaking in which the lover becomes unconscious of himself, enveloped, as by sheet-lightning, in the pleasures of his beloved. For the pleasures of women are not only temporary and physical; they are that— and they are permanent, the source of all things, the center of the world, a beauty that calls from the inside of our lives, the reason this earth has a come-hither look. Where do we find these things, if not in the pleasures of a woman?"

"Where, indeed?" inquired the educable Muscovado. She had hit upon his deepest belief; in fact, his only belief.

"And so, to the *scherzando,*" said Chiara with satisfaction.

Muscovado was thinking, Hey, maybe graduate school wouldn't be such a bad idea.

Petals of flowers moving around them wrote in air the midnight ideas of wind.

"What is the body of a woman, because of the prolongations of her pleasure? She is, in lovemaking, become full of soul; what is the movement back and forth she makes with her lover, at the far reaches of pleasure? A coming to the world now as body, then as soul, back and forth—"

"Is this your idea of motherhood?" he inquired with real curiosity.

"I love my Izzy," she admitted.

Muscovado looked this dark woman up and down.

"Heaven knows what you would do with a son," he said with a smile.

Chiara touched his face—and resumed: "In the *scherzando,* that man who has in his touch a simmering and a teasing, comes to his lover in full meditation on her: that is, in meditation of her come, how she can come, and then come again, how from a spinning in midair that is her first come, in her birthright of pleasure she begins the passage-making natural to any woman's plain fantastical rooted beauty. When a lover devotes himself to seeing our beauty come into its own: this is the beginning of the *scherzando.*"

"The beginning!" exclaimed Muscovado.

"You think the beauty of women has an end?" she inquired of her student.

"I don't know," he admitted.

"It is in the *scherzando* that you will find out," she said.

"Say then, that I have made my beginning," he hypothesized.

"And so at the beginning of her beauties, her soul, like a flower, opens with the pleasures of her body—" Chiara left the path and went to pick a wide-open flower.

Standing close to Muscovado, she held it up.

"Look at this opening," she said. "Even as this flower is petaled, so does he petal her with pleasure. Each petal is one way of pleasuring: each has its own fragrance and softness; each moves her toward her whole beauty. So it is she has these visitations, different each one by his teasing and the prayer of his playfulness, different because of what he says to her of her beautiful lips, her hair, her waist; his praises of her skin, her hands, her pussy, by her giving of the bud in the centermost of herself. He travels far inside her softness, and by the opening of her soul again, with her petaled body, by the slow sure turning she does to pull him inside her once more"—here Chiara held up for Muscovado the opened flower—"she draws them, petal by petal, into the midmost of her beauties, until in that lustrous country"—she took some pollen from the middle of the flower and traced a gold streak across Musco's cheek—"they are made over with remembered light—the soft light that shines in souls."

Muscovado looked at her, the streak of pollen giving its gold to him.

"And that is the light he needs to see her," said Chiara.

Muscovado was silent; his thoughts moved with the rhythms of the night. Chiara stood watching him; the evening streamed from her hair.

"When can we meet again?" he asked.

"It may be," she hypothesized, "that you will become curious about the fuck *capriccioso,* best conducted in the kitchen, during an afternoon-long preparation of dinner."

"I may well become curious."

"Then there is the *sostenuto e vivace,* which in little mountain towns, in the high clear air, comes to lovers as they return to their inn and its feather beds."

"Surely there are no more varieties," he said, laughing.

"Only if we leave aside the *piacevole*—best found in bringing quick graces of pleasure to rooms tucked along the streets of big cities."

"I love you," said Muscovado.

"And, loving me, you may well ask: what of the *adagio*, which may take many days?"

"Is there a simple one?" he asked.

"The *dolce!*" she said triumphantly. "In which the lovers easily and happily settle one another into the sweetness of the world."

"What about the *reggae?*"

"Sir, you will have to invent that for yourself," she said. And she was content.

Muscovado looked at her; she stood in her vestments of cool wind, in a kind of smug motherhood; and he concluded that his Great Basin excursion had strayed beyond conventional journalism.

Listening to her, though, he wondered what he could give her back. For Chiara, as Muscovado sensed, and as we know from her florescent past, sprang her surprises and made her demands.

In the long run, she succeeded in surprising even him; even herself.

He stood, and in the desert sky that crowned Chiara the falling stars fell toward Izzy.

He turned to walk toward the ranch house. As he went, Chiara called after him.

"Muscovado, you are a brave man!" she cried. "There's one more thing!"

"There's nothing else," he said, not breaking his stride.

"One more: if I find out that you have mistreated my daughter I will hunt you down and hold you on the ground and as if you were a sacrificial animal I will cut your throat."

"I know, I know," he said softly as he headed for Izzy, her small hands, her sass, her cream.

SO BEGAN at the house of the angels a week celebrated with many a musical cadence.

Izzy and Muscovado had gone off to the back of the ranch house, to the room that looked south into the big valley where the days ran clear, bearing into the room a warm lotion of light. No one went near except to leave outside the door hot meals on a tray. An occasional bottle of whiskey and bowl of ice cubes complemented these efforts, to which the household, under Peggy-Sue's and Cookie's supervision, smilingly devoted themselves.

"Lucky this place has provisions," cracked Peggy-Sue as she stood over the stove making the breakfast muffins.

"Oh my this is one musky ranch house," said Cookie, as she dished up some steaming eggs-taters-cheese-and-meat and set it in front of Juha, who received with his food a buss on his muscular neck.

"Eat up, you burly thing, now I ain't having you complain of no starvation on my account."

Juha, who by this time was so much in love with Cookie that he could hardly concentrate long enough to hold his fork, looked gleefully at his lover.

"And stop starin' at me like you been struck dumb, fer chrissake!" remonstrated Cookie.

Renato was out painting the swirl and simmer of the flowers.

Ananda and Chiara thought, given this hiatus in their journey, that this would be a good time to take stock. And what better way than to consult with the daughter of angels?

They surrounded Peggy-Sue.

"How about a walk up the top of the hill to the east, where we can look down on the ranch and talk a while?" asked Ananda.

"Right-o," answered Peg, "I reckon we got some more stories to tell."

"I was afraid of that," mumbled Juha between bites.

"I still got work to do fixin' that shyness of his," explained Cookie to Chiara in a thunderous sotto voce.

"I see real progress," observed Chiara.

"He's so *solid.* It's like loving a tree."

"Is he the kind of tree that broadcasts his seed?" asked Peggy-Sue, who, as we remember, had been paying attention in her biology class.

"Hmm . . . broadcast . . . now that does 'bout sum it up," mused Cookie with a slow grin.

"Maybe I'll take him into high school and use him as a science demonstration," proposed Peg.

And she winked at Ananda and Chiara and went with them out into the morning air.

Walking among the fields of flowers, the three of them felt the gusts of desert silence, as around them the petals flashed and flashed in the sun. The sharp blue Great Basin air gathered in their breaths, and the sagebrush watched as they walked.

"Come now, Peggy-Sue, is it not so that angels are just some hackneyed made-up religious thing?" Ananda, ever the attacking attorney, said.

"That idea was put out as a trick by the angels themselves; they got tired of being bothered by a bunch of nosy self-seeking beggars—wanting this and that and not doing shit for themselves." rebutted Peg, who was not about to be faced down by a goddam big-city securities lawyer.

"When did you pull that trick?"

"Long ago. But it works well. Look at us here: everybody thinks we're just a family of crackpots."

"When will we meet your parents?" asked Chiara, who as we know was concerned always with the social proprieties.

"On the way to the Lost Coast, they'll come around. Maybe by then Musco and Izzy will have oozed out of that back room."

"This love affair *is* rather sudden. Why ever do you think that man was in such a lather last night?" inquired Chiara sweetly.

"Couldn't have anything to do with what you were telling him, academic that you are," said Ananda.

"Was I completely off base to imagine that he might want my ideas on Socrates and Diotima?"

"Maybe I could talk to him about corporate tax law," suggested Ananda.

"I love you women," said Peg. "You're so full of bullshit."

"So what is an angel?" asked Chiara.

"An angel is someone who has become human," said Peggy-Sue immediately.

There was a long silence.

"You want to run that by us again?" asked Ananda.

"People are born, everyone assumes they are alive. It ain't so."

"So we're *supposed* to become angels?"

"A purple-sage seed is supposed to turn into a purple sage," answered Peg. "It's just that plants have an easier time than we do, doin' what they're supposed to."

"Now who's to say this isn't just one more sack of new-age horseshit!" exclaimed the worldly Chiara.

"Have you gone to the newspapers with this information?" asked Ananda.

"Hell, everybody already knows. But they've got ideas, so many fucking ideas about themselves, thinking they're this, thinking they're that, and never seeing it's just jerking off the brain. This is how they feel good. They think it's a life—"

"Will you hold down the invective for a minute? And what makes you so special anyhow?" challenged Ananda.

"Sorry. Hey, I'm a novice."

Chiara and Ananda looked at each other, and then out at the acres of flowers. A couple of pros and a teenage sprite.

Chiara spoke first. "You know, I just did want to get away from the university, to have some time with Izzy, to pal around and see some of the big country. Now here we are, off the map."

"All I know," Ananda said, "is that it puts a woman in a play-ful mood. I'm going to stick around. Besides, at the rate this group is going, somebody's going to need a defense lawyer, and I think I'd be passable," she added.

"At least Izzy has found a way to lay down on the job," threw in Peggy-Sue.

"May we follow her lead," suggested Ananda.

Chiara was looking out again over the ranch of flowers, mulling it over. "Being an angel, I take it, is to have the chance for days and nights that are a kind of long pillow-talk with the world," she said.

"I don't know much about pillow talk myself—but I think you're on to something," said Peg.

Above their heads circled a big golden eagle.

"So now we're going to find angels all the way to the ocean, aren't we?" asked Ananda.

"You would have anyway. But now you'll recognize them," answered back Peggy-Sue.

"Oh my," sighed Chiara, "we'll have to get down and dirty and celestial."

They told Angelica she was their first bitch. The original bitch. They were her men. Anyone hurting her is dead. Dead. No one gave a living shit anymore about anything, but here were two men who could make them understand.

Grimes thought he knew what was wrong. Men were afraid to judge. Nobody was willing to stand up and be a judge. And Grimes knew why. Because once you judged, then you had to punish. You had to. But everybody was too lazy and afraid;

it was easier to put a ring in your nose, or build a big house.

It happened when people were young, they got in the habit of being scared. It was like they had some operation and the guts were taken out of them. Maybe that's what happened in the universities—you handed in your guts, they gave you a diploma.

When you can see the world straight you have to do things.

Angelica looked at them lying around on the floor of the gun shop lit by the neon from the street. They were smeared with her lipstick, sweaty and streaked with lavender, they lay among the pillows and comics, and she thought with relief, They don't smell like garbage. What do I care if they can't shut the fuck up?

Tabby and Grimes stayed naked after Angelica left.

"She is the best," Tabby said.

"The Innocents—one of the Innocents," said Grimes.

Tabby got loud: "When do we start? Are we cans of meat? Canned pork? I'm telling you, Grimes, I want to start. How long are you going to let my old man sell the bodies? Don't you have any feelings? Huh? Why do we have to practice at the dump again? I thought you said we were ready."

"To the dump tomorrow," said Grimes, pressing Tabby's shoulder. The neon still flickered through the gun shop. Tabby lay there and watched Grimes; his friend was keyed up. Tabby liked that—his friend always got like this in the dark after Angelica.

"—To the dump right on our regular schedule. I taught you. A schedule. I'm teaching you to be smart, like me. Who got that history prize at school? Alexander at Tyre. The Venetians at Lepanto. Agincourt. The Battle of the Bulge. Okinawa. Don't they want me to go to college? Isn't that what they say? But I'm too smart for my teachers, what do they know? They're Innocents. Not all of them, there are some working in a stinking high school because they're wimps and bitches and cowards. But the innocent ones. The decent ones. Who's out fighting for them? Who's going to do something about the slime? You know why the world is all slippery with slime? Because kids went to school and stuffed their heads with snot and didn't think they owed anybody anything. They're too selfish. They didn't go into the world ready to fight. They don't have a plan.

Grimes stroked Tabby's hair and went on. "I've taught you to use every one of the guns," he said, gesturing to the walls. "To stand straight. Polite. Look like class. Ready to go. Sharp. We'll drill, sweat. You know what history is about? It's about good men. Not about the scumsuckers on the streets, about the filthy donkeys on television and the rich people in their offices smooth and shiny as pus—they're just fillers. They're just waiting.

"And what are they waiting for? They're waiting to get punished. They know they're doing wrong, and they know it's only a matter of time. A good man will come, they'll be able to tell by his bearing. He'll be sharp, he'll see into them. And they'll want to be judged. They'll know he's right about them. And they'll beg him for punishment, they'll beg him. Inside, they're already begging."

Here it comes, thought Tabby—he loved to hear Grimes talk like this. Even though he had heard it lots of times, Tabby always got choked up—this was so important. There was so much work to do.

But his friend was interrupted when into the glass door of the gun shop an old man from the park pressed his face, seeing the two teenagers. He rattled and rattled the door and pounded on the glass, pounded as he shouted at them, the shouting turned to a raspy cough—

"A Maggot. He must have heard us talking about the dump."

Tabby laughed and stood up.

"There's no place for you in here, Maggot! Dog food!"

"You can't help but wonder what happens to their ambition and dignity," Grimes said, shaking his head.

In the middle of the sagebrush Renato lifted his brush: the desert, he thought, was like a sea—his painting a little harbor where moved, in colors, the wind and current of what he meant.

The blue-gray oils on his brush glistened in the sun.

Painting there, letting the air and water of his soul work into his brush, he reflected that if desert and sea were akin, then not only people, but regions of the earth might fall in love—why not a tryst between the hazy springtime Great Basin valleys and the archipelago of the South Pacific, for instance?

Renato was, helplessly, a painter of many centuries. He produced oil paintings using pigments he mixed himself; his lapis, ocher, umber, gold leaf, everything he made with his own hands.

He loved the transcendental colors and gilt divinities of the early Sienese; but then again, he loved Kandinsky. If Duccio had had the young Kandinsky for an apprentice, that would have been Renato; that is, he was a realist who thought that no resource of color, form, and subject should be denied him—and when he painted figures, they were illumined only by the light of their souls.

If the early Renaissance, on a canvas stretched over wood, could give us a Gabriel striding along passages of air to deliver an Annunciation, then Renato reckoned he could paint a cowgirl in Big Smokey Valley at that moment when the beauty of the season is delivered all at once into her hands. Instead of a proud and ruthless Doge of Venice, Renato set down in angular exact lines a young prospector with his burro on a dirt road at dawn—a man snarled and hopeless in the intrigue of his own dreams.

And he painted box canyons whose stone was colored with the wild shimmering of desert silence.

Just now, he was finishing a painting that would after some years being passed around junkyards and secondhand shops, after twenty years in the basement of a house in Paradox, Colorado, would with some ceremony be hung in Paris. And so he did not expect to be swept up in

THE STORY OF THE MERCHANTS OF JUNK

Down the dirt road to the ranch came an old flatbed with thick pine slat sideboards; on the panels of the cab, both sides, were painted the words JUNK TRUCK. The truck roared past Renato, made a few loop-de-loops in front of the house, skidded to a stop, sounded off with an irresponsible series of toots on the horn—

oompahs, snorts, ditties, and whoopees. The racket brought Cookie and Juha, Peg, Ananda, and Chiara all outside. Renato, brush still in hand, curious, sauntered up.

"We're glad your truck piped down. We'd be even gladder to see you head straight back out of here," shouted Cookie to the woman grinning in the cab. Cookie and her compatriots were having such a good time, she thought, that the last thing she wanted was some vagrant and her damned sales pitch. Even out in the West, the days were becoming one long sales pitch.

At the taunt, a door opened and the woman swung down to the ground, quickstepped to the back of the truck, and vaulted up into the incredible mass of junk there.

She began to speak: "Junk you say! Not so! From going ranch to ranch all over the West, I know it's a rare house that cannot use a choice bit of my collection. Need to fix an old pipe? I have the coupling you're missing! Need to snip an umbilical? Clean scissors, I've got 'em! Need a herding-dog to bring in the cattle? I've got this puppy, who will grow up to be the best herd-dog of all time! I say of all the world!"

"When do you shut up?" inquired Juha, who always had hated hucksters.

She went right on: "Need to shut up unwelcome visitors, hucksters from nowhere? Huckster repellent!" She held up a plain battered can. "Just spray this can in their direction!"

"How much?" asked Juha with a smile.

"Very expensive if you buy it alone—but cheap if you buy just one other thing. How about: a cowboy, toughened by a life on the range but honest as the skies, ready to say what he learned from the stars, still lanky and still curious: and here he is!"

And out of a bedroll laid out just at the back of the cab, rose a tanned clear-eyed man who looked them all over, tipped his hat.

"Name's Bret," he said. "Howdy, June," he said to his companion on the Junk Truck; and, social obligations satisfied, he promptly lay down and stretched himself out once again.

"Now what about that?" June asked in satisfaction. "That's no junk, there!"

"How much for the cowboy only?" inquired Chiara.

"I'll split the cost!" offered Cookie.

"Cookie!" admonished Juha.

"Just kidding, you big bruiser," comforted Cookie.

"Who the hell *are* you?" asked Ananda.

"A junk merchant," said the woman. "I buy and sell the whole world."

"So what is your story?" asked Chiara, who could hold out no longer.

"I can see into the future," said the woman simply.

"Why didn't you tell us sooner?" asked Ananda.

"You didn't ask sooner."

"What the hell are you talking about?" spouted Juha. "What does the future have to do with that pile of junk you've got on that truck? And if you're so smart, why are you driving around selling shit?"

"Most junk salesmen serve the present needs of their customers. I serve their future needs," said the woman simply.

"So give us an example," suggested Chiara.

"Let us begin with the ranch," said the woman. "I can see that in two years a dust storm will come through this valley and blow sand all through the ranch house. What you'll need to clean it up is a big broom for the wood floors and a little broom for getting into the corners, the nooks and crannies."

"Great," said Chiara, "so we'll be spick-and-span. Commerce to the rescue. You're holding something back."

"Maybe I am."

"What is it, what?" asked Peggy-Sue impatiently.

"The third broom."

"This sounds like a courtroom drama: The Case of the Third Broom," cracked Ananda.

"Now this third broom you will use for sweeping out the house once you think you have it clean—this is a special broom that you can only buy from us."

"No surprise there," asserted Juha.

"This is the broom that will sweep for you the special residue left from the visitation of the wind, the dust from the farthest reaches of the night sky, the sand so fine that it is like grains of light. And you will collect these leavings of the storm, and keep them: a hope, your gift; it is a magic dust."

"And then measure it out and bake it in little cakes, right?" jabbed Cookie.

"With this dust," continued the woman, "you can repair the broken legs of horses, or make a shy child sassy. You can make a salve that reconstructs broken hearts, you can with a handful restore a streambed so the water will run clear again, as in paradise; you can put some in the tank of your tractor and it will repair the engine; you can, by placing a minute quantity on two men in a fight, get them to admit they are just two shitheads."

"I like the part about the tractor. Does it work on chain saws?" asked Juha.

"What happens if I put it in my coffee?" asked Cookie.

"It puts you in an amorous mood."

"Hell, coffee always did that to me anyway."

"And one more thing: in the back of the house where the light streams into the room all afternoon, you take a pinch of this dust into your palm and blow it into the air. There the motes will dance, and if you watch that dance you will see written for you in the air the sentences of heaven, that tell what the soul must do."

"Well, well, too bad—the back room in this ranch house is occupied just now," observed Peggy-Sue, smiling her big teenage smile, and the cowboy rose again from the bed of the truck, and he and the storytelling woman looked upon her long and sure, with easy mischief and the lit gaze of affection.

"How we have missed you, Peggy-Sue!" exclaimed the junk merchants together; and they jumped down from the truckbed and hugged Peg again and again.

"It's lucky you have a daughter who knows how to keep a straight face," said Peg between kisses.

"Well, it's good to have some help," said Cookie, "because we're probably goin' to be leavin' hot meals on trays outside of closed doors the rest of our natural lives."

"What natural life?" inquired the angel-junkman.

"All right, all right—" said Cookie.

"So what about a brewski, Peg?" asked her mother.

"You bet, let's roll inside—"

"Where are your wings?" asked Juha brusquely. Juha, even though he was learning fast, was still a tad literal-minded.

"You're a general contractor. You're supposed to be able to hammer together anything," shot back the junkman.

"Let's get into that kitchen. There's nothing that can't be understood in a kitchen," said Cookie with justice. And so they went.

And so they stayed. For days our nonplussed ramblers talked to the angels and their daughter. The angels, Bret and June, were at first always breaking off the conversation to fire questions at Peggy-Sue about the flowers at the ranch, about school, about certain residents of the town. But slowly they turned their attention back to the travelers, answering their questions; and their lives as a ranch family, as junk merchants, as celestial creatures, as pig farmers and planters of flowers, they wove into ordinary afternoon-and-morning chats. The cooking went on; one person or another might leave the room to attend to some chore; the meals for Iz and Musco were carried to the back of the house in what was now a hallowed tradition; and everybody felt neighborly.

All during this shootout of astonishments, hints, and curiosities, Renato painted, his easel stand perched sturdily in the kitchen. He wanted to set down the angel family, full of food, beer, and light, arrayed around their own table, and then he wanted to head outside and treat, from a number of angles, the outlandish junk truck.

June fired out at one point: "And why not? It's not just a word! Why not a paradise right here: a paradise of rustic frolics? Did you think it would be solemn? What, did you think that in heaven the beer is warm?"

No one had an answer.

And another day Bret: "And this business with the damned

flowers is over! We're going to go back to the way we started out: we'll plant alfalfa, drink heavy on the weekends, and have the neighbors over for beans and rice."

"Just so I don't have to take up the deaf-and-dumb routine again," rejoined Peggy-Sue.

"How 'bout a peg leg?" suggested her mother.

After four days of this, Chiara and Ananda huddled to set down a mercifully brief list of questions, with the idea that they might move these humdrum enchantments toward an even more wild horizon. And so they did—though not in the way they intended.

THE LIST OF QUESTIONS FOR THE FAMILY OF ANGELS

1) You say that wings may grow, but only because of love. What kind of flying is this anyhow? What about air traffic control? How are we to make sense of this?

2) You say that angels are everywhere, since to be an angel is simply to have certain capacities of soul. But how do we recognize them? Do they carry ID? Get speeding tickets? What about farting? Are they all lackadaisical like you? And how many junk merchants does the world need, anyhow?

3) You say that it's not that bad a strategy, to set forth with a wing and a prayer. And if ever there was a bunch took that approach to heart, it's this one. Do you think we should continue on to the Lost Coast? Or is this like the ship of fools?—A truck of fools?

4) How on earth are we going to get Muscovado and Izzy out of the back room?

5) Why do you think that time is just another element in the world—like color or shape, sky or taste? And that we must take hold of this immaterial movement, this subtle rhythm, and make it our own music?

6) What do you mean when you say that we ain't seen nothin' yet?

7) Does everything *have* to mean something else?

8) OK, OK, we'll come back for the dust storm and collect the magic powder or whatever the hell it is. But for newfound friends, you're a little quick on the draw—

9) We hate to be the ones to break the news, but this idea of destiny—c'mon!—we haven't heard anyone talk about that one for a *long* time. Are you sure? The idea that each person has destiny, if only the playfulness and resolution are present? If only we go forth with just the right rough-and-ready lighthearted charge? The world exists partly to present us with this chance? Are you pulling our legs?

10) What do you mean when you say that the arts of love are an introduction to the arts of life?

11) And even if that's so, shouldn't Musco and Iz come out at least once and take a bow? Like acrobats or something?

12) Other than being cosmic, how did you raise such a pistol of a daughter?

13) When you say that the movement of light is the thinking of the world, and that we are meant to make our lives in harmony with such luminous storytelling, are you making a metaphor? Or is this just another cryptic declaration?

14) Would you like to come with us to the Lost Coast? We think your junk truck would make a magnificent addition to our fleet of vehicles.

The questions having been duly conveyed to Bret and June, the group took a deep breath and decided just to loiter for a few hours.

Ananda and Chiara had fallen into one of those strange unreserved partnerships, like air and light, okra and soup, cheese and wine, time and space—a friendship so unusual for both of them that they each wanted some time apart to consider their easy confluence of energies.

Juha wandered out of the house and up to the hill overlooking the valley, where he sat down, and as was now his fixed habit, wondered what had hit him. Was he not a builder? Yeah, maybe it was a little quiet just now, but shouldn't he be looking for the next job? On the other hand, why not a spell as an itinerant contractor? Why not stay with this group? This trip he had meant to be a long weekend, his lark with a pack of hysterics. He had figured to be back in Eureka by now, getting his equipment together and planning the next project.

But here he was. Cookie still covered him day after day with lather and her own honey; Renato he liked—a pro who had painted old Hansel and Gertie's ranch house with so winning a fanaticism that Juha had resolved to offer him every painting job he had forever; Ananda and Chiara were like double suns, sometimes one behind the other, sometimes side by side in brightness; he was even getting to like Izzy and Muscovado, and he was happy when the two of them vanished into the raptures.

Juha, strong as a grizzly, looked out over the ranch of the angels, and he thought that being a contractor was the perfect preparation: for he was man enough to know that, no matter how many skills he had, there was some way he was just an empty lot.

Maybe, with these friends, he could go ahead and put in a foundation.

He got to his feet and looked out at the attentive desert. The stone and sage made a slow dance as far as he could see.

At the back of the house Izzy and Muscovado lay in each other's arms, holding on as through them moved their meteor showers.

AFTER TWO MORE days it dawned on our earnest group that Musco and Iz had no intention of returning to society. And so they all decided to be on their way.

Peggy-Sue, who was by now getting attached to our ruffians, did not want them to go.

"What about your daughter? What about her need for maternal advice and comfort?" she asked Chiara.

"It is my hope that her sense of propriety is everything we would hope for in a young lady," replied Chiara. "Besides, I think I smell smoke."

"How will she find you?"

"Why, she and Musco will just ask you where we are. You aren't going to tell me you angels, seeing into the future, are blind as bats about the present?"

"OK, OK," said Peggy-Sue, who knew when she was cornered.

"And when they come to find us, why don't you come along? You can chaperon them, or they you, or something—"

"You're on. See you down the road."

And Chiara went on out to join the rest by the truck. It was late afternoon.

Renato had finished his meditations in oil. He covered his canvases and put them in the wagon, which they were leaving there at the ranch for Musco and Iz. One canvas of the desert he bestowed upon the family, who promptly hung it in the bathroom.

After his days of work, the painter looked like he himself had only this minute emerged from a room of long musky loves.

Ananda came over to him. "Glad to see you among us again," she said.

"I'll pretend I'm not painting in praise of you."

"Don't pretend."

"I'm painting in praise of you. When Musco came for Iz, I felt like a cheerleader; I felt like rooting."

Juha got ready to take the wheel. The family of angels came out and gathered round him.

"Well, I guess it's time to make the obligatory trip to the junk truck," said June.

"I knew we weren't going to get away clean," replied Juha.

"We have some things you're going to need, you big thick oak of a man," whispered Peggy-Sue, with her hand on the massive shoulder of the contractor.

Juha, followed by his fellow pilgrims, went dubiously over with Peg and her parents.

Bret, June, and their daughter clambered up in the bed of the junk truck as if they were tumbling on a playground. They rooted around, whispering and nudging, tossing things carelessly, toppling little piles of detritus, and in general making a mess and having a high time.

When the dust settled, they vaulted down with three objects for the giving.

"Hooo boy, will you ever need this!" said Peggy-Sue as she handed over a dented, water-stained, decidedly crooked trumpet.

"A trumpet?" queried Juha.

"And that's not all!" exclaimed June. "Here for an accompaniment is a little bell."

Juha took into his gigantic palm the bell, which was in even sorrier shape than the trumpet. A little dot of a thing, the bell was so corroded by weather and abuse that when he shook it the sound edged out weaker than the chirp of a little bird.

"I just can't wait for the third present," he said in a huff.

"And here it is!" said Bret, placing in his reluctant hand a truly disgusting harmonica. Juha's first thought was that it had spent a year in the belly of a jackass.

"And somebody's supposed to put their mouth on this?" he asked with what was for him a notable politeness.

"Maybe it plays angel music, doofus," said Bret cheerfully.

"I don't know how to thank you," said Juha truthfully.

"You may thank us by gettin' back on the road," said Peg kindly, as she approached Juha and gave him a lusty adolescent hug of, he had to admit, distinctly angelic energies. And he felt much better.

Cookie, watching this show, cracked to Chiara, "A regular musician, huh! A good thing. I was already gettin' good an' tired of the animal-noise routine."

Chiara glided closer to Cookie and put her arm around the rough strong Eureka woman. "Thanks for cookin' up all those meals for my wayward daughter," she said.

"Well, to tell the truth, I was feelin' kinda protective of the love-struck little filly. I wanted her to have some fortification," said Cookie.

"Let's head out!" cried Juha.

"Good-bye, all you angels," said Ananda.

Chiara passed some hugs around. Juha looked quizzically at his trio of instruments as Cookie steered him toward their truck; Ananda tossed her hair and sent some lightning bolts around the yard; they made a hubbub of good-byes and whispered speculations on when they would all see each other again—for it was twilight again, the desert twilight, and in that inevitable beauty they knew it was time to ramble.

They piled in the truck with the house, made a few honorary passes around the ranch house, and headed off into the violet amorous evening.

*   *   *

Juha and Cookie rode up front, and the other three took up lounging positions in the house on the rear of the truck. Renato's continuous working at the ranch had loosed his soul to radiate wildly through his flesh. And so just now he needed the steady presence of these women.

And besides, Renato, with a force that surprised even him, knew something that even the two women did not know: he knew that Ananda and Chiara were in love.

Grimes couldn't imagine being without guns. They were like playmates. His parents gave him a more expensive gun every year: what's the use of having a child if he could be taken out by a scumbag? If a child couldn't defend himself, you might well be just sending him out for sacrifice. Someone would mail you his head in a bag.

Grimes had grown up with firearms; taking them apart and putting them back together, cleaning and oiling, he understood their mechanism. He studied each new gun when it was intro-duced—the autoloader revolvers, lever-action and pump rifles, semiauto carbines with conversion kits, gas-system autoloaders; he knew all the grips, the scopes, the silencers. He kept a snub-bie with him always. He liked the feeling of it under his arm. The snubbie just fit in his hand. It made him feel happy.

He had learned so much in the shooting competitions, he had met so many veterans and sportsmen and policemen. They were everything to him. They weren't just fucking talkers, god-dam spitheads. They were people who counted, because they saw the world as it was. They saw how bad it was, and they were ready to defend their families. So innocent! They loved their families, you could tell. It was so moving, the way they stood guard.

But it wasn't enough anymore to guard. You had to judge and punish. Every day, get up, go out. Judge. Punish.

He was glad Tabby had the money. In these last months the two of them had ripped out the backseat of Grimes's Chevy and in the space they had welded a beautiful steel rack; and for the trunk too, a special rack. They could carry sixty-four guns, all their ammunition, special scopes, conversion kits, everything they needed.

They had tried it out; driving around in the sun with the whole car weighted down with their favorites, everything from sweet little derringers to a simple autoloader Grizzly pistol, the Mauser he loved, their three pump-action shotguns, to the big carbines they could use to hose down a whole house, until the sleaze ran out—

Even at seventeen, Grimes felt sick with waiting. The only times he felt good were in the shop with Tabby, or with Angelica, or riding around in their car.

With their speedmasters on full auto, they spent all afternoon shooting the shit out of the dump.

When the stream of bullets stopped clanging, they stopped to see what was so soft. They had to walk in a ways, but they found it: a cow, monstrous now, the body open and swimming with larvae, in the spreading guts, the eye sockets.

"It's San Jose!" said Tabby, and they laughed and stripped their shirts off; they were bright with sweat, Tabby felt so happy. They had the guns at their hips, swiveling around; they tried synchronizing their fire to cut up the carcass with bullets. It took a long time.

Not two miles down Interstate 80 headed west, Juha felt pulling on the truck a force that, to call titanic, would be litotes. It pulled them north, away from Reno, off the highway into the little town of Wadsworth, where they stopped, killed the engine, and got out to take a breath and consult the sky. The truck was shaking with some insistence of the country, and they went into a tavern in town—where else—and asked what on earth was going on.

There was a Paiute waiting for them, tending bar.

"Oh, that's just Pyramid Lake," he said with a wave of his hand, "the meeting ground of the spirits of the high desert. It's twenty miles north." And the Paiute smiled.

"Do we have to go there?" asked Juha, who liked the idea of a nice highway.

"You don't have to. But if you are called there, as you seem to be, and you refuse, then you run certain risks."

"Like what?" asked Juha.

"Untimely death by decapitation," replied the Paiute happily. Juha sighed.

"Straight north?" inquired the practical Ananda.

"You can't miss it," said the bartender.

Walking back out to the truck, they noticed the engine had started by itself.

Twenty minutes later, coming over a rise, they saw it: in the middle of pale gold hills, more than merely blue: the thunderbolt of blue, breaking over the truck and its house, rocking the sky, cracking their vision for entry of a color; the lake was the custodian of blue—where the pigment from all over the earth went for refreshment; it was the history of blue, calling the beauties of the past to the shining of the present.

The lake moved there, turning into itself, coming for them, clamorous, quiet.

It was too much, even for Juha, who pulled right over to the side of the road, onto a knoll overlooking the water. He *knew* they should have stuck with the highway.

Renato was the first one out of the truck. He looked over the scene, and wondered where he would find the courage to lift a brush. There was no hope of success; but there never is any, hence his lightheartedness, and the prayer he made that the waters might use him and his canvases for some unpredictable coming-forth.

The five of them stood watching as the stories of the lake were readied.

In the room at the back of the ranch of angels, Izzy, with Muscovado wild and deep inside her, felt how in her coming her eyes went gold again and again.

Ananda and Chiara held on to each other, black and gold hair mingling; Cookie pressed against Juha. The mountains moved around the lake. But Cookie in her practical way knew they had to keep going; some places on earth are doorways to the next world, and that was that. It didn't take all that long to get used to.

"Well, well, it's a helluva lot better than decapitation," she said loudly.

No one replied.

"What, am I on a trip with four stumps? Four posts? Let's get back on the road, I see a little town up ahead. And I'm hungry anyway."

And she stamped back over to the cab of the truck, putting everyone else in motion. It was a short drive into Nixon, the Paiute town just at the southeast corner of the lake. Out in front of the little grocery store were two Indians, who, in touch with a certain Shoshone auto mechanic, snickered to see them come down the road.

"What a crew!" said one.

"All the same," said the other, "I love to see coming down the road people all in a shambles."

The truck pulled up beside the store, bringing out the wondering multitudes within. They circled round the house with its turrets and dormers.

"Serious crackups," opined one.

"They coulda used it to haul gravel; but no, they had to hammer up a fancy-pants house."

Juha got down from the truck, and stamped among the onlookers. And such was his physique, his let's-get-it-done emanations, that soon he and the Paiutes were debating loudly the fine points of construction on flatbeds. So boisterous and manly became the exchange, that the Indians swept Juha into the store for a sixer of beer, so that their ideas might effervesce together. Thus was Juha, who had put up with such irregular incidents, mercifully spared when the two Indians that had been sitting in front of the store walked over to the rest of our travelers in order to set them up for the telling of

THE STORY OF THE HIGH SCHOOL MARCHING BAND THAT PLAYED A CONCERT FOR DEATH

"Now I am sure glad to see you come down the road," said one.

"All right, how much do you want?" asked Ananda immediately; once she knew the rules, Ananda was an impatient negotiator.

"I can't tell you until later," said the Paiute.

"I was afraid of that," she said.

"Now just you settle down, we got a story here, and you got to help us. We've been waiting for you." And the two Paiutes guided them through town, across a little pasture with some cottonwoods, up to a knoll that overlooked the lake of stories.

Ananda and Chiara did not even notice the continued mingling of their hair.

And so it began—

"It wasn't a week ago that the band from a high school in Reno came on out here looking," said one of the Indians. "They were looking for someplace to leave their grief, because two days before, one of them, a fifteen-year-old girl, had drowned out here at the lake. They found her body by the shoreline just as the turkey vultures were coming for her."

"I was afraid that this trip would get serious," remarked Chiara.

"Don't count on it," rejoined Ananda.

The Paiute went on: "Now the students were in the band, and they thought they would get together and play for the girl, play out here, because all of them were lonely. There is nothing like the solitude of the living."

"I like it so far. No moral uplift," ventured Chiara.

"And so they had decided to get the band together and come back to Pyramid Lake. Just last week, I tell you, they got their horns and drums and right out there"—the Paiute gestured toward the shoreline—"along that beach they assembled, all in their best uniforms; it was the whole band decked out. They formed up in their lines and started out along the beach right down there, playing the slowest songs they knew. There was a wind off the lake and they had the feeling the waves were listening. They marched on, playing, all the way around the far bend, and there they rested, to have some time in silence to pray. But nobody felt any better."

Cookie, during the telling, could almost hear the high school band music, fading as they went down the sand. But she dismissed the hearing, figuring that the Paiutes were driving her batty. That was the idea, wasn't it?

"As they rested, one of the kids, wandering in the brush out there around the bend, found a freshly dead pelican: a white pelican with a six-foot wingspan. Someone had shot it. He took it back to the band, who by the waters were looking for the spirit of the drowned girl. They gathered round the bird. And they spread its huge wings, and, with two students holding the bird in front of the band, they took up their instruments and began to play, and bearing the bird came along the beach around the bend and onto the long stretch of sand—"

"Oh my heavens!" cried out Renato—

Ananda, Chiara, Cookie, and Renato scrambled up to their feet, and there they were: coming around the bend in the beach, in their uniforms playing, the high schoolers so hopeful, with the pelican held in front of them—

"What are you doing to us?" demanded Cookie of the Indians, as she watched the band move toward them.

"I was afraid of this," said Chiara: she knew they might have to help them, and didn't know how.

"They are marching too far toward death," said one of the Paiutes.

"They need a messenger to death. It could be anything. It could be anyone. But that is what they must have. They cannot be denied," said the other.

Cookie went several steps toward them.

"Not yet," warned one of the Indians.

"Just watch," said the other.

The group of high schoolers played on, as if they thought they could by what they did save something. They marched bedecked and beribboned down the beach toward the knoll; a breeze off the lake moved the feathers of the dead bird and the tassels on the uniforms of the band. They came slowly.

"They have come so far, to be here," said one Paiute.

"This is a lake of sorrows," said the other.

The band came halfway down the beach when the ones holding the bird aloft ahead of the rest stopped and put the white dead beauty down on the sand. They surrounded the bird, and in a semicircle they played, facing one another. And except for their hands on their instruments and the moving air, there was now a holding in of things, all things slowed in the circling of the hour. Behind them, the lake with its powers charged the stillness; and upon the stillness that small music tossed.

"They are so young," said Chiara.

"They're crazy to come out here," said Renato quietly, even as he memorized with his eyes the scene on the beach.

"You can see they want the bird to take their message to the land of the dead," explained one Paiute. "And so it may."

As he finished speaking, the bird moved. A few more awful blasts from the band, and the pelican stood on its feet and shook its head.

"Well, isn't this a goddam miracle," commented Cookie.

"But there's a catch," the Paiute went on.

The bird took a few steps and raised its wings. The band cheered as the bird stepped down the beach and lifted into the air, they cheered as it made a turn down the beach and headed back toward them, and so emotional and fulfilled were they all that they were not prepared when the bird faltered in flight and fell like a rock among them, plunking down on its head in the sand.

All at once the whole band turned toward them. There was no sound now but the sound of the wind streaming off the waters. The teenagers looked steadily at them.

"What are they doing?" asked Cookie nervously.

"You will see," said a Paiute.

"Why don't they move?" asked Ananda.

Ananda later remembered thinking that they were going to be eaten alive, just as in some lousy Los Angeles drive-in movie. And it made a certain kind of sense: if anything could kill, it was the music of high school bands.

The band lifted their instruments and began to play again at the bird, as though it didn't have enough problems, being dragged from the next world into this one, and back again. It's tough for wildlife.

Chiara burst out: "So what the hell? What is this insistence on visiting the land of the dead? Isn't the band asking a little much? What is this, Homer? OK, Odysseus, he can visit the land of the dead, but a pelican? C'mon!"

"They're only in high school," explained the Paiute.

The band was grating away again, tooting and honking, trying their damnedest to bring the bird back to life, so that it could take off and bear their message away.

"It's not so dumb," said the Paiute, "the bird would know the way. Who else around here knows?"

The band played on, whistling and rasping, clattering and banging, and the pelican moved again, stood again, stepped and once again was airborne. Only this time it made a few turns, careening around above their heads and then like a warplane brought down by ground fire it slanted out of the sky and dunked into the water just offshore.

"So what's the catch?" asked Cookie finally.

"Glad you asked. This is the catch: if they can't send the bird, one of you travelers will be chosen to die and go see the girl in the next world. Too bad for you," said the Paiute sweetly.

The teenagers were in a panic, and five of them rushed into the water to retrieve the bird, dragging out the wet and heavy body, their hands slipping on the feathers, lugging it onshore where they dropped it.

"It's spectacles like this that make me wonder how anybody gets to college," said Chiara.

But Renato knew he was fading: he couldn't help but wonder about the other side of death: the colors: he wanted to know what it was, in the next world, that could take the place of a beauty so sensuous and abstract at once.

The band—wet, cold, grumpy, desperate as only teens can be—played on. Ananda was getting bored. She was so tired. So many years. The persistent ugliness of the music pressed upon them like the weight of water, it was as though the lake was being constructed over their heads.

All of them would remember it—the pressing of death, so homely and persistent.

Back at the grocery store, others among the Paiutes mulled it over.

"This is a funny one! Do you think that they can figure it out?"

"It's a little early in the game for a death. It would kind of cut the story short—though Pyramid is a kind of Lost Coast."

"Going down with lousy music. A bad one—even for whites. And they don't have long."

Juha came out of the store that minute but of course didn't notice a thing. He was still talking lumber and tools, plans, and what it is to have your whole work in your hands. They talked happily, and death kept its distance. Juha would be tough to kill, anyhow.

It was Ananda who figured it out. She pushed past Cookie and Chiara and headed for the truck, her step strong. From the cab, she brought out the dented trumpet they had been given back at the ranch of angels, and with the instrument in hand she strode back up the knoll, straight by her compatriots and down along the beach.

Juha was just at the moment explaining his ideas on the placement of casement windows.

"You can't just throw them in anywhere. They're like eyes. Would you put your eyes just anywhere?" he asked with burly rhetoric.

"I'd like to have a spare set in my ass," suggested one of his interlocutors.

"Now, with a house, you can do just that," rejoined Juha enthusiastically.

On the knoll, Renato was growing weaker, and he stretched out in the dirt.

On the beach Ananda, having shouldered her way through the still-dripping band, was standing over the pelican.

The drowned band member had played the trumpet.

It had been a long time since her days in the clubs. But she lifted the trumpet up and turned loose a riff, it made her smile, she turned loose another one and then came through with a few trills, a few cuts and bursts, and then it came back to her, she lashed out with a long raw flourish—standing in the sun she blew bright passages of sound, lifting up her instrument she turned through a devil-may-care burn of notes, she cut a wild run deep down into the air, she knew what to do with the trumpet of the angels: she knew death was their sidekick on this trip.

A rush and sparkling burst upon the pelican: it stood on the sand as though reconstructed from within. It stalked over the sand, looked out to the blue clear horizons everywhere, gave Ananda an arrogant stare.

Out in front of the grocery store, Juha got the sudden idea that it would do him good to have some beef to chew on; and so he went in for a handful of jerky. Where the hell were the rest of them, he wondered. Was he the only one who ever got hungry?

The teenagers gathered round the bird, and every one of them put their hands on it.

The pelican spread its wings and the wind off the lake lifted it into the sky, and as they watched it flew faster and faster, until it left the wind behind.

Watching the curve of that flight far out over the lake,

Ananda didn't see the Paiute next to her. The man pointed to the trumpet.

"That belongs to us," he said.

"And why would you need it?" asked Ananda.

"Did you make a dead thing live by asking a lot of goddam questions?"

She handed it over.

Up on the knoll, Renato stood shakily, together with Cookie and Chiara. Juha, espying them from the store, had made his way through town and clambered up the hill to them.

"What's doing, guys?" he asked cheerily, as he chomped on his jerky.

Ananda was coming along the beach toward them; behind her Juha could see a flock of pelicans wheeling over the lake.

"Maybe we should get some lunch, huh?" pressed Juha, puzzled by the silence of his traveling mates.

Ananda joined them.

"Let's eat," she said.

They headed down the hill. Chiara longed to see Izzy. More Indians joined them, they had a conversation of their own, pointing and laughing at our journeymen and women, until they came round to the table in back of the store. There were more Paiutes there, and their leader looked them over and said: "Well, you did it. But you're not the swiftest bunch I ever seen."

Ananda was by now feeling a little combative. "Was all that really necessary?"

"We were supposed to get something from the angels. You were the messengers. You let us see the trumpet do its work. On certain occasions, we need to be able to make the dead live. It is one of the tasks of angels, and one of ours. Now you have helped us."

"Why didn't *you* help *us?*" asked Chiara.

"We did help you. We showed you the band. We trusted you."

"We almost didn't figure it out," said Chiara angrily. All she could think about was seeing Izzy.

The Paiute turned to her. "Well, you should be good for something."

"Maybe we'll stay around for another story, the first one was such a humdinger," broke in Ananda.

"You're on the road, and you have to stay on it," said the Indian, chuckling.

Chiara looked him over, and then looked at Ananda, who winked at her.

"Hold on now, whoa now, just a minute," broke in the stumped Juha. "What in the hell are you talking about?"

Cookie went over to him.

"While you were talking in the store, we were out by the lake playing with death," explained Cookie.

"Death?" exclaimed Juha in his big baritone. "Do you feel OK? Do you want some jerky?"

"And besides that," the Indian went on, "we needed to find out from Juha certain things about building for a special lodge down near the lake. It will be the House of the Travelers. Whenever we have work someplace in the world, we will enter the house, and when we emerge, we will be in that place. The house will not need to move, but we within it will move."

"Is that what I told you?" asked Juha with incredulity.

"Have you not built for your fellow travelers a strange house that moves? Who else would be qualified to advise us?"

"I guess you're right," admitted Juha.

"And why would you need to go somewhere else?" asked Chiara.

"To use the trumpet, of course."

"I think I'll go sleep," said Renato; and he headed for the truck. He felt confused. Colors mingled in his vision.

"You sure do know how to show your visitors a rock-'em sock-'em good time," said Cookie.

"Just you wait," said one of the Indians.

There was a long pause while our bedraggled group thought *that* one over.

How 'bout some sightseeing?" suggested Cookie brightly. "Or do we have to stand around chewing on death all afternoon?"

And with that unanswerable inquiry, the gathering broke up.

It was a hot day in the city; the air smelled remarkably like vomit.

They had the car all packed.

Grimes wanted Tabby to go through the whole story again, it was an exercise for him, he needed to know all about their target, it was like reconnaissance. And besides, he knew Tabby wanted him to have the same feelings.

Tabby went through it—

Everybody knew that Ben, Tabby's father, the preacher at his pentecostal church, had done well; having the plate in his head gave him a certain cachet with his congregation. Ben's real regret, though, was that he didn't figure out this scam earlier, it would have saved him all that time wasted on robberies. So dangerous! No one praised you for them. No one looked up to you. It would have saved him the gunfight, the head wound, the brain hemorrhage, the operation. But at least a nice social worker had introduced him to her pastor.

Ben loved it right away. Religion was about getting other people to kiss your ass for stealing their money. It was a scam of genius, something that really worked, that would get you all the sucks you want.

A con who had died in prison had told him about the trafficking in bodies that went on with the churches and hospitals and funeral houses. It was great, the way people kept right on dying. Death was the business of religion, making big money, for centuries, too.

Ben got out of prison and started his own church—they were easy to kick off and he had a Christian upbringing anyhow. He got a reputation for laboring among the downtrodden, there were some articles in the paper, and the city council had given him a certificate. He had a framed letter from the governor.

He had been working it for years.

He directed the families in his church who had lost someone

at home—it happened all the time, there were so many fucking old people in church—to give over the body to his partners at the mortuary. He got a piece of the action everywhere. He had a deal with orderlies in the hospitals to deliver corpses to the funeral houses where he had a percentage, they sold off some bodies to medical schools, he had an interest in the crematoriums. Cremation was good, not so much stink.

Sometimes for a joke they would burn cats alive, no more than four or five at a time, and give the ashes to the family in little urns they paid good money for. They loved to pay. The human ashes they sold to a compost firm; recycling was important to California.

Ben had seen scams, but nothing like these profits. And he loved to comfort the grieving relatives, they were always there to remind him of his holy calling, of the solace he could give. He comforted them with his gentle hands and deep voice. Sometimes he cried with them.

Being a preacher's son, Tabby had a good time growing up— at least for a while. He could see how people respected his father; they would turn to him in any crisis, they were so needy. In his teens, he found out about the trafficking in corpses. Ben used to have him go around and collect commissions from the undertakers; he'd have a checklist of corpses and where they had been delivered. He'd have to go to every one and check them off and bring back cash.

One time, when Tabby was thirteen years old, he forgot to stop at one of the undertakers. His father counted the money and saw that it was short. Ben rose up from the table and stood up tall over his son and and said he was a thief and slapped him down to the floor. And when Tabby got up Ben told him to go into the bedroom and get some underwear the whores had left. Ben made him bring it back and he made Tabby take off his clothes right in front of him and put on the whore's panties and walk all around the house with them on.

He had to wear them until he got down on his knees and begged God for forgiveness. He had to say over and over he was a thief who stole from his own father.

* * *

Tabby and Grimes had a special category for Ben: A Maggot of
God.

"I never really thought he was human," Tabby explained. "If
you opened him up, you'd find no heart, you'd find a dead piglet."

They were ready.

Tabby and Grimes took Angelica over to the church and spent
an hour screwing until the preacher showed up. He was a man
who had seen a lot. But he had never come back to his place of
worship to find a tired hooker and two big teenagers.

Grimes held him with a nine-millimeter submachine gun while
he handed the snubbie to Tabby.

"Dad, I love Angelica," said Tabby politely. He was deter-
mined always to be polite, just as Grimes had taught him. "And
I don't think you treat her right. And besides, you're a thief. Did
you think it was going to go on forever? Did you think that no
one would stand up for this innocent whore? That no one would
come to punish you, you with your pig's heart?" Tabby paused.

"I'm going to put on some music now. Then Angelica is going
to watch me pistol-whip you."

Tabby went over to the preacher's stereo, the one that fed the
whole church, and as the cello sounded he hefted the pistol in
his hand and walked straight toward the poor bastard.

"I always wondered about that plate in your head," said Tabby.
"I mean, whether it would ring."

At Pyramid, over by their truck Ananda and Chiara leaned on
each other, and Cookie held Juha's arm. And it may be said that
our strange group was looking more disheveled than usual.

No one was really surprised when, upon opening the back door
of the house on the truck, the coyote peered out. For a minute

she just sat there, framed in the doorway, looking at them with her golden eyes. And then she took her gold back into the shadows of the house, to hide herself from Mike and Jeb, who came around from the front of the truck, one with a pistol drawn, the other with an automatic weapon pointed at five tired people who had turned away death once already.

Which brought to their minds a question: what is worth doing twice a day?

9

MIKE AND JEB had had enough of their job. While they stand with weapons trained upon our wayward band, let us recount the adventures of these two detectives. We remember them being shat upon back in the Toiyabe Mountains; since then their fortunes had declined. After watching the coyote chase Izzy, they had followed the whole dissolute bunch into Fallon. The road into town, however, was in the flyover zone for the big navy base outside of town; from this base pilots took off to practice their bombing runs. In parts of the Basin they even got to use real bombs. And, with real bombs, it was hard for some pilots to resist a car headed along the lonely roads of the big high desert. And so, driving along, grim and professional, Mike and Jeb were flummoxed to see high in the sky an attack jet make a long, lazy curve in the sky, and moving eight hundred miles an hour at two hundred feet off the ground head straight and unmistakably for them.

"Naw," said Mike, "he couldn't be—" as they watched the rocket leave the wing, and, spurting orange and blue fire, zip toward them with incredible velocity.

"No way," said Jeb, as the weapon angled in for the kill.

* * *

The explosion was powerful enough to have made of our stalwart investigators two flaming stumps; but, strewn along the sides of the road with their clothes and snacks, they held together. The rocket had hit not their truck but the trailer they were towing that contained their guns, ammo, and sporting equipment. From the detonation Jeb took in the shoulder one of his very own whizzing bullets, and was peppered in the ass by shrapnel from an exploded bowling ball. As for Mike, his very head was nearly engulfed by a burning creel, which he fended off clumsily, only to slip and fall smack into the molten lead of his melted fishing weights.

Yet, both of them on their backs, they were able to watch a spectacle talked about for years by the birds in the Great Basin: the duck decoys catapulting through the air—on fire and looking stunned, but finally in flight.

From their ignominious roadside posture, wounded and blaspheming, they were rescued by a passing farmer who chuckled as he heaved them into the back of his pickup.

"You boys should drive more careful! Cain't you see the mess you made! Jesus!" he remonstrated.

And, shaking his head, he drove them down to the nearest spot where medical care was available: Salt Wells, a lively bar, social club, and legendary house of prostitution.

The farmer, who knew the place, rang the bell and swung open the gate, whereupon a number of strong women stalked from the house, hefted Mike and Jeb like a pair of sorry corpses, and toted them into the back room with the Jacuzzi.

Looking around at their saviors, Mike and Jeb felt much better. Mike was assuaged by the gentle handling he received from a statuesque brunette named Sultana, to whom, through the shocking pain of his burns, he pledged the reform of his disrespectful attitude toward women, and went on to swear oaths that he would earn her love with decades of virile devotion. This, he declared, would be his privilege.

"I've seen it before," observed Sultana. "When a man is in pain, his mouth fills up with shit."

Jeb, who was also feeling weepy and dependent, at least had sense enough to keep quiet and let his suffering like an ardent shadow extend through his flesh.

By the ambulance crew they were removed from the cathouse, carried out through the bar to the bray and razz of the keyed-up crowd of johns.

"Kink City! The Capital of Kink! Kink-o-Rama!"

"Looks like a couple o' used-up fireworks—did you go off by yourselves?"

"You get what you pay for—"

"What do you call *that* one? Whew!"

"It must have been Gasoline Sally!"

Mike and Jeb, bandaged and furious, were plunked down in the ambulance by the two paramedics, who on the way to the hospital announced to them that in their honor they intended to stop at a bar called the Double Eagle for "two stiff ones." Neither detective thought the joke was funny, though the bartender, our weathered old boy Stumper, cackled like a loon.

At the hospital, they were given a room together. This, of course, made them sicker. But it was there they decided to attack our infamous group and kidnap Izzy and deliver her over to one or another—according to the bids—of her putative fathers. It all sounded masculine, forthright, propitious: as history has demonstrated, not even guided missiles will bring men to their senses.

With fresh dressings on their wounds they had stalked from the hospital.

Standing there at Pyramid Lake with their pistols and rifles aimed at our nomadic five, they wondered what to do next.

"All right, where's the girl?" cried Mike.

All five of our threatened party burst out laughing.

Chiara stepped forward. "Let me give you a mother's guess:

she is, even as we speak, in a distant bed whose sheets are full of flower petals, naked and happy in the arms of that fragrant and muscular Jamaican, Muscovado Taine."

Mike and Jeb paused. Distinctly in the air was the sound they had been hearing for over a week: the sputtering of their lives.

"Where? Tell us where!" demanded Jeb.

"In Fallon at the ranch of angels. Just ask anybody in town where the angels live."

The two detectives tried madly to think. Sex among angels? Was there a law?

"While you're thinking, could I ask you a question?" said Ananda.

"Sure," replied Mike amiably, glad for the distraction from his vague cerebral efforts.

"What is that loud sputtering I hear?" she said sweetly.

Cookie put together some salad and chops and cornbread; the hot food sizzled up over a big fire Juha built up on the beach. The lake studied the stars.

"Are you always this good to kidnappers?" asked Jeb as hot butter flowed out of the cornbread down his hand.

"I guess it was all them bandages," said Cookie. "It's hard to get too hepped up when you're being threatened by crippled mummies."

"Besides, we had earlier in the day met death, who always tells the truth; so we knew you were full of shit," said Ananda.

"I just haven't felt right since they blew up all my fishing gear," admitted Jeb.

"Me, I'm still thinking of Sultana," said Mike. And he was.

They turned morosely upon Chiara.

"Why do so many men fall in love with you?" asked Mike. Mike had, in his background work on Chiara, heard from a generous selection of her suitors, who to help him had formed a committee.

"It's because of my tattoos."

"Where are they?" he asked.

"Hidden," replied the animated Chiara. "It takes years to find them."

"I'd come over to your side, if you'd pay me," said Mike after reflection.

"I don't pay mummies. We've already done enough trafficking with the dead for one day."

"Where are you all going?" Jeb asked.

"To get lost," said Renato.

"Maybe you need your own security force," ventured Mike.

"Maybe you need an escort," seconded Jeb.

These faltering offers were registered by our travelers with astounded silence. But Mike and Jeb had never been so lonely. It was Pyramid again, brushing away their simpering conceptions of themselves, reducing them to their own strange raw materials.

In other words, they were maniacs even more dangerous than before.

"No, no, no, you're being paid to spy on us, harass us, make us sorry, and in the long run to win for your clients custody of my daughter, are you not?" asked Chiara.

"You're damn right!" said Mike, suddenly proud once again of his role upholding familial integrity.

Why are all maniacs contradictory? wondered Chiara.

Renato shook his head. "I laid out a couple of sleeping bags down by the water. Why don't I show you where they are, and you can let yourselves and your wounds down to sleep."

And so he did, and they did. Everybody knows that sleep and death are brothers: at Pyramid Lake they are twin brothers. And so did Mike and Jeb fall into black regions of unnatural refreshment.

—Refreshment they needed. For the next morning they woke up alone, except for flocks of pelicans that turned and turned over their heads.

As anyone who has pistol-whipped a family member will know, it's easy to go on too long.

Tabby left his father half dead, and he and Grimes had a few more rounds with Angelica, bending her over a chair, making her thank them and thank them, she was so grateful, just like they knew she would be. They stopped every now and then to give Ben a few kicks in the face.

"Someone had to do it," said Tabby.

"This is our day," said Grimes. He was proud of Tabby, who hadn't said a single harsh word. "I liked how you handled that. Like a hero."

"This is our day." Tabby stood with good posture, he liked the sweatiness of it, this fucking and pistol-whipping, it was a workout! He wished there were some mirrors in the church, maybe even some way to record it all, especially the clanging of his father's head.

They had to move now. Grimes had it all planned out.

First, a phone call to the newspapers. Angelica would tell them just the kind of fucking the preacher liked and how he paid her right out of the safe at the church, and how Ben had attacked her. And how she was saved by two brave young men. Finally someone looked out for her. Stood up for her.

Tabby and Grimes took all the money in the safe, so they could give it away. They had this part all figured out, this doing good, this setting things right. Tabby couldn't wait to start handing it out. As for the rest, Grimes had explained it all, how they didn't have to look back. The work was begun, the world was begging for it; and there would always be grateful people around to wash up after they left.

They went out, checked all the guns in the special racks in the Chevy, made sure they had enough ammunition and cleaning oil, clapped each other on the back a few times, and traded a few high-fives. They had cash. They strutted around. Tabby felt charged and wild and happy—to finally do something that counted! It was so simple, it felt so good. He knew that once they were on the road, the world would look better—it would look thankful.

The city pressed upon them like a suffocating blanket. They were ready to throw it off.

They headed up Highway 101, wanting to drive straight through to the north coast. But they had a stop to make first. They had to buy some clothes, that would be the proper thing, Grimes thought. And it was—Brooks Brothers, downtown San Francisco. He loved watching Tabby in the mirrors; his big shoulders barely fit in the sport coats. They spent two hours talking to the salesman; the way he helped them on with the coats was so respectful. He would hold them out, slip them on, then touch the material into place, check the length and cut. He really cared for them. He could tell they were special, and that they had important work to do.

They turned contemptuously away from the suits, and settled on blue blazers and charcoal flannels, only the classics for them. They took a long time picking out the ties, they had to be just right. There aren't any ugly heroes, everybody knew that.

They wore the clothes out of the store and found the car and headed for open country.

Two days up the road, north of San Francisco, past the Lost Coast, through the beautiful redwoods, they drove with the top of the car down and the trees high as their hopes. Way up by Crescent City Tabby called Angelica and she told him everything—the problems getting Ben to stop bleeding, the questioning by the police and the arrest, the newspaper articles and the charges filed to disband the church and put his father back in the slammer, his fulminations against Tabby, the spittle always on his face. They were thinking that it was something about the plate. Ben wasn't talking right. Scratchy, like a kicked radio.

Angelica laughed, and then sighed and said how much she missed them and how happy she was to have the money they left her. They were so kind, she said. She felt better about things, knowing the two of them were at work.

After he hung up, Tabby turned to Grimes, who, with his tie still knotted carefully and his coat on, leaned casually against the side of the car.

"We're on our way, fella!" Tabby yelled. And he did a little dance and a strut. He wanted to be able always to swell up just like this, just because someone was so grateful to them. Because they'd helped.

"And I could use another workout before too long! It's justice time!" Tabby went on. "They'll beg, won't they? They're going to beg, I know it."

Grimes just nodded, he was thinking ahead. There was so much to do, so many responsibilities.

The cello boomed from the car stereo.

Our troupe was traveling along the west side of Pyramid Lake, past the cutoff to Reno and past Sutcliff, toward the dirt roads that led to a pair of deserts in love: the Smoke Creek and the Black Rock. As they came over the rise whence they looked over the Smoke Creek, Renato, up front with Ananda and Chiara, said, "The world is a ragbag of beauties."

And, a raggedy bunch themselves, they went on north into the silence of the two biggest alkali plains of the Basin.

Some new lovers, after a week, take their hours and thread them together with pleasures; and that jewelry they hang upon one another, the bright remembrance of affection.

Some lovers, after a week, know that pleasure is a country, and that love may travel far; but to claim that country lovers must learn perfectly an ecstatic patience.

Some lovers, after a week, are just warmed up.

Besides, Izzy and Muscovado liked the food.

Just at the beginning of the desert, in the southwest corner of the playa, they came upon a ranch.

Renato parked the truck beside the peacock, a common bird on rural Nevada ranches. There didn't seem to be anyone around, and so they spilled from the truck and sat down on some benches near the water pump, in the shade of a half-dozen black locusts.

The silence had changed. While Pyramid Lake had a silence rapt in power, as though the air held within itself heat lightning from another world, the Smoke Creek desert had a winged silence, a silence that gave a weightlessness to the morning.

Given all this, no one was especially surprised when the peacock strutted over and told them

THE STORY OF THE WILD LIGHT OF GOD

"Look," said Chiara right off, "I've had about all the eschatology I can take."

"Let me give you a tip," said the bird. "Never try to argue with a peacock. I'll swish my tail, and take your breath away."

"Thanks anyway. I prefer other tails," riposted Chiara.

"Are you always this friendly to strangers?" inquired Ananda, copping a line.

"I don't get to see many. Almost nobody goes through the Smoke Creek. And even when they come, they don't bring their own house. Such as it is," said the peacock, looking skeptically at the truck with its ornate habitation.

"I was inspired," explained Juha.

"You are all mad as birds," pronounced the peacock.

"Look who's talking," said Chiara.

"But you are only in part mad as birds; as for the rest of your souls, you are plain as hens, even as I was myself once. I'm telling you, at the rate you're going it will be an eternity before you get smart. You just think you can go cackling on, and everything will be terrif. You're a sweet bunch, but pathetic. You need the counsel of a peacock."

"I like this," said Cookie. "Nice and straight. No spooks."

"Let me start with some simple introductory material: In the beginning, in paradise, there were in the world more colors than you see now. The ones you do see now are meant as an introduction to the real, original colors."

"Now you're talking my language," said Renato.

"Please go on," urged Chiara.

"Are you friends with those junky angels?" asked the suspicious Cookie.

"No, but I hear they are friends with you," replied the peacock, who, although his tail still was folded, was beginning to stalk around with a rustling and a shuffling.

"And so to my story," said the peacock, settling in under the locusts, near to them all, glancing with bright avian eye at his audience.

"Once there was a bird in the desert, and he wanted to have a wild life. What is there, after all, up here?" The peacock gestured around with his remarkable claws. "The whole playa is short on nightlife, no? I mean, where would you go to cut loose? Go out and pick up on a rattlesnake? Peck on a badger? Taunt a bobcat? I mean, the old chestnut 'All dressed up and nowhere to go' was *invented* for me. But here I was, a ranch peacock."

"And so what does this have to do with us?" asked Juha in his brusque and admirable way.

"I was sort of hoping that the lot of you would help me solve a riddle—you should be good at something!" shot back the peacock.

"You're saying we're not good enough?" asked Cookie.

"We'll see, sweetheart," said the bird. "Now listen up: I was, as I said, sitting around here at the ranch when I heard a voice speak to me, and it was a voice of a certain gravelly authority, I've got to say even his little whisper sounded like someone had touched off a case of dynamite. And wouldn't you know against all the odds it turned out to be God. And God said, 'Peacock! You've done a good thing. You've accepted your lot! Took you long enough. Most of you living creatures never see that you've got to find out where you are and what you're really doing, without a lot of goddam—if you will excuse the expression—embellishment and expectation, without a lot of pretending and out-and-out bullshit. Yessiree, you have come round! You're just a lowly ranch peacock. Too bad for you!' "

"Now whoa, wait a minute. This is God talking?" queried Juha.

"You betcha."

"We haven't gotten to God yet; we've tried to keep it simple, you know: coyotes, sex, magic dust, death," explained Ananda.

"But this is just the kind of thing that perks up God!" The peacock felt like he had scored a point.

"So go on with your story," said Chiara resignedly.

"Thank you, I will!" cried the peacock.

"Are peacocks good to eat? As good as turkey, maybe?" speculated Cookie.

"A gamey, almost divine flavor," guessed Chiara.

"Could I have some order here?" said the peacock. "Don't you remember we're in the middle of a conversation about God? Fer chrissake!"

"We will listen reverently," said Ananda.

"At least for a while," added Chiara.

"Now then," the peacock went on, "God didn't stop just yet. She went on! He said, 'And so, peacock, let me see—what fate will I visit upon you? Hmmm . . . I've got it!'

"Now lemme tell you, I wanted to hear this. Who knows? Maybe I was going to get my own show, and get to take that show on the road, or something. And then God said, 'First of all, let me tell you what you do not know: you have the most beautiful tail in the world.' "

"What a common line," cracked Chiara.

" 'And second of all,' said God, 'this beauty, through all your life, must have one quality: it must remain invisible to you.'

" 'Wait a minute!' I protested to God, 'you mean I never get to see it? Or even just feel dressy and stylish? Ever?'

" 'Nope,' said God, 'but there's one more thing: you have to find someone who will tell you the true story of your tail: that is, where you got it, what to do with it, etc.; but most of all, tell how we can use that radiance of feathers to return to the world's original colors, the true colors that here you represent to us—if you can find this storyteller, then you get one other thing.'

" 'OK, OK, OK, so . . . what is it? What? What do I get?'

" 'Well, it's *obvious* what!' said God grouchily. 'You get to flourish over all the earth the wild light of God.' "

There was a long pause.

The peacock looked at them all.

"And so—" ventured Chiara.

"So there!" said the peacock.

"You mean that's it?" asked the indignant Juha.

"What the devil does that mean?" quizzed Cookie.

"I was hoping *you* could tell *me*," replied the peacock.

"Do we have to?" sassed Chiara.

"Maybe it would help us think if you opened that tail, instead of just talking about it," suggested Ananda.

"What makes you think you get to see it?" said the peacock with hauteur. "Besides, I pledged to God that I would in all my life open my tail under one condition only."

"And what is that?" asked Juha with anxiety, since he thought he knew the answer.

"I will open it only if I hear the ringing of a bell of the angels," said the peacock proudly.

Juha relaxed. He had been afraid he was going to be called upon to play the revolting harmonica.

"Just a minute," he said, and he lumbered over to the truck and plucked from the dashboard the tiny bell.

"You're kidding," said the peacock.

Juha held out the little thing between thumb and forefinger, gave it a shake, and the sound brought the bird toward them and everyone in the Smoke Creek Desert could have heard the rippling and cracking of the light as the colors of his tail arced across the sky.

No one moved. Not even Renato for his easel.

The surrounding world went pale, because there is only so much color in the world, and the demanding iridescence of the feathers needed some green from the sagebrush and some blue from the sky; some black from the eyes of rattlesnakes and some yellow from veins of gold spiraling out of the earth.

"Foolish bunch!" reprimanded the peacock. "Did you think that the peacock was just a bird, that his tail was just a spectacle, that beauty is just an idea?"

AND AS IF to confirm that ideas will only take us so far, just then behind them they saw grind to a halt a dilapidated ranch pickup with a rifle slung in the back window. Dust was spewed all over them.

"So thanks. Think I'll be moving along just now," said the peacock, as with haste he strutted away.

It was then our wanderers realized that the big muscular driver of the pickup was taking the rifle from the rack and stepping down into the dirt, where she took aim at them one by one, as if in drill for a mass shooting. But our dear travelers were getting tired of having guns pointed at them.

"We've seen it all before," said Chiara hotly.

"Besides, you look too much like Gertie," added Cookie.

The rifle-wielding woman smiled.

"My sister," she said gruffly. "She told me about you rip-snortin' crazy-ass bunch, and it don't surprise me to find you here messin' with the Peacocker."

"I must say I do love Nevada. You look every bit as sweet as our dear Gertie," said Renato ceremoniously.

"O fer blessed sakes!" said the woman, and she swung the rifle around and fired off a shot that rang the big bell by the barn; then three more shots to spin the weather vane at the top of her house; swiveling around, she squeezed off a pair that blew open the door to her chicken coop, releasing two fat hens she dropped with two quick shots; for lagniappe, she picked up the spinning in the vane again, whizzed a bullet through a little window in the house on the truck, picked the hood ornament off an ancient pickup abandoned near the corral, and for punctuation clanged the bell again three times.

"You ring a little bell, all the bells in the world want to get in the act," said Juha.

"Shut up," commented Beulah.

And she took a bullwhip from the cab of her truck.

"Maybe you should get into the act, meathead," said Beulah.

"Try me," challenged Juha.

"Toss that little bell into the air, I'll show you some swipin'," promised the big rancher.

Juha flung the tiny thing into the air.

Beulah all in one motion uncoiled the whip and smacked it so just the tip caught the bell, which catapulted high, then turned with little spins and descended light as a little chick back into Juha's hand. Beulah then pivoted—an awesome sight—and with several strokes snapped the latch off the barn door, wrenched on three valves to irrigate some alfalfa fields, and wrapped up the handles of two double-sided axes that with a jerk of the whip she sent cartwheeling toward her. As they went end-over-end through the dust, she dropped the whip, and snatched out of the air the two axes, one in each hand.

"I think I'm going to like this woman—" began Ananda.

But she was cut off by the ax that came rotating across the yard. Beulah had let go the first one with an over-the-head heave; as it spun the blade passed directly in front of our wanderers, who were of course standing at attention. With a terrific explosion of splinters, and a rocking of the whole fence, the edge slammed into a post just above the peacock's head.

The bird folded his tail. Color in the area was restored.

Beulah reared back with the second ax and whipped it toward the front of her house, so that instead of the blade the flat end of the ax head crashed into her front door and blew it wide open.

"Well," she said with a shrug, "it's a lucky thing I made all them raspberry pies this mornin'! Damn you all!" And with one sweep of her arm she herded them toward the house.

"Does your hospitality always have this same razzle-dazzle?" asked Chiara on the way in.

"You're going to tell us that the pie's already cut, right?" inquired Cookie.

But Beulah had questions: "And who the *hell* are them two mummies chasin' all you fools? I shot out all their tires just north of Pyramid after one of 'em called me 'Missy.' 'The name's Beulah', I said jes' as I opened fire."

"They're used to it," Cookie assured Beulah.

After hot raspberry pie and coffee, which they one and all found made a very satisfying breakfast, Beulah continued her questioning.

"Now, I want to know some things right off. First, where the hell is your sassy-ass daughter?" She looked at Chiara.

"She is in Fallon dedicating her sassy ass to spring frolics," said her mother.

"I thought so," mused Beulah. "Now fer seconds, tell me— ain't it true the world has gotten unloosed head-scratchin' hell-puzzlin' heaven-sent plain-jane crazy? Now ain't it?"

"A fair statement," answered Renato, who at this point half expected his brushes to jump like snakes out of his case.

"Jes' like Gertie predicted!" crowed Beulah.

"Give your sister a big smacker from us," proposed Juha.

"Now fer thirds," demanded Beulah, "how good are any of you at diggin' ditches?"

There was a long pause. They were, as a group, getting good at pauses.

"Enough is enough, and it's time you came down to earth. A little fun goes a long way. Besides, I need a big channel dug from over the main water ditch to the new garden. I need some labor. *Free* labor. I'm glad you came along! Come with me!"

And she marched them out and put them all to work.

"And don't be takin' too many breaks, neither! Exceptin' of course for Cookie and Juha, who might need to go off and feed on each other. As for the rest of you, if you ain't workin' steady, you ain't workin'!"

The peacock looked on with a smirk.

"Tastes like the elixir of life," said Muscovado to Izzy. "Has this always been true?"

"It needs a stirring to bring out the full flavor," replied our Iz.

Mike and Jeb were beginning to get the idea that they should spend a little more time letting their wounds heal. The Paiutes by unanimous tribal vote refused to replace the tires, so the detectives had to send to Reno. A shop there had agreed to bring them out. And so, at Sutcliff, looking out over Pyramid, they waited.

"You know," said Jeb, "it doesn't even look like a lake. It looks like blue plastic."

Mike knew this was a mistake.

"It looks like the blue lint fuzz you take from a dryer," he corrected.

A pelican, spiraling down out of the zenith, plunged into the lake. After a minute, twenty pelicans surfaced.

"Maybe we should shut up," suggested Jeb.

Tabby and Grimes were headed for the Sierra.

"It's because we're good! It's because we just can't help ourselves," Tabby was saying to an irritated Grimes. "Just think of the stories that people will tell about us. They knew that we loved them. That one girl, she even cried, she was sniffling like a puppy. Nothing will ever be the same for them! I think they really liked the clothes. You should be proud. You're not backing out, are you?"

"You weren't supposed to give away so much of our goddamn money," said Grimes. His friend had just dropped four thousand dollars cash on a brunette in a booth collecting for children with leukemia. The money was used to buy toys for them, give counseling to the parents. Tabby had talked to her a long time, such little children. There were pictures of them in their hospital beds, they looked so bewildered. Tabby wished he could walk in, tall and strong, to every one of their rooms and let them touch his big hands. He'd show them what they could become, give them something to live for.

Earlier that morning on the coast, in Crescent City, they had sorted a couple thousand into envelopes and sealed them up, and then gone out on the streets and just talked to people. Of course, even up North there were a few Maggots living in shacks they had hammered together out in the woods, they begged in town in the fog. Tabby and Grimes shoved them off the sidewalks. There were a lot of Chumps, too, looking so serious, the suckers.

But the Innocents. Just waiting and hoping—

They had looked hard and talked it over, and they had given the envelopes of money to just the right people: three to single mothers, one to a lumberjack in a wheelchair with a broken spine after a fall from a redwood, one to a little boy who was dirty; and then one each to a mailman who worked hard, a woman who ran a lingerie shop, a carpenter whose wife had just given birth to twins, and a sixteen-year-old girl they thought had nice eyes.

Envelopes gone, they had headed back to the motel to clean up, and Grimes had them take off their clothes and he hung them up in the bathroom and turned on the hot water to steam out some of the wrinkles. Then later they went again into the town. They felt colossal. They were polite to everyone; Grimes was so proud of Tabby then. He really did see that you always had to be vigilant. There was always someone who wanted help; and always someone who needed punishment.

Heroes are so good it's as if they're from another planet.

They had sat and talked with lonely people. They had visited the police station and looked around for whores. Signed petitions to buy bigger parks and save some trees somewhere. On the outskirts of town, to keep sharp, Grimes had taken his .357 Magnum and blown up a dog sitting stupidly in the middle of the road. A big ugly fucking dog—probably belonged to one of the Bone People, one of the sentimental ones. They had left three years of tuition as a tip to a waitress who had winked at them; she was just starting her studies at the state university in Arcata.

At the end of the day, they had found a gym, stripped down, worked out hard. It was good to get in front of the mirrors again, so bright and pure. Grimes thought, as he watched Tabby posing: It's like the two of us come from there—shining, come out of mirrors, out of a better world.

Powerful: making a difference; and the air so beautiful along the coast, the big trees full of mist, the little towns set along wild Pacific bays, the coffeehouses, the quietness. It was as if they had escaped from an inferno, the whole south bay with stinking air, the lying streets, the klaxons of greed, the whole city like America sinking into the toilet of its cowardice and ignorance. Tabby and Grimes wanted to flush it all to hell, be done with it; then live here at peace with the Innocents.

They headed south, then east. Tabby wished he'd seen the north coast sooner.

They felt full of the months to come, the future was out there, all they had to do was walk into the light meant for them. Everyone was waiting, everyone knew they were coming. They were all waiting in the dark, watching the lights of the stage and hoping.

The waves rolled out of the sea; and the two boys rolled inland, along Highway 169, headed toward the Trinity National Forest.

Out at the Smoke Creek Ranch, there began a week of manual labor. The clear spring days brought round their restored colors; the Smoke Creek rose into the warmth of the season, the meadowlarks remembered all their music; one and all labored on Beulah's ranch.

As they worked the peacock came round and cackled at them, occasionally letting go one of his remarkable shrieks.

At night, the black sky was brushed with the passage of meteors.

"You're like a night sky," said Izzy, moving her beautiful small hand slowly down the chest of Muscovado Taine. "I have left long hot bright marks."

The smell of baking pies wafted from the ranch house. Beulah chopped wood over at the side of the barn. The new ditch was about a third of the way to the new garden; all of them swung picks and shovels, filled wheelbarrows, cursed at struck rocks. The work had advantages: they hoped for a time to avoid the questions thrust upon them, which had each of their souls looking curiously out in the world to see what would happen next.

"Some vacation," complained Ananda, who, aside from her ridiculous fussed-over prettified garden in Los Angeles, had not done that much digging in her life.

"Get your city ass in gear," suggested Cookie.

"We need a break from the stories, anyhow," offered Chiara, her hair pinned back, lifting the heavy pick.

"You bet we do. I thought we were jes' out headed for a randy time. But no, animals talk, Indians come round, death drops in. I feel kinda stunned, like I been horse-bit or somethin'," summed up Cookie as she whipped the pick into the ground.

"You do some bitin' of your own. Scratchin', too," teased Juha.

"I got to say that you ain't totally useless yourself. I mean, it's better than gettin' in the sack with them men that jes' flare up and go out: them kind, it's like fireworks: they smell burnt up afterward."

"I never seen anything like it," continued our Juha. "You are carrying one free-flowing hive of honey on you, woman."

Renato, Ananda, and Chiara looked with wonderment at these two stocky lovers. And so they should, for Cookie and Juha had in their brusque and muscular way come into that province of love where the world, renouncing its neutrality, sides with the lovers—with their pleasures and promises.

Even the raspberry pie had a more comprehensive tang.

For Cookie's part, her early interest in this giant contractor had been mere intrigue: who on earth, she had wondered, was this great hulk of shyness? Are mountains sheepish? Do storms mince? Are stallions punctilious? What was going on here?

Cookie, with her usual straightforward techniques, had, sure enough, with her early-morning fucks blasted Juha out of his habit of holding back. And then without any further prompting from her, he had proved to be a lover of muscular improvisations: a feral trustworthy sumptuous lover of such sustained gentleness that, after bewildering enravishments, he would hold her face in his big hands and kiss her to sleep.

How did Juha get to be so strange? Ribboned with muscles, yet still so tentative? It was more than just natural shyness: Juha looked out on other people with a kind of affectionate confusion. He was on their side. He didn't understand what they were up to, but he wanted to, in order that he might himself have some clue how to get along. And so, devoted, he watched and watched everyone. Among some people, like some ranchers and the Indians, he could move easily enough. But with most everyone else—Cookie saw this now—he was bewildered. So he worked hard, made his own way, and felt curious all the time. But he could not carry out the male compulsion: to stamp upon the moment his idea about himself.

This was of course because Juha *had* no idea about himself. None. Zilch. Zippo. Blank. Hence the strange sense of possibility about him that so drew Cookie.

Besides, Cookie liked the way he swung a pick—high enough to pull down the noontime.

As for Juha, he had to admit that Cookie had totally disheveled him. Ever since the astounding striptease in his little room at Hansel and Gertie's ranch, all through her wisecracks, her straight-in-your-face challenges, and shameless coming on to damn near anything that had happened to them all in this wild trip, Juha had been amazed at her. It was her mix of erotic constancy and gritty practicality. It wasn't just that she wanted, and took, all his seed; it was his sense that, whatever happened, she knew what to do.

And Juha was right: she *did* know what to do. If, say, the Four Horsemen of the Apocalypse were to come riding across the desert, Cookie would know what meal to tempt them with, so that they would all stop, dismount, and come into the kitchen to glut themselves. Destroying whole cities and countries is a lot of work. They would find a ranch meal so flavorful that none of the Four would realize he'd been fatally poisoned.

And then she would confiscate their strong horses: destiny should damn well be some help in the ranch chores.

As we all know, it is only by such methods that the world dodges catastrophe.

Cookie threw down her pick.

"Look," she said, "I've had it with this shit. Now I've rode the spring brandings in the freezing rains, I've had a goddamn steer bolt off and yank my arm out of the socket, I've stuffed full of food all day, day after day, a ranch full of stiff-pricked cowboys, I've seen men gored, electrocuted, horse-bit, and four-year-olds stomped all over by bulls, but I'm still rollin'; and I'll be damned if I am going to dig with a bunch of weak-assed stick-armed slowpokes like these three, so that me and Juha end up doin' all the work."

She looked fiercely at Renato, Chiara, and Ananda.

"Stick-armed?" questioned Chiara.

"Now you know I love you bitches, and I've known you, crazy painter, for years. But hey, you're on your own."

She turned, walked up next to Juha.

"Let's get some mares from the barn and ride, you big sweet-tastin' fool."

And Juha tossed down his pick, and they stalked off together. Left behind were only the three: abandoned, despised, exploited. They too threw down their tools.

"Well, I don't see why we should continue this effort, with our best and brightest no longer with us," reasoned Ananda.

But just then a double-bladed ax came rotating across the yard, and with splinter-blasting report slammed a fencepost at one corner of the garden.

"Donkey-faced candy-assed jerkoffs! Work!" shouted Beulah.

"Maybe we should examine the social context, and *then* plan our long-term strategy," Ananda surmised in her best voice—her voice of counsel.

Chiara and Renato both looked at her.

"You're more than just a dizzy blond," said Chiara.

"You're more than just a painting," added Renato with a wink.

Ananda walked over next to Chiara, and with a few gibes and elbows in the ribs they picked up their tools.

And Renato understood that this time was arranged for him to watch Ananda and Chiara sweat.

And sweat they did, for days. They did not understand that the uncanny agitation of their souls required a physical corrective; that the emergence of visions needed days of open spaces; that the beauties loosed in their blood wanted time to spread all through them wild clarities.

One thing was sure: both women admired the over-the-head ax throw so happily practiced by Beulah. But they recognized they needed more strength if either of them were to make their own double-enders sing through the air.

As for Renato, he was memorizing again: memorizing the sight of the two women working together: the way the sunlight searched their movements; the way the hours, one by one, lined up on the edge of the trench to watch them.

Even the peacock wandered over.

"This will give me new qualifications: Ditch-digging 101, the Archeology of the Soul. It'll be a survey course," cracked Chiara.

"I'll say to my clients: I'm not afraid to get my hands dirty; and then I'll give them muddy handshakes," returned Ananda.

"I'd like to watch you work sometime," said Chiara.

"I'll come to your classes; a combative student if there ever was one," mused Ananda.

"I gave you a story, and so I'd like an answer now to the puzzle of God, OK?" said the peacock, who had wandered over. "You're guests here. You shouldn't be totally useless. If you can do all this digging, you can answer God. C'mon."

Chiara flung a shovelful of dirt at the bird.

A meadowlark sang from the fencepost.

Renato watched them, and remembered.

Renato: during these many years in Eureka, even given his status as the town oddball, he'd had as visitors in his life and bed some very strange women indeed. Cowgirls with plugs of tobacco in their lips had given him demanding hours that left ribs bruised and sheets stained; and on one occasion left him with a case of blueballs so severe he had to hike a hill and by delicate crouching dip the affected tissue in a cool mountain stream.

A whimsical red-haired field geologist, happening upon him painting high in the Toiyabes, after around an hour of tale-swapping and banter, had taken her field hammer and in an astonishing display of professional dexterity, stripped the belt right out of his pants. This charming gesture he answered by passing his mink brushes for a half-hour over her face, her neck and breasts. Thus acquainted, they had a summer which to call orgiastic would be *deminutio*.

And yet the very next summer he devoted to a certain professor, a historian known for her work on early Nevada mining towns. She had gone to dinner with him and then the next day posed for a portrait by the side of a big cottonwood. So excited was he by this project, and by her air of subtle and elaborate passions, that as he worked, quite against his intention, a thick new brush was brought to prominence. The professor, taking this as a touching aesthetic gesture, came straight over and brought immediately to this phenomenon kisses of historical sweep and savvy; and, their professions brought into happy alignment, they sighed and roared all afternoon in the dry grasses.

Then there was the college martial arts instructor, a young woman with a thick leather belt and a big club. She was driving through Nevada to school and found him in Eureka in the middle of the street painting the courthouse. Her smile sent firecrackers going off in his bone marrow, which made it difficult to hold his brush steady. She noticed this wavering; and, as his emanations of strangeness did not cease, she was intrigued. Besides, why worry? If he was too weird, she could always kill him.

And so it was with assurance that she suggested that with her legs around him he might explore her most sweet nectary, her delicious adored darkness. She spent two weeks in Eureka, and in the midmost of her pleasure the exuberant arch of her back was so beautiful—bend of sky, camber of moon, arc of story line in the female season of the world—that he included that exact curve somewhere in every single painting he did thereafter.

If these women loved him, as long as they loved him, it was because of his strangeness. Ever since the adolescent bedtimes with Ananda, Renato had thought that women, day by day, actually gave the world its form: that is, just as Ananda gave him a body, so women, as they lived, as they worked, made the world with their hands.

How otherwise could the world look so good?

He had gone to Nevada, and on driving through had happened upon Eureka; the high desert wilderness had moved far into his visions, and he was home. He had been in Eureka twenty years, and still he had, day in, day out, just two thoughts: the women he loved; the work he loved.

Hence that strangeness.

And now this trip—

"Think of yourself as a bottle of rum," suggested Izzy, "and I'm taking sips of you."

After five days Beulah tramped along by the side of the ditch, looking critically at the work. Privately, she was astounded, even to her very gristle. She had not expected such passionate labors from city women, whose soft bodies she thought of as insipid rotten things.

Ananda, Chiara, and Renato stood near, now tanned, strong, rough, and sore. But they'd be damned if they were going to let a country matriarch make them complain.

"OK," said Beulah, "I'll teach you two gals how to do the overhead heave."

And she did. Because of the weight of a double-sided ax, Ananda and Chiara needed to bulk up even more than their week of digging had allowed. But ax-heaving is so alluring an enterprise, and results in such immediate gratifying demolitions, that they were patient—as well we might expect from two pros.

In the ensuing week many a double-header was flung, in more than one case requiring evasive action from the peacock, who with indignation lurched and darted around the yard.

In the meantime Cookie and Juha had taken one of Beulah's pickups and roamed all over the Smoke Creek. It was tough on Cookie: during all her years working on her ranch, and over the stove, she did not have any reason to presume she was developing transcendent capacities—and now she could decipher the writing of juniper branches against the sky.

"Oh, what the fuck is going on, Juha? Everywhere we go, it's just one more match on a gas leak."

"I don't get it myself. I thought I had a future as a big dumb happy guy."

"Well, not *everything's* changed, Juha."

Right about then Renato began to paint so much no one saw him except for an occasional meal. He would paint all day, and then at night in a tack room with some lights he had rigged, until he was too exhausted to stand. Then he would kneel down, spread out a bedroll, and sleep in front of his easel.

It was the way of working he loved best: painting souls.

Do souls become visible only when loved—like diamonds in a cave at night, ignited by the light of a torch?

Beulah would come to look at his doings.

"I'm keeping two of them things," she announced. "Room, board, and rent of the tack room."

When he had about seven canvases, all of Ananda and Chiara, Beulah stopped again in the tack room and considered them all, long and hard. She became slowly more surprised.

"Well, well," she said, looking at Renato critically, "and to think you'd turn out to be a man! Jes' goes to show: you never can tell!"

"Beulah, do you know any stories?" asked the painter. He surprised himself: but it had been too long.

Beulah considered him.

"I was goin' to tell you a story. Don't rush me."

"I'm not rushing you. No, ma'am. You take your sweet time."

"All the same, you *need* this story," continued Beulah. "I mean, when you need my boy the worst, that's when you'll see me again."

"Your boy?" asked Renato dubiously.

"Yes. My boy!" she said, taking the brush from his hand and pushing him into a saddle. And, leaning back against the side of the barn, she commenced to tell

THE STORY OF THE INFANT FALLEN FROM THE SKY

"Sometimes when I was out on the desert I used to find little birds that had fallen from a nest, or had been attacked by some varmint, and I would take them back to the house and nurse the damn pecky little things back to health, even though I'd have to listen to all that peeping and chirruping. I liked it, though; I liked the little falcons the most. They had them bright eyes that made you think that they knowed everything that was goin' on outside the room and inside your head. I'm tellin' ya: falcons even when they're little can dive right into the middle of what you're thinkin' on and carry it away in their beaks. And a good thing too, since thinkin' is not so much damned use."

"One time, though, I was out in the east Smoke Creek and I saw this small gleamin', a little slip of sparkles, like a snake on fire. And I went over and there was this crooked little piece of light, I mean no longer than my forearm, but blazin'! I mean like dynamite goin' slow! Bright as a noontime packed in a stick—I mean if you took a rope and sowed gunpowder all though it so's it was more powder than rope, and lit the thing up, and it never stopped burnin', that's what it would be like 'cause this thing jes' kept firin' steady, crackin' and sizzlin' and singin' in its own heat."

Beulah paused and looked fiercely at Renato.

"Now what was I s'posed to do with the damn thing?"

"My guess is," said Renato, "that you're a good woman to have around when something weird happens."

"You're goddam right I am!" shouted Beulah, who looked like she was going to cuff Renato a hard one out of sheer happiness of recollection.

"And so this shining thing . . ." said Renato quickly, to get her back into the east Smoke Creek.

"And so," Beulah went on, "I was thinkin': now this ain't no rotten old bone, no old longhorn all polished up, no sir, and it's the kind of thing that mebbe I could use to rout out some of my old pipes, and so what are you goin' to do, Beulah?"

The ranchwoman glared at Renato.

"And so what did you do, Beulah?"

" 'Bout time you asked, pussyface!" she retorted. And she stepped up and leaned her muscle and gristle against a saddle and looked out the doorway as she talked.

"I roped the little sucker and dragged it back to the truck and hoisted it in the bed onto some blankets; I left it on the rope and tied it down and then headed out. And as I was drivin' back to the ranch, with this thing fizzin' and sparkin' all over the place, all of a sudden I started to hear."

"Hear?" inquired Renato with extreme courtesy.

"That's right, hear! Are you calling me a liar?"

Renato envisioned Beulah writing her name in his flesh with the horsewhip. But we recall that the painter loved women; and so he had the good sense to shout back: "Beulah, you're a rock of a woman; but I know it's rock candy. So knock off all this bull-shit!"

Beulah, who had stood forth in fury, now leaned back again.

"Don't you tell nobody!" she said grudgingly.

"What do you mean, hear?"

"I couldn't help listenin' to all the fizzin', and it were pretty soon that I could start to make out it was sayin' somethin'; in the fits and bolts and burstin' out, I could start to hear what the little thing meant. And that's not all. Because the ornery little thing had slipped off the blankets in the back."

"How could you tell?"

"I could tell because the whole truck was glowin'! I looked like a comet comin' down the road! And then I knew! I knew what was what! It was a baby lightning bolt! The cute little thing had fallen out of a nest of clouds and jes' couldn't strike back up into the sky. And *now* what was it going to do? Come home with me, that's what ... So's I had a big grin smack on my mug, I ain't never brung no lightning home off the range before. And then I thought, Beulah, you got a problem: how the hell am I going to get out of the truck without being fried?"

"It would take a lightning bolt to fry you, Beulah."

"I'll take that as a compliment."

Renato bowed.

"The trick is not to get grounded. And so when I pulled into the ranch I jes' threw open the door and hurled myself clean out of the cab, slammin' right down far out in the dust and rollin' away."

"Now *that* I would like to have seen," exclaimed Renato.

"And laying in the dirt I thought to myself: what does a woman do with a baby lightning bolt? Course, I knew right away what to do! 'Cause for the first time I was bustin' out with that mother-feelin'! Me, Beulah, I had got myself the baby meant for me. Mine! And there I was, all proud with lookin' at the way it made my truck shake, ripple, and glitter! My child!"

Slowly Renato got it.

"You mean that's what you've been doing out here all these years? Raising a lightning bolt?"

"You betcha!" said Beulah with satisfaction.

Renato paused to mull this one over.

"And so how many years ago was that?" he wondered.

" 'Bout fourteen years now."

"So you have on your hands a teenage lightning bolt."

"Lanky. Wild. Strong," said Beulah with gusto.

"They say parents learn a lot from their children," he ventured.

"You betcha; he taught me how to strike out at things, if you know what I mean." And Beulah gave him a smile so hearty and strong that Renato felt like a little pipsqueak.

"And so . . ."

"It's a good life. I was supposed to be a mom. I done what I set out to do."

"And so where is he?" burst out Renato.

"Come with me," said Beulah, twirling Renato around and shoving him out the door of the tack room.

"Maybe it wouldn't be so tough to be angels," speculated Izzy, "now that we can fly."

They walked, the painter and the ranchwoman, out in back of the ranch and straight through the sagebrush, moving toward some low hills.

"At first I didn't know what to do—hell, I hadn't had no kid around before. 'Sides, this was a boy that was goin' to take some figurin'. First thing: what the hell is his name? Well, what about Bolt? It says what it says. It is what he is. A good name for an impulsive boy, anyway! Next question: what does he eat? Then all at once it hit me. He eats everything standin'! If it stands, he'll eat it. Easy enough. So the next afternoon I took him out to where there was some little saplings in a draw of a canyon, and right there I jes' flipped him out of the blanket up in the air. It was kind of a windy day, the trees whippin' around, but that little bolt just hovered a minute and blammo! He made *ashes* of the tallest skinniest one! And I thought, don't turn this little sucker loose in town! You don't want to be the tallest cowboy in the room around my kid, nosirree!"

Renato measured his height against Beulah.

"And so I took him home and laid him out in some insulation in the back room, he was a-sparklin' and a cracklin', the dear little thing, a sizzlin' and beamin', the sweet thing, that was my boy! Now I always did want a child with some energy, some zip. And there he was. And so's he and I jes' settled into our life together out here on the Smoke Creek. It's been good. This was the perfect spot—when you're raising up a lightning bolt, you need some room! It's jes' not something you could do in some piddlin' little house in town. What a little beauty he was. Wait till you see how he's grown! It's been wild. It's been a blowout. I don't know how it coulda been stranger."

Renato thought: every orphaned piece of lightning should have such an upbringing.

"There was one time early on when I took him out to the Sierra in the truck—already he was gettin' so big that he would barely fit in the bed of the pickup, and I had always to cover him up with blankets, otherwise his light would damn near blind me as I drove. I remember one time when a police car pulled me over for speedin' on one of those faraway straight roadways all over the state, and this cop he came a-stridin' up to the car and Bolt knew that he meant me no good. And he always was kinda protective. And so he started thrashin' around in the back of the truck, fizzin' and sparkin' heavy, clangin' on the sides of the bed, and the whole truck was shakin' with electricity, glowin' there in the road, the brightest thing in the Basin, in the middle of the day a star sittin' there in the high desert—the truck shinin' and buckin' and throwin' off sparks. There was a thumpin' in the air and the cop was standin' there wide-eyed and all of a sudden the thunder cracked right in the road, I mean *blasted* this guy, it was like thunder growed out of the ground and the cop turned and he hightailed it to his car and drove the hell out of there like somebody who had seen God! But it was jes' my boy Bolt! Sweet thing! How we laughed about that one for years! And what a day that was, like so many other days. We went out in some open valleys where no one would see us, and Bolt would dart around, jes' snap and zip around, rambunctious thing, what a beauty.

Sometimes I would stay all day with him waitin', waitin': fer there ain't nothin' prettier than to see him play in the dark. I would jes' sit back, jes' sit back: and when twilight was gone he went sparklin', I mean sparklin' all through the valley and did his flashin' and jabbin' into the little canyons and shootin' down in caves, firin' back out, the black sky over us an' the whole valley singin' with light, my boy, my boy, he could *rock* those valleys, he could. He'd wear hisself out playin', he'd be plumb worn out and I would take him real soft and slow and I'd lay him in the back of the truck and cover him real careful and do a long slow drive back to the ranch. I don't know how I coulda been happier."

They were approaching the hills. Renato could see little whirlwinds of dust over soil and rock where it rose from the desert floor, and there was a movement—the whole hillside was rolling, and steam piped from fissures in the stone.

Beulah smiled.

"Just how big is he now?" asked Renato as he heard the rumbling.

The two women, at the end of their work day, were stiff, burnt, dirty, and from the sweat drying on them, cold. They headed for the ranch house, for their room with the bunk beds. In the little shower with cracked tiles Chiara turned on steaming hot water. Neither of them was thinking about anything but getting warm, the enveloping pleasures of heat in the late chilly afternoon; it was natural to get in the shower together, natural to use the rough bars of soap to wash each other, and in the long moment after their breasts touched and each of them, watching now, slowed down the soaping, it was natural that their first kisses were a little shy.

But these were not women to whom shyness came naturally—

They stayed in the shower until the hot water was gone, and then led each other to the lower bunk bed. Chiara lay with her hands in Ananda's hair; and Ananda said, laughing, "We are the world's two most unlikely virgins."

Chiara touched lightly Ananda's lips, her neck; she followed with her fingertips the surprise and desire in her newfound lover's face. They had each of them conjured for herself, from their liaisons with men over the years, what a woman in the best of worlds might want in an embrace—how much, how long, the manner of delectation, its surety and incendiary hopefulness, how exactly the heart might have its way. These studied embraces, the ones they had most wanted themselves—they gave away now to each other.

A seasoned female wildness—this is what they knew. The certainties of lovemaking—skylarking languorous promised offerings, blessed fluting and foldings and arcs of flesh, wet drawn-out mantic brawling pleasures—the wisdoms of a woman's life enveloped them, as the blond hair of Ananda fell over the olive skin of Chiara, and Tupelo at the end of the bed fell on her side and snuggled up, licking and nuzzling Chiara's feet.

Cookie and Juha were watching a rattlesnake bask in the late light.

Juha leaned against her. The snake settled its beautiful head on its coils for a snooze.

"Cookie!"

"Juha."

"Marry me! You have to! I want to!"

Cookie laughed.

"Juha, fer chrissake, there are laws against bestiality."

Izzy, sitting up, looked out into the Basin. The afternoon came softly, and scented with sage, into the room. Muscovado was asleep, his head cradled in her hips.

* * *

Renato and Beulah stood at the base of the smoking hills. Before them, the entrance to a cave. Renato could see flares.

"Bolt!" called Beulah.

—Stampeding of air, shuddering of hillside, parting of sky: even with a story to ready his vision Renato could not keep his feet before the roaring of the light.

IN FRONT OF how many ranches will our reckless voyagers stand, saying good-bye? And to the mother of a thunderbolt?

As many as they have to: but this farewell had a certain pungency, since it was accompanied by so many discoveries: that Beulah was a beaming mother; that the peacock had climbed into the house and intended to travel with them "and cackle at God the whole way, too"; that the house still held the coyote that had peered out at Pyramid lake; that the tousled, the sparkling, the bestirred Ananda and Chiara, holding hands in front of the truck, bore the unmistakable grin of the recently incorporated; and that Juha and Cookie wanted to head into town to find a justice of the peace.

"Fuck if I know why," said Cookie, "but you never know: maybe in the next town he's the bartender."

Renato was smiling. "Well, well, Beulah, a lot of shenanigans here, I'd say. Must have been those raspberry pies."

Beulah, who had spent the last night with her son, filling up some Basin valleys with thunder, just wanted to be left alone with her offspring.

"Next town is Gerlach. Jes' up the road. At the foot of the

Black Rock Desert. It's real quiet out there on the playa. I mean it's a thick quiet—like butter."

"Good for cooking. We'll cook up a life. C'mon, Juha," said Cookie, and the two of them got in the cab of the truck, and Renato climbed in with them, leaving Ananda and Chiara, our noontime and midnight, to head into the little house and, still hand in hand, lie down together across from the coyote and peacock.

"And so maybe it's time we told *you* some stories," said Chiara.

"I'll just watch," suggested the peacock, who really did want to.

The two lovers, the two animals, the house where they lived, moving through the Smoke Creek: in the distance they could see Beulah and her bright ranch.

The coyote came over to Ananda and Chiara and they reached out their hands to her and cradling her head looked long into her golden eyes.

It was just about then that Mike and Jeb, with submachine guns, bazookas, flamethrowers, and various imported field artillery, with engine revving and pride so much restored that it was under pressure leaking from their pores, so that the very odor of pride—rather like rotten mint sauce—was detectable; it was just then that our detectives made their showy entrance into Smoke Creek Ranch.

Beulah, however, was too busy in the garden to give them an open-hearted welcome, or even to heave an ax or two.

"Bolt!" she cried.

It was early evening when Juha pulled into Gerlach, and motored right up, no surprise here, to a bar: the Jalisco Club.

—A bar distinguished by the most beautiful neon in the world. Renato loved the colors.

"Barhopping across the cosmos," he said.

From the door of the bar poured forth shadows full of opals and a rough inexplicable scent of allspice.

"Izzy and Muscovado!" cried Renato, and rushed inside to

where they were leaning with insolent and thankful exhaustion against the bar.

"Took you long enough!" said Iz. "We've been here in Gerlach for weeks, waiting for you. Shoveling sand. Playing checkers. Peeling potatoes. Walking around with empty beer bottles. What a drag."

Muscovado had a certain glistening to him, a sense of gratitude about him—as though he wanted to spring into the sky and with much exposition and apostrophe thank every last blessed perilous star.

In other words, one more ordinary lover.

Chiara hugged and hugged her daughter, and took her off into a corner for some whispering and jokes, some winks and digs.

Ananda came straight into the Jalisco Club and cruised up to the side of Muscovado.

"It just could be said that you and I are sort of like family now," she noted mischievously.

The coyote dashed into the bar, went straight over to Izzy, and sat by her side.

Juha and Cookie ordered a couple of shots.

The peacock stalked in, strutted around, and shuffled over to examine Muscovado.

"Who the hell are you?" the Jamaican asked.

"I am the peacock seeking the answer to a riddle, which has to do with the wild light of God," answered the bird, as with a spare feather he buffed his claws.

"I should have known," said Musco.

The coyote, sitting a little apart, watched them all. And this is what she saw:

—She saw Izzy stroking her mother's hair; and as the two of them traded stories of love, she saw how the opal in Izzy's soul had spread to her shadow: an iridescent darkness.

—She saw the soul of Muscovado Taine, that curved like an arc of islands, each island one day in his sunlit rigors of loving Iz; the whole scene covered with the girl's beauty, as the Caribbean Sea is covered with warm light.

—She saw Ananda, whose soul was reaching irresistibly for the world, as a flock of cormorants along the Lost Coast will explode into the air, spreading over the sky as they rise.

—She saw Renato's soul, made lean and supple by being in a bar with three sets of lovers; Renato who knew he had to learn more than the movement of light: he had to learn the origin and destination of light. Just for a second the coyote let him see the brightnesses of the lovers: the rough-and-ready flashing between Juha and Cookie; the soft auroral envelopments around Ananda and Chiara; the full oil-painted flood tide of tropical light that streamed between Muscovado and Izzy.

By Izzy's side the coyote sat quietly.

Ananda said, "I don't want to get too far into a 'like mother, like daughter' kind of comparison, but all the same I have some questions I would like to ask," and she grinned as she took Musco to the bar, the peacock following behind.

At the bar, Juha was laughing.

It turned out the bartender *was* the justice of the peace.

Renato set up his canvas in the corner of the room.

"You two want to get married? Here? In the Jalisco Club?" inquired the bartender.

"This very minute!" boomed Juha, and the bottles deep in the cooler in the far corner of the cellar all rattled.

Tupelo the cat inched into the bar.

"You're crazy," commented Cookie. "You might as well go out in the open country and jump on the back of some mustang filly, and call her your own. You're goin' to get bucked over the edge of the earth, fool man."

"I know how to hang on tight," retorted Juha.

"So far, anyway," she admitted with a sigh. The last thing Cookie had wanted on this trip was to be a damned cowgirl in love.

Izzy, with her hand on the coyote, wondered aloud, "Has Tupelo started to talk yet?"

"I thought no one would ever ask," retorted the cat. "What is this, everyone thinking that only wild animals can talk? If you will permit a comment by a mere domestic animal: this is one worn-down bunch. I mean, at this rate, soon you will all be soft as cats."

Izzy winked at Muscovado.

"Not only that: some men play like kittens," she said.

Muscovado, wide-eyed with the revelations given him by Ananda concerning a recently charged smokiness in the Smoke Creek Desert, could not help but overhear Juha and Cookie.

"*Somebody's* got to marry. Otherwise, we're talking meltdown," he said with a sort of ecstatic desperation.

But was meltdown certain? Or could there be, so much against our expectation, right here in this bar a whole new helpful range of irresponsible splendors? Of course there could: for in Gerlach lived the twelve Daughters of the Moon. They were cooks and metaphysicians—a very common mix of labor. And, after all, such genius was to be expected in this little town, for as Athens was to classical Greece, Baghdad to classical Islam, Florence to the Renaissance and Paris to the Enlightenment—so is Gerlach to America.

Just then, before anyone could do even one more foolish thing, a Daughter of the Moon, wearing a fresh white apron, stepped from the back of the building. She was Amanita, the main cook; and she had the darkest eyes in all the world. This was because at birth, the powers of the world had, for eyes, given her two new moons, in all their shocking glossy blackness. And it is with that incident, however trivial, that she began as she told them all

THE STORY OF THE IMMACULATE CONSUMMATION; OR, THE COOK, HER KITCHEN, HER BODY AND SOUL; OR, TRY EMPARADISEMENT FOR A FUN TIME; OR, THE HUMDRUM MYSTERIES OF LIFE #1—YOU'VE GOT TO START SOMEWHERE

"My name is Amanita: I am a woman with moons for eyes."

Cookie elbowed Juha.

"See that? I'm tellin' ya, Juha, cooks are a secret society. See what you're gettin' into?"

"And so I want to tell you my story," said Amanita, "a secret given to me."

"Once I was walking at dusk in the desert by some hot springs near an old ranch, and noticed that the steam off the water was following me. It found me, wreathed me, passed itself round and round, and condensed upon me; so that with its warm mistings I was enchanted.

"And why might this happen to me? Now, to a cook, this was obvious as an onion: it was because I was in love."

"Happens to cooks all over. It's an occupational hazard," cracked Juha.

"The steam is like the body: enchanted but temporary. And my body, in the middle of the steam, was like a soul: that which gave meaning to the wreathings of flesh we have as our gift.

"The mist made itself a temperature just like mine, so that I felt dissolved inside it; and in the twilight the mingling of myself and the mist was so complete that I was a woman married to the air. It reminded me of my love—because in love, in bed, at our best times I cannot tell my body from the body of my lover.

"And so it was as plain as a chile pepper: loving is a kind of practice: we practice turning our bodies into souls. This is why it has always been rumored that real lovers get to stay together forever."

"Now this Amanita can roll through those sentences!" spouted Izzy. "She clips right along!"

"When I returned to town, I thought about these things as I cooked. It gave a certain style to the simmering of my beans, the slinging of my *rellenos*. And one night I was serving someone from Reno, and he had a book. He read to me; he read the lines

> *Then, as all my souls be*
> *Emparadised in you (in whom alone*
> *I understand, grow, and see)*

and I understood—

"It's undeniable as garlic: as I am emparadised in my beloved, my body is emparadised in soul. As lovers are made one flesh, so body and soul are made one substance. When this occurs, our lovers are emparadised in the world. This is the unity that is called the Immaculate Consummation.

"It is true, as well, that this world is emparadised in another. But that is another story."

"Well, well, *well,*" said Chiara professorially, "this does button up a number of sticky issues in theology and philosophy."

"But there remains one important question," said Amanita brightly.

"And what's that?"

"What would you like for dinner?" asked the woman with moons for eyes.

And with that, the whole raucous band crowded into the little back room, where there was one long ramshackle table and a number of others ranged along the walls.

"I have never been so hungry," said Juha with good reason.

"Let me help you with this pack of beasts. Besides, I need to know more about all this body-and-soul hocus-pocus," said Cookie with the good cheer she took always to the kitchen. She slung on an apron and walked with the moon-eyed woman to the grill.

Izzy and Chiara went off again to a corner. It is not often that the world gets together a mother and daughter who are both so recently in love.

Chiara said, "She's very tough, there is a raunchy sweetness to her. After all those strange male creatures—I loved them, loving men is like teetering at the edge of the world, there is an exhilaration to it; but no constancy at the center of it. Of course, there was more than that, better than that: there was you at the end of it, Izzy."

And Chiara looked at her, a girl cherished for weeks in a room at a ranch house of angels, she of candent shadows and opalescent recklessness; she whose skin was darkened by a dusting of allspice.

Izzy, whose cocky smile was not in the least diminished by her sunlit acrobatics, said, "Well, love ain't bad. And then to leave the room and get kisses from angels, not bad either. I needed their kisses, my bone marrow had turned to burnt sugar."

"Did he sing to you?" asked Chiara.

"In a low voice, in the dark . . ."

Chiara sat back before the certainty of her lustrous daughter.

"Does she sing?" asked Izzy suddenly.

Her mother thought it over. "Not yet. We both have to learn some new songs. I hope it'll take a long time," she answered.

In the kitchen, steam was rising from the grill, beans were frying, tortillas heating, hot sauce bubbling; on the counter were bowls of bright vegetables.

"So what happened to the lover?" asked Cookie of the woman with moons for eyes.

"He will return. Two years from today he will come here and take me away forever."

"And you trust him?"

"Do I trust sunlight? Do I trust the stars?"

Ananda had her head on Renato's shoulder. He whispered to her, "So it's new. You have friends around. Me and Tupelo, for instance."

"What about those brushes?" she asked.

"I'm using them. Every day," he said.

She pulled up and looked at him.

"Maybe you should become Chiara's lover—"

"I am both your lovers."

Little did *he* know. More, much more, would be required of Renato.

The coyote stayed close to Izzy.

The peacock roamed around the room, pecking and watching. Now and then Juha would take the little bell from his vest pocket and ring it, and the whole night would go quiet for the unfolding of the peacock's tail. But as the time for the meal approached this delight had to be recalled, because the tail drained the crimson from the hot sauce, sucked the green straight out of the peppers, and stole the brown away from the beans, so that they looked like oatmeal. And who could eat food like that?

The peacock swept up his feathers, and the cooking went forward.

Tupelo nuzzled Ananda.

Izzy and Chiara still sat together in their easy beauties.

Muscovado Taine sent glances down the table at Izzy that to the amusement of all left heat ripples in the air.

The bartender brought in a tray of cold beers.

Cookie jumped up and ran into the barroom to make a quick call.

"Kenny, how are ya?" she said when her husband back in Eureka answered the phone.

"Well, I bet you're findin' that travelin' is a dirty dull business, huh, sweetheart?" asked Kenny immediately.

"Well, not exactly," admitted Cookie. "It's been more shitkickin' and strange. *Real* strange."

"Well, it's been pretty lively around here, too," said Kenny. "First, I moved in here that strawberry blond bronc rider from the Fiddleback Ranch. She's wiry, she's tasty, she thinks I am one handsome bronc. As for you, I divorced your ass yesterday. Now ain't I somethin'?"

Cookie was quiet for a moment, with her eyes shut.

"You know what I always loved about you, Kenny? You ain't one to sit around and grieve. You ain't one to dillydally."

"That makes two of us, darlin'."

"We wasn't so bad, Kenny. At least when we made smoke, there was fire."

There was another long silence. And then they both hung up at once.

Cookie winked at the expectant bartender.

"Well?" he said.

"I hope you're working tomorrow, bud."

With a sort of contented steaminess Cookie helped the moon-eyed woman serve up plates of food to the table.

"What's for dinner!" cried Juha. And all of them, from the difficulty of their adventures and the exertions of love, were seized with a hunger they doubted could ever be satisfied.

The moon-eyed cook emerged.

"We have Tamales Colorados and Corundas, the triangular tamales of Michoacán; we have Pipian de Oaxaca, for which my grandmother has sent pumpkin seeds from Mexico; and then there is the black bean paste, and Papas Chirriónas, whose chile sauce will fire your bellies."

"That's been done, thank you," noted Izzy.

"And at the same time a fava bean salad, with Legumbres en Escabeche, and Chileajo, whose cold chile sauce will turn your toes red and make you sweat like ditchdiggers."

"At least we know what we're getting into," said Chiara brightly.

"And don't forget the potato cakes and the Nopales Asados."

"Nopales?" asked Cookie.

"Grilled cactus paddles," said the moon-eyed woman with satisfaction.

"We're ready!" exhorted Juha with gusto.

"And then after you're done with this first course, I'll tell you about the main dishes," she said as she took Cookie away to the stove.

"I think we're going to like it here," said Muscovado.

The phone rang. The bartender, who was dusting off the beer-and-tobacco-stained pages that bore the wedding vows, answered and nearly had his ear blown off his head. He poked his head into the dining room.

"Juha? Somebody on the phone for you. Goddam voice like a cannon! Jesus!"

Juha strode with machississimo to the phone. "What in tarnation do you want, woman with a mule for a brain and a brick for a heart!" he shouted into the receiver.

"What the hell did you do when you built this ranch house? What?" roared Gertie into the phone. "For one thing, the day after you left I found a coyote sleeping in my goddam bed! My bed! How can I shoot something in my own bed?"

Juha put down the phone and took a quick look at the long table. Sure enough, the coyote was right by Izzy's side, rubbing her cheek against the girl's bare arm.

"Don't blame me," he said to Gertie, "the animals here are all accounted for."

"And what's more," shouted Gertie, "a junk truck came through here and sold us some old horseshoes, and when Hansel shod the mare and got on her she rode off like a damned comet down the valley. Hansel clean disappeared on me, and there was a sonic boom, and I ain't heard from him since! Juha!"

"Look for him to ride out of the sky about dinnertime. Ain't no way he's goin' to miss out on the beef stew. And Gertie!"

"What, you puffball!"

"The joke's on you, you tough old broad. See ya!"

And he hung up. Back in the dining room, he sat down alongside Cookie and the two of them, in a rare display of agility for a couple so robust, played footsie as they ate.

The smell of chiles billowed in the room. Steaming plates of food were taking over the table.

A man in a short black coat, and carrying a trumpet, came through the back door.

"O fer chrissake, it's the trumpet of death again," moaned Juha.

"It is not," called the moon-eyed woman from the kitchen.

The man with the trumpet tootled briefly at Juha.

It was Muscovado's turn to answer the phone when it rang again.

"Muscovado," said a voice with the savor of auto grease and the silence of canyons.

"Antelope on the Moon!" exclaimed Musco. "We have a coyote with us and I don't know what you started but we're all here in Gerlach and man you wouldn't believe it! The angels! Izzy!" There was a whirling in his thoughts, a common hazard when you are in love, have consorted with angels and animals, and then begin talking to a Shoshone auto mechanic who is occasionally an eagle.

"Listen up," commanded Antelope on the Moon. "You have been flying with the girl because you know how to fly and now you have taught her, she has the air under her wings and the land spreading out under her, and now you are not thinking how to help her fly away, are you? You are not helping her to be on her way, are you?"

"Hold on a second," said Muscovado, and he went to look into the dining room at Izzy, there with the coyote; the peacock was by her side and Tupelo had moved to her lap, and Izzy gave Muscovado a smile that covered him with her love. He went back to the phone.

"You're crazy, you're wrong, it's cruel, and I won't anyway," he reprimanded the Shoshone.

"I've been living, flying, and working here in the Basin for forty years—of your time, that is. I have been the wind. I have been an animal. I know the stones by name. You're going to have to let her go. You're telling me that I cannot see the wings on a woman?"

"You can't see her all the way from Austin. We're in Gerlach," reasoned Musco in the way of desperate men everywhere.

"Look across the room!" ordered the voice.

And across the room, at the other pay phone just by the front door, he saw Antelope on the Moon. Antelope winked.

"I still won't!" yelled Muscovado into the phone. But the Indian had hung up. And when Musco looked over again, he was gone.

Another man in a black coat came through the back door, carrying an accordion. He tossed off a few bars.

Musco felt a little better.

As the accordion player laughed and his instrument laughed back at him, both phones in the barroom rang at once.

Ananda and Chiara leaped up. To the surprise of neither of them, they were calling each other.

"It's just like being in bed with you. No one in the world, I mean in all the world, would be able to say we planned this one," said Chiara.

"But there's one thing I don't understand. Why, in such unsought-for rough-and-ready sex, do I feel we're so responsible?" asked Ananda.

"This puzzles me, too," admitted Chiara.

From the kitchen wafted the odors of tomato and garlic, onions and chicken, toasted chiles and stirred spices.

June and Bret, the angels of Fallon, broke in on the line.

"If we may interrupt," they said, "most love affairs are not about the lovers. They love pleasure, they love their future, their excitement they love; but they do not love each other. Now, you two *do* love each other: hence, that strange responsible feeling. Now if you will excuse us, we've got pigs to feed. Do you think you could leave us alone for while? For heaven's sake? Good luck."

The men were stamping around with the trumpet and accordion, checking things out, trying to romance the two callers with hair like midnight and hair like noontime.

Ananda and Chiara let the silence on the line run for a minute.

"Maybe we should get into farming," suggested Ananda.

"I'm going to plant you with a cinnamon stick," asserted Chiara.

"Chiara, Chiara," said the brilliant smiling Ananda, "on this trip to the Lost Coast—"

"Yes?"

"There has to be a long way."

They walked back to the party together, these two women: indoors, but knowing the stars in circulation close and dense over the roof of the Jalisco Club.

"No one ever calls me!" complained Izzy in what she thought was a good imitation of a teenager. Everybody clapped. The phone rang. The bartender answered.

"Phone for Izzy!" he cried. Everybody clapped again.

All the animals followed our Iz into the bar.

It was Peggy-Sue. She had her own complaints.

"First of all, the window in the back room is always fogging up. It doesn't matter what we do. Leave it for an hour, a tropical mist forms on it."

"Hey, you were the one feeding us. What did you expect?" riposted Iz.

"Second of all, if you look out the window in the morning, the desert disappears. There's a sea and reefs and a long arc of islands under clouds like cream."

"Tasty cream, too," commented Iz. The coyote rubbed along her legs, the peacock rested its head in her hand. Tupelo was perched on her shoulder, exploring with a raspy tongue and cool little nose the inside of her ear.

"And you two left whispers all around the room. The words are still there, very soft. But I know what to do with them."

Izzy, remembering those whispers, was embarrassed for the first time ever in her life.

Peggy-Sue went on: "We take some of the whispers, a handful, every night late out onto the porch, and toss them in the air."

"You listen!" accused Izzy.

"No, goofy. They don't *stay* whispers. When we throw the words of lovers, each one turns into a firefly, and the whole porch, the whole ranch house, is enveloped in little arcs of light. If there were no lovers, there would be no fireflies."

"You angels have an explanation for everything," commented Iz, who had gooseflesh from her memories and from Tupelo's tongue.

"Let's have those main courses!" cried Juha.

Three more musicians walked in the door, with more trumpets and a guitar. They milled around, strumming and tooting, sniffing at the food, giving hard stares to Izzy.

"Peggy-Sue, why don'tcha come on up to Gerlach. I miss you. We hardly got a chance to talk."

"From the number of these fireflies, I'd say you talked plenty," teased Peggy-Sue.

The accordionist tossed off a few bars.

"C'mon! what about a little teenage fellowship?" insisted Izzy.

"I'll catch up to you, it won't be long," promised Peggy-Sue, who missed Izzy. "The thing I like about you and your mom, is that you got no middle ground. I mean, you women *need* an angel along on this trip, sweetheart."

"OK!" said the excited Izzy. "I'll see you! The Lost Coast. Think of it! If you can make the party tonight, do it. The food! Here, I'll hand you over to Tupelo, so you can hear about it."

And she gave the receiver to the cat, who lay with it on the floor and wrestled it in her paws; she nuzzled and licked the mouthpiece, she swiped at the phone cord and wrapped herself up, did some dodges, feints, and somersaults.

The whole band had sat down at the main table, and were tipping beers back and dipping their fingers in the hot sauce.

"And for the main courses," announced the moon-eyed Amanita, "we have Mole Negro Oaxacan and Mole Coloradito. Yucatan smoked sausages and Biftecs en Chile Pasilla. Then there is Chichilo Negro—that is the best food in all the world, and is the one dish eaten by the angels in Oaxaca."

"We have experience in this field," commented Renato, who had the feeling that all this food had been bubbling for decades, to get the sauces just right.

"What a relief *you* are," said Ananda to the guy with the accordion, "the last music we heard was from a high school death band."

"All to be accompanied," went on Amanita, "by the flour tortillas I pounded out this afternoon, and the raw tomato sauce, and my private salsa picante. It melts iron, so I have to serve it in a steel caldron."

"May I have the first dance?" inquired Renato.

"Let's see how you do with the picante, first. Then, if you are a man, I will allow you to eat dinner with my youngest sister, Maria-Elena. She also has moons for eyes, as do all my sisters. Good luck, Renato," answered Amanita. And she went back to the kitchen followed by the hoots, the low whistles, the oohs and aahs of the whole table.

"You're going to need luck, Renato. These are stately old-fashioned decorous women," said Ananda, slugging down some beer for emphasis.

Renato began downing tortillas soaked in salsa picante. It made him more hungry. He shone from his own sweat.

The musicians seemed to grow in number all the meal long, until the room was crowded with their instruments. Cookie and the Daughters of the Moon kept bringing huge plates of food, steaming and sizzling, the salsa and the mole sauce provoked

shocking delectations in everyone at table; and the accumu-
lated romance of the last week made the room move like a vault
of the heart.

Someone distributed along the length of the table fresh bottles of ice-cold tequila.

"OK, OK, I give up, I'll marry you tomorrow," said Cookie as
she sat back down by Juha.

Juha put a giant arm around her and hand-fed her some chiles
and some fragrant beefsteak.

"Very endearing," commented the moon-eyed Maria-Elena as
she sat next to Renato. She was slight, with the same light step
and dark eyes as her sisters. Renato began to see in this Latina
how the moonlight she held inside came forth as silvered radiance hidden in her black hair.

"So you have moons for eyes, and can see all the earth?" he
asked.

"Right now I just want to see you," she said as she threw back
a glass of tequila and gave him a full double-lunar shot.

"How many sisters are there?" he asked, in hopes of keeping
his senses.

"There are twelve of us. One for each of the new moons in
the year."

"There are thirteen new moons in a year," corrected Renato.

"One of us is yet to be born," said Maria-Elena. And she
looked at him with curiosity.

"And what about the wild light of God?" asked the peacock.

"It would be a good name for a band," answered the man with
the trumpet.

Izzy, who could taste the allspice in one of the sauces, said,
"Muscovado Taine, let me tell you this: you sure know how to
draw out a proposal of marriage. Whew!"

Ananda and Chiara didn't need to talk. They could hear each
other's thoughts.

Suave propositions of spices, storytelling of peppers, strutting
of peacock around the room and padding of cat down the table;
women who held the night in their hands, men in love; fireworks
that broke in the room as the band struck the sparks of their

music, accordion and guitar and trumpet in the irresistible swing
of a ballad: it was an ordinary night in a little bar with beautiful
neon far out in the lonesome deserts of the Great Basin.

Muscovado and Izzy were the first to dance.

Renato and Maria-Elena stood together, not moving, except
for the painter kissing her fingertips. They talked and leaned into
each other. When they danced, she led, slow and sure as the
moon in the sky.

Izzy's shadow still shone with opals.

Ananda and Chiara began to dance, going slow and mingling
their hair.

Cowboys and railroad workers crowded into the bar.

The sound of the band blew open the doors of the building
and rattled the bottles behind the bar in a way that matched the
beat of the song.

More tequila was uncapped. Hours swept round, singing.

Juha and Cookie danced in and out of the doors.

In the smoke of the bar their stories glittered.

The town readied itself for an outbreak of fireflies.

The cat slept on a barstool.

From the corner the coyote watched.

BRUNO'S MOTEL in Gerlach, just down the street from the Jalisco Club, was a concrete-block compound painted gray-blue. At night, it disappeared in the deep blue light of the desert sky. But in one room there was a shining: not of the glare off the concrete blocks, nor of headlights from the car of some late-night arrival. Neither of neon nor lamplight: one room held behind the tawdry drapes the radiance of the moon.

—A light that held a heavy sweetness. Maria-Elena, the youngest of the Daughters of the Moon, ran her long fingers down the chest of Renato.

We will ask the obvious question: why did the painter find lovers who lit his room with their own female radiance? Easier than lighting a candle, but still, won't he just be burnt to a nubbin sooner or later?

Renato had gone too dangerously long without giving pleasure.

"Come with us to the Lost Coast," he whispered after many hours as he wound his hands in her moon-bright hair.

"I cannot," she said, "but we may have our rendezvous. The Daughters of the Moon have been waiting for you, I have been waiting for you, much-loved man."

"I will not leave here without you!"

"You must," she said as she curled the long crescent of her body along his. "You must go work. If you paint a world where we could live, I will come to you."

The police car chased Tabby and Grimes through the Trinity National Forest, and when they spun and rocketed up a dirt road, the cop got interested. He was a cop who loved a chase, a small-town cop. He had seen the two punks pass him doing twice the speed limit on the winding road.

Up ahead, he could see they had pulled over. He made sure he had the cuffs ready.

He had no way of knowing that their car rode low in the back because it held one of the most impressive collections of weapons in northern California.

The cop got out of his squad car and walked up to the Chevy. Grimes was behind the wheel, he had checked out his clothes, not too wrinkled. Grimes was so relieved. Finally, a cop! A brother. Look at that uniform!. They didn't have any uniforms yet, but at least the cop would be able to see they dressed right. He'd be able to see how serious they were. Grimes sat up straight; he was reverent, grinning. He had his big polished deer knife at his belt.

The cello boomed on the car stereo.

"Our first recruit!" said Tabby. The music flooded around him, he could see that it was a big cop and he was so excited.

Morning in Gerlach:

A mist of tequila lay over the town. In the air here and there hung colored bars of Mexican music. A truck sat by the side of the road, five of its big tires blown out because in pulling over it had run carelessly through a pool of *salsa picante* someone had discarded. By the side of the railroad tracks lay the accordion, occasionally throwing out a random blast.

It was an easy day. Everyone lingered in the motel. From the Black Rock Desert a sunlit quietness flowed into the town.

The hours gathered close and held hands. The lovers ate in Bruno's cafe, or hitched a ride with some desert hands in a truck going to the Calico Mountains for a breather; they stopped by the still steaming and vibrating Jalisco Club, where the sisters moved smoothly among the wreckage of the party, preparing for the nuptials set for twilight.

The woman with moons for eyes held Renato in a persuasive conjugal embrace.

"With me you have more than a painting," she teased him, who could see nothing in the world but her supple lunar beauty.

"Let me stay here with you," he said.

"I told you, my lover—you must work up a world for us," said Maria-Elena.

"I cannot paint without you," said Renato, uttering a sentence that had never in his life occurred to him, even in theory.

Izzy and Muscovado Taine, out and about late in the day, came upon Juha and Cookie and gave them hugs.

"We've done our part to contribute to the nuptial spirit," said Izzy. "Muscovado here, the things he can promise! And the moments he chooses to whisper those promises, right at the tiptop of things!" And she nipped Musco in the earlobe.

Chiara glided up. "The important thing for a wedding is to have in attendance a small amorous band of guests," she said.

"Though I assure you we will all conduct ourselves with great dignity," offered Musco.

"Does that mean you'll stop putting out that allspice smell? Goddamn, is someone cooking you all the time?" questioned Cookie.

"Not all the time," remarked Izzy. "Sometimes he's done. I mean really done. You wouldn't believe the flavor."

"Izzy, for heaven's sake!" protested her lover.

"C'mon, Musco, stop being such an old lady," she teased.

"I think he'd make a helluva'n old lady," opined Cookie.

Renato came into the group. But Renato had changed. For one thing, there was no brush in his hand. For another, even though the day was somewhat advanced, there were no paint specks on his clothes. And most worrisome of all, Renato had upon his face the glazed expression of a man in a funk.

Cookie, who had no patience with funks, chimed right up. "I don't see any wedding photographer. How 'bout a wedding painter? You know, somethin' to hang on the wall, make your kids shake their heads with regret."

But Renato said no word.

"Great!" said Cookie in disgust. "We'll be having a goddam zombie at our weddin'."

"Are we the only marryin' kind in this whole bunch?" demanded Juha.

"I'm too shy," observed Izzy.

"I'm too surprised," said Chiara.

"I want to. But what does the moon want?" murmured Renato.

And as though to explain everything, coming out of the motel Renato's moon-eyed lover strode up and said, "I *have* what I want. Thanks." And she gave Renato a moon-bright smile and headed for the Jalisco Club.

Chiara, in whose black hair there were plainly visible some blond strands, with raised eyebrows said, "Renato! One of the Daughters of the Moon? Very suave! I guess you passed the hot-sauce test."

"Good! A good thing!" boomed Juha, who had been worried that Renato, amid the rather high temperatures of this group, had been getting cold and lonesome.

"Like riding through the sky?" wondered Muscovado.

"Well, well!" cracked Iz, looking at her mother, "not the only one doing some skylarking."

"She won't come with us," said Renato—in so miserable and droopy a way that all of them might as well have been looking at some fleshy broken-down old basset hound.

Even Muscovado, for whom everything that lived in the world was a permanent and irretrievable good, was alarmed. He walked up to the troubled Renato and took him in hand and led him off toward the bar.

"You probably think you *have* to be some kind of sad-ass lunatic now, huh? Not necessarily so, guy . . ."

The cop stood tall. He knew city boys when he saw them. It was another goddam joyride.

"Could I see your license?"

"We'll go over everything!" Grimes said. He was excited, he was eager, finally a cop—it was only a matter of explaining things. "We don't *need* licenses."

"That's why we came all the way up here. Your country here—" Tabby broke in. "We knew you'd understand. Something had to be done."

Tabby and Grimes—they had it rehearsed—both got out of the car. Grimes loved cops. He went straight to him with a friendly expression and held out his hand for a firm handshake.

"Let me introduce myself, sir. Grimes, from San Jose—Grime's Gunshop and Ammo. I'm pleased to meet you and I want to do business. But I need to know we can count on you. I know that you see innocent people get trampled on. Well, you don't have to watch it anymore. It's time to protect them. Let's talk about it. Let's talk about standing together and doing something for them."

"Are you going to get mad?" asked Tabby. He could see the reflections of all of them in the shiny surface of the police car.

And the two of them alternated, they had rehearsed the patter.

"The Innocents. They need protection."

"There's no use protecting the Chumps, they like the world. They like having a mouthful of piss."

"Nothing to do with the Suits, in their big houses, paying other people to wipe out their asses and making them eat it."

"But the Innocents!" Tabby was thinking of Angelica, and all the people they'd helped in Crescent City and Arcata.

"Have you heard stories about us?"

"The legends?"

"Giving it away—"

"We're fed up. We got mad."

"We're not afraid to judge."

It seemed to Tabby, watching their reflection in the glossy patrol car, that they were sparkling. It was such a beautiful scene, with the big trees all around and just the three of them there. The sun slanted through the trees, it was just like he thought: stagelights.

Tabby reached in the car and got their ten-millimeter submachine gun, such a beauty, a little five-pounder that would hold thirty rounds. He held it out and walked towards the cop.

"This is the kind of stuff we've got. You'll love it. You'll love having your hands on it."

The cop's eyes widened and he took a step back. Jesus! he thought—How the hell could they have gotten a hold of that weapon—but his hesitation made Tabby suspicious.

"Oh no! You're not a Chump, are you? Not afraid, are you?"

Even a country cop knew that maybe this was not going to be his best day ever.

He drew his service revolver.

"Both of you kids, turn around, your hands on the hood!"

"Right-o!" said Tabby, and he felt so good. It was decided. Back in the dump in San Jose they'd practiced a move for just this situation. It would be very smooth. Did the guy think they were so stupid? That they hadn't figured it all out in advance?

He vaulted over the car and kneeling down out of sight behind the wheel frame he raised the rifle and with a burst took out the window of the patrol car, blew up the tires, and with a few rounds set the engine on fire.

"Heroes have a rough time. They have to be showy, know what I mean?" yelled Tabby, his heart drumming, as he stood up and spun around, tall and graceful. What a scene!

The cop did know what he meant, because Grimes had walked right up to him as Tabby was firing. Rural cops have a disadvantage, in that very often they haven't had to shoot anybody. Especially, they haven't had to shoot a teenager. Grimes just walked up and knocked away his gun and kicked it into the scrub at the side of the road; and then stood behind the cop with the deer knife at his throat.

"You shouldn't have done that. We come to help, then you go and be rude. This is a bad thing. You've been bad," suggested Grimes.

"Bad boy!" said Tabby.

Tabby was thinking how much fun this was, and how much he wished Angelica was here to watch them.

Electrocution, if the victim survives, has no permanent effect, save to vest its subject with an astonished look. So Mike and Jeb, after their unfortunate encounter with Bolt, walked into the wedding party with the appropriate expressions. Everybody was glad to see them.

Beulah had left word at the Jalisco that Bolt had scored a direct hit.

"Surprised you could make it," said Ananda as they walked through the door.

"Hell," said Mike, "we spent a while just laying around Beulah's ranch smoking like two pieces of charcoal. We even looked like charcoal. It's the second time in a week we've been blasted. We've come to surrender."

"You'll have to surrender to Chiara and Izzy," noted Ananda.

"You mean directly? To a couple of broads?" questioned Jeb.

"Shut up, Jeb," rebuked Mike.

At that moment Chiara walked up and enfolded Ananda in an unambiguous embrace.

"Sweet goddam Jesus!" said Jeb.

"You can provide security for the wedding," suggested Ananda. She and Chiara both laughed at the notion that Juha and Cookie needed security.

Chiara was right. Nothing improves a wedding like amorous invitees.

It was twilight again. Such were the currents turned loose in the Jalisco that the owner, Jose, was able to pull the plug on his beautiful neon, which stayed lit.

The bartender *cum* justice of the peace roamed around the room, pouring margaritas according to his rule: straight liquor for parties, mixed drinks for weddings. Jose was tired from his labors of the night before, and all the afternoon had been taken up by a wake for a local cowboy. The Jalisco Club was much in demand.

Jose handled it all according to his rule: mixed drinks for weddings, beer and ribs for wakes. Besides, the cowboy, whose name was Lonesome Bob, had not suffered the indignity of burial in a cemetery; they had put him down in the high country, overlooking the whole Basin. It was common knowledge that from such spots the souls of the dead spring immediately back to life. The last of the wake was taken up by heavy betting as to who would see the dead buckaroo first.

So vociferous were the bids, that the ranch hands refused to be shooed away for the wedding; and so, in the interests of economy, the wake was combined with the nuptials.

"And a good thing too," said one of the cowboys. "There's nothing I like better than takin' home the bride."

But he changed his mind when he saw the mammoth Juha.

Juha and Cookie had entered into a state of prenuptial bliss so kicked-back and easy-in-the-flesh that to call it languorous would be hyperbole.

Juha in his shyness and Cookie in her worldliness both knew one thing: their marriage would make an old-fashioned center to things.

The cowboys milled around, ready to get on with the party.

"You know I really did take a likin' to Lonesome Bob," said one. "But fuck 'im, he's dead."

"Stands to reason that jes' like all them big changes, death makes a man smarter," said another. "And a good thing, too, in Bob's case."

"That hand could *ride*, though," said a third. "I saw him ride that palomino o' his up a tree alls the way to the top and down t'other side."

"Thet was his problem," commented the second cowboy. "Now Bob, he rode like thet 'cause he thought he was doin' his job. He never could figure why he didn't find no cow in the damned tree. He'd come down lookin' all stumped an' bewildered."

One of them turned to Izzy. "Don't listen to them," he confided to her, "they're just storytellin'."

Izzy had a good laugh at that one.

"You guys think that it's probably the dream of every sixteen-year-old girl to fuck a cowboy, huh?" she asked.

The mustachioed, the brawny, the wind-and-sun-polished bunch of them looked at her in a transport of lust and astonishment.

"Sorry, I think about nothing but vector calculus and the poetry of Hafiz. You got *no* chance." And with that Izzy swaggered over and took up a post behind the bar. She was, after all, experienced in this work. And the other bartender had pressing responsibilities this evening.

"I sure would like to serve you guys some slow drinks, though," she said as she looked happily out with her practiced and opalescent savvy.

As the buckaroos crowded around, Muscovado, watching from the corner, rolled his eyes. Then he continued his ministrations to the hangdog Renato.

"Hey now, the moon always comes round again," he reasoned. And out of nowhere a country-western band formed up and began crooning its stupid songs. But of course just at that moment in that bar they sounded as good as the *Iliad* and the *Odyssey*.

Cookie didn't see any reason to wait. She walked back to the regular bartender, who was in the back kitchen with three of the moon-eyed sisters, all of them together pounding away on flour tortillas.

She yanked him up by the collar.

"Let's go, asshole," she said in her affectionate way.

The flour-smudged bartender came out into the barroom and everyone gathered around.

On either side of Juha and Cookie, the peacock and the coyote. The animals, everyone supposed, were giving away the bride and groom to each other. Someone had to.

Ananda was there in her lightning, Chiara in glistening certainty; Musco in a torrent of satisfactions, Renato in his lunar devastation; and beyond them, Izzy regaling the cowboys with their own hopes, the band clanging away, and outside the stars falling all over the high desert.

"Well?" said the justice of the peace when the band was between songs.

"What?" asked Juha.

"Do you or don'tcha?"

"We do!" piped Cookie and Juha at once.

"I pronounce you husband and wife!" shouted the JP. Even he was starting to get into the spirit of it. He motioned excitedly toward the kitchen.

"It's done!" he cried out.

And because of love, because of the honest traveling of our little band, all at once from the back stepped all twelve of the Daughters of the Moon, who ranged themselves like the beauties of night itself before the wedding party.

Like the beauties of the night: our dear wanderers were stunned to see all of the sisters together. They stood there, plain, formidable, fabulous.

And everyone felt hungry.

Maria-Elena, the youngest of the Daughters, stepped forward and very delightedly went to Juha and Cookie with the news that they could take their nuptial bliss and go straight off by themselves, while the Daughters would stay and entertain the wedding guests. Ideal for a wedding: the betrothed aren't forced to stand around on display, grinning like idiots, but for everyone else the party goes on.

Juha and Cookie cruised out the door of the Jalisco. The desert had been waiting to embrace them.

And back in the bar, our wandering band gave themselves into the care of the Daughters, who moved among them with lunar grace. And to each of our travelers, that last night in the little bar with beautiful neon in the middle of the high desert, the Daughters brought tequila and then they brought stories—for they knew that this was a group that needed provisions.

As Maria-Elena explained it: "These are," she said, "the private nuptial gifts of the Daughters of the Moon. To you, our compatriots, we present them tonight, in secret. For they are the finest we have, and we would not have you leave us unless we knew you carried away with you our best treasures."

And so in the course of the night, as the drinking and singing went on, Chiara and then Ananda; Muscovado, and then Izzy, then finally Renato were taken back one by one by a Daughter of the Moon into a corner of the bar, to be given a story to take on the road.

And it would be much later, as our travelers neared the Pacific Ocean, that these tales were given away to strangers, tales about paradisiacal machines, the origin of chile peppers, the creation of the earth—

And in the giving away, one of them would save a life.

But that is another story.

All through these shenanigans the bar had been filling up, with prospectors coming in from the country, and the maids from the motel down the street stopping by; geologists looking for gold and hunters for antelope; townfolk wanting a party and others wanting harsh liquor for sweet solitude.

Renato had watched hungrily his Maria-Elena, but she just looked back at him lingeringly and then went off with her sisters. And so he took the logical next step and passed from funk to deep funk. Musco abandoned his rescue efforts—he had some sidling up to do, some subtle provocations for Izzy; and what was he supposed to do anyway, sprinkle some pixie dust of happiness on this poor bastard?

Izzy had circulated all around the room during the wedding party: sometimes coming with embraces to Musco, sometimes brushing by; sometimes stepping outside to the desert air she had so much come to savor; desert air that had come to savor her.

The stories of the Daughters of the Moon had braided together again the midnight-and-noontime hair of Chiara and Ananda.

Tomorrow they would all be back on the road.

Tabby and Grimes would always remember, as though it were drawn in florid colors, the next minute. Both of them in action, muscles standing out, looking good. People who cared. They thought later that it would have been even nicer if they'd had some costumes that were more contoured to their bodies, so that there was more of a sense of action, more a sense of the way punishment really worked. How it was like a dance.

The cop was mad. Having a punk hold a knife to your throat, who did they think they were? Did they think they were in the city? Nobody got away with this shit up here.

The cop spun away from Grimes, drew his billy club and knocked the knife away; and for the benefit of Tabby, who was watching, swatted Grimes once across the face, then back across the face once more. When he had Grimes down on the dirt road, he very regrettably kicked him in the head.

"Fucking punk city kid! Who do you think you are coming up

here with this shit? I'm sending you home handcuffed, you little bag of shit—"

Grimes with his teeth clenched rolled away; holding his face in his hands, he rolled over and over, crying out; he was still for a minute, then he got to his feet and with bloody face smiled at the cop. He stood straight. His new coat and shirt were torn and there were dust and bloodstains. He knew his chest was showing. Nice. Why hadn't they brought along a photographer, dammit!

The cop turned, sweating and red-faced, and swore at Tabby.

"This isn't playtime here, kid. Now put the gun down before I give you the same welcome—"

Tabby looked at Grimes.

"Tabby, you see he's dirtied my clothes."

"A bad temper."

"A Monster."

"A Monster! You think? You really think so?"

"I can tell."

"How can you tell?"

"See that shine on his face?"

"I see it."

"That's a little scum-shine."

"Exciting!"

"—Scum-shine. We should have looked closer to see if he had the mark: scum-shine. A Monster."

"What to do? Is there work to do?" wondered Tabby aloud.

"Get him before he breeds," suggested Grimes.

"No! A breeder! Exciting!"

"Little monsters everywhere."

"I'll have to fix it."

"A breeder."

"I'll fix it."

"A breeder, too bad."

"Fix it!"

"Fix it!" ordered Grimes.

"I think you're right. No use even giving him the chance to

beg. It would be too disgusting to see him on his knees," commented Tabby.

There on the dirt road under the big trees the cop was still furious, and because of such a mood was not really as thoughtful and prepared as he could have been when Tabby let loose a burst of fire that blew an important part of his head into the bushes.

Tabby came over to Grimes; they both felt upset. Why couldn't they make him understand?

Tabby looked down at the oozing cop. "You shouldn't have kicked him. Why did you kick him? He was nice to you! I hate to see people doing bad things! It really hurt my feelings! You hurt me! We've helped everyone up here! We liked you! You should have been happy to see us. Why weren't you happy? We've been so generous"—Tabby straightened his tie—"What about all that money we gave away? What about it? You could have been a hero and now you're not worth shit except maybe in a photo with us, you are some kinda bleeder—" Tabby did a few turns and flexes, struck a few poses, spun and strutted, hit a few more, he could hear his heart pounding just like in the shows under the lights. "If we had a picture you'd be in a fancy coffee-table book sometime, because someone is going to tell all about us. We want them to tell. They're going to write that you were rude. Too bad for you! Too bad! Rude! But we'll be good to you. Want to know how? I said"—Tabby kicked the body a few hard ones—"I *said*, do you want to know how? This is how: we won't even crap on you now that you're dead."

Tabby thought of all those envelopes they had given away. The chance this guy passed up to be a good person! The idiocy of it!

Grimes looked down at the cop; and then he stooped down and took his badge and gun.

"It's funny—they even look like his real fucking brains, I mean, they even *look* stupid," he said, and he was glad he thought of it. He should write these things down, they really should be keeping a scrapbook.

It was such a beautiful evening, they could see stars, and the mist rose in the redwoods.

Tabby and Grimes high-fived each other and got back in their car and put in a tape and when the cello sounded they turned it up loud. Tabby closed his eyes and Grimes reached over to rub the back of his friend's head; his buddy.

"It's not easy, protecting people," Tabby observed. "It's just as much work as I thought it was going to be."

13

AS THE BATTERED station wagon was restored to the troupe, so the caravan was restored to its former glory.

Ready to take their place were Mike and Jeb, who had given themselves over with gusto to the job of armed guards. If the group needed help, they needed it now—they were leaving the Great Basin, a region protective of outlandish souls.

The animals, joined by a kitten that Tupelo had improbably adopted—marriage parties will make even a cat hospitable—all clambered in the back of the house on the truck. Into the middle of that bestial party our voyagers tossed Renato, who still had not wised up. In fact, they had to truss him down, so that he wouldn't try to stay at the Jalisco and make a pest of himself.

The kitten went to him and got under his shirt.

Juha and Cookie, as a result of their marriage, were designated with some ceremony the Responsible Parties. This, after a rebuffed attempt, inspired by the nearby town of Empire, to designate them Emperor and Empress. These titles were rejected as too obscure.

Everyone felt good to have straightforward plain-grit leadership. And they took action: ready to go, Juha and Cookie threw open the doors of the wagon driven up to Gerlach from the ranch of the angels by Muscovado and Izzy. Yet from that ride such were the vapors still circulating in the wagon, that the whole bunch of them had to stand back while a fragrant mist— an allspice-bread-and-peppers, musk-and-mint, cinnamon-and-sugar elixir-of-life mist—cascaded from the front seat and made its viscous way through Gerlach.

With a grin the newlyweds got in and set off, followed by Musco and Iz and Ananda and Chiara all crammed in the front seat of the truck with the house, with Renato in back all by his lonesome—so he could think, as everyone generously put it; then bringing up the rear of the caravan, in their four-wheel drive, Mike and Jeb.

Once on the road, they all thought it was time to just take their ease. Ax-heaving, talking peacocks, partying in obscure little bars, celestial ranchers, metaphysical trumpets, marriage, the exultations of the soul, free-flowing tequila, and so forth—shucks, it wasn't stuff you could absolutely count on for *every* day. And so, at their ease, on the road, what might they do?

They chatted.

"I'm not sure I like this," said Jeb.

"You know, for weeks we've been going by what we like and what we don't like. And so we get bombed, shot at, shit on, and struck by lightning. Maybe we got to rethink, you know?"

"And who the fuck are you, Mr. Philosophy?" inquired Jeb amiably.

Up in the wagon, Cookie turned to Juha.

"Well, this is my plan, Juha: you build, I'll cook. Then after a year, I'll build, you cook."

"Well now, I was just thinking that maybe I should be buildin' us a house before too long. We ain't going to get to live in the house on the truck. If it ain't full of animals, it's full of Renato, mooning away back there."

"So let's get to buildin'. No dillydallying. Where do we put it?" Cookie wanted to know.

"Well, let's find us a river bend, maybe with a little meadow, put up a log house, a simple thing, just for two."

"A river? In Nevada?"

"I just want to be roamin' around with my wife, and us lookin' for a place to settle. I 'spect we'll know it when we see it."

Cookie looked over at him. "You know I always did reckon I had the fixin's to be a wife; but far as I could see there weren't no husbands in the world. Men, you know it's like God jes' dumped on earth his sack of idiots, spilled all over, bluster and peckers, I tell you now they're everywhere and it's too late, we can't get rid of 'em."

"So what are you doin' with me?" asked the befuddled Juha.

Cookie laughed. "You *are* a husband. You're jes' *disguised* as a man."

"Cookie, you know how in Nevada the valleys kinda settle down between the mountain ranges, deep and solid down in between the ranges?"

"Yep."

"That's how I'm settlin' down with you. Deep inside you."

"Well now, I happen to like your disguise, Juha."

In the front of the truck, Ananda and Chiara cozied up with the feral Izzy and Musco.

"Maybe you should open the window on your side. We don't want to pass out from the vapors," said Chiara.

"Maybe we should open all the windows," shot back Izzy. "It's obvious I didn't chaperon you close enough."

"A mother-daughter tiff, isn't that cute!" gibed Ananda.

"I'm not sure we tiff," reflected Chiara, "but we do rollick."

"What I want to know is, am I sort of a mother-in-law now?" speculated Ananda.

"Sure. Let's have some weepy conflicts," chuckled Iz.

"Ananda, this romance of ours, is it right? Is it true?" said Chiara mockingly. And what she meant was: how long could all of them get away with teasing the world? Teasing it, that is, with their good fortune?

"Uh-oh. They're going to jam," observed the prescient Muscovado.

"We've got to figure that one out," affirmed Ananda, "because this is not how it's supposed to go, according to contemporary studies."

Ananda had some questions about the bearing of modern psychology upon their adventures. Important questions; for, as we know, psychology floats on the modern narrative like pond scum.

"This I want to hear." Chiara could see the attorney getting revved up.

"We have to ask ourselves what we *really* are doing! For example: What about heartfelt, honest communication? What about our past, the family influences that guide our actions, govern our impulses, set our very character? Should we turn aside this opportunity, that comes maybe once in a life, to get confessional? And maybe even to cry, without the holding back of a single droplet, the tears of true revelation?"

Ananda was coming quickly into her rhetorical stride.

"Let me put this another way—"

"Oh, please do. You have struck the gong of my deepest concerns," said Chiara with piety.

"Thank you. As I was saying, let us make full disclosure, each to the other, of the key experiences in our lives. Let us air the grievances of the past, and not just the big-time emotional whipsaws; what about, piling up like dirty dishes, those small but cumulative disappointments, huh? Everybody knows we can love at all only if we are willing to scrub out the filthy sinks of each other's psyches. Everybody knows that! Let's do it! Let's scrub! Thank you very much!"

And Ananda slumped happily down in the seat.

"You must have been irresistible in the courtroom," commented Chiara. "If I was a judge I would have blown you kisses."

Ananda and Chiara looked, they paused.

"It really is so much better putting together a life from scratch," said Iz.

"But can we? And just how? I think we need some advice," said Ananda.

She looked over at Muscovado, who had been doing a bass-note laughter at the women's skit. He had that look you see on the face of someone who thought you'd never ask.

"Sure, I'll advise you. If I was alone with Izzy, I could really concentrate, and come up with just the right thing," he said, grinning.

"As a matter of fact," suggested the obliging maternal Chiara, "why don't you stop and let me and Ananda check on Renato? We don't want him to go from deep funk into subterranean funk, or even into the dread abysmal funk."

And he did stop, and the two of them climbed back into the house to check on the painter.

Izzy and the smitten Muscovado Taine rolled along the highway alone now in the cab of the truck. There is no security like being able to take your own house wherever you go. Besides, they liked driving the balconied, the corniced and crested house, complete with its tiny weather vane pointing here and there.

"What on earth am I doing in the middle of the desert going from story to story and in love with a sixteen-year-old? I mean, was this the agenda? Is this journalism?" the Jamaican wanted to know.

"It's OK, Musco," replied our Iz. "I like older men. What am I going to do for a lover? Take younger men?"

"How about a boy your own age?" he suggested.

Izzy laughed herself crimson. When she caught her breath, she said, "Have you had a look at any of them lately? Their nervous system is slow to develop. And I mean *slow*. They go step by step through the whole evolutionary tree. They *lag*, you know what

I mean? At sixteen years old a boy has the range of a swamp fungus. On a good day."

"And so you picked me out?"

"Look, I'm out and about. We didn't come out here to play fucking cribbage. My mother once told me, she said, 'Iz, remember this: you love 'em—let somebody else trust 'em.' "

"You and your mother are cynical bitches," commented Musco in a sweet way.

Iz gave him a shot of the double opals.

"Muscovado Taine, I love you. You look like a lover, smell like a lover, you sing into my hair like a lover, you're a born lover, Muscovado, and I love you. It's not just the way with your hands you tease the honey from me all night and lick it off in the morning; not your strong back where I cut you up with love, not even the allspice that runs from your cock. I wanted a man. We have found out that the desert is a house of angels, my lover, with how many men could I have done that? You're the man I love, Muscovado, I love you so much that it'll make a dazzle of the whole rest of your life because Muscovado Taine, I'm going to rub your soul until the genie comes out."

Musco, rocked in these supple energies, was with pious vows turning to her when she went on to say, "And so you can see how much I'm going to miss you."

In the back of the truck, the animals, ignoring Renato, came straight over to beguile the lovers. First the peacock—"If you keep me I'll tell you one of God's proverbs," he proposed, giving the two lovers a big peacock wink.

"We'll keep you, if you tell us now," said Ananda. Lawyers can't help negotiating.

"This is it," said the peacock. "Unless your soul can tell a joke, you're just one more big dummy."

"Why is it that God when he's talking to you is such a sassy-ass?" inquired Chiara. "He's supposed to be august and solemn."

"Well, she ain't. She's robust and sarcastic."

"Do you have a whole collection of God's proverbs?"

"You bet," said the peacock.

"So let's hear a few more."

"If in the months to come you both take the time to kiss me about the head and stroke my lapis breast, if you feed me little somethings and wink at all the eyes in my tail, then I will tell you the proverbs," promised the peacock.

And without waiting for an answer the bird nestled up between the smiling women.

In the corner of the pickup's bed, the coyote rolled her eyes, since coyotes are, of course, in wit and flesh a direct extension of God's body.

But who could attend fully to the animals when Renato was hallucinating? He spoke from the shadows: "Why is there moonlight here in the back of the truck?"

"I just can't help doing things. I want to build things," Juha was saying. "I feel naked without my tool belt on. If I was in paradise I would want to add on a room."

"I'll bet you've always fooled people," said Cookie. "You're so big, no one would expect you'd be goin' here and there and tinkerin' and fiddlin'. They'd think you'd be more like a block of concrete."

"Why do I love you so much?" asked Juha suddenly.

"I expect it's 'cause there ain't two more practical animals in the world. We'll put the days in our tool belts, and work up together a whole world, you big lunk."

"Yep," said Mike, "we're definitely foot soldiers in this one."

"You know, I always wanted to be a pro," said Jeb. "Going out, getting the job done. Staying straight. Paying attention. And now you've signed us up as guards for a goddam troupe of orangutangs, a pack of bozos who don't know where they're going, or what they're doing, talk funny as cats, and are always flopping into bed like so many hot tamales. Great. Why don't we go work at a zoo?

Bouncers, maybe, in a club at a nuthouse? We could toss the really bad droolers."

"So maybe you want to do a few more rounds with Beulah and her son?"

"So maybe I'll stop bitching."

They had turned left onto a dirt road, and after a few miles Juha and Cookie, with much horseplay and honking, got the whole ensemble to pull over and shut up. But it couldn't last.

Chiara stepped out in front of them all.

"I don't see anybody to tell stories out here," she said, "so I guess we'll just have to tell 'em to each other. And by the time we get to Honey Lake, we'll have a strategy."

"A what?" inquired Mike. Mike and Jeb would always ask the short questions.

"She means," said Izzy, interpreting for her mother, "that we are going to have to figure out something to do. Except for Juha and Cookie. They know what to do. As for the rest of us—we have to get back to society sometime."

"We do?" inquired Jeb. "I thought I just gave all that shit up."

"Just follow our lead, Jeb," shot out Izzy. Jeb ground his teeth.

And since everybody was getting bored with the funkathon that had gripped Renato, Chiara thought she would try to give him a jolt. She went over and banged on the door of the house on the truck.

"Renato: you first! Put everything you know in the world into one little story, one and one only. Go for it!" commanded Chiara.

And Renato emerged, looking pale and sad, as though he'd been recently drowned. But these were his friends, and, lovelorn or not, he had to deliver. Though he had to cogitate a while: for some reason, it is uncommon in our historical period to be asked to put right there on the spot all things one knows about life, death, and love into a little story. It is more common to be asked to, say, pass the potatoes.

But it happens. And Renato commenced

Renato, who had on the drive from Gerlach been wreathed in his meditations; Renato, for whom the radiance of night and day now had gone dark, no longer the cascade of colors he knew and loved—Renato looked at them all, and said slowly, "I'll tell you all I know, as near as I can figure:

"First of all, you have to have a work to do. It's just the way things are. It's something you learn about; if you can't keep learning, you need a new work.

"Once you're at work, you see that it changes you; because what you do gives you something to love with. Something to hand over.

"So you do this work, and then what? You hand it over. However much your lover takes, you hand it over. You have your work, you have your lover, and then you come to the day you have nothing left.

"What happens? You have gotten rid of yourself, you have given away everything entrusted to you by love, at long last. There's nothing left of you but soul; but that was all there was to you in the first place.

"Of course, at death, we get rid of ourselves anyway. But if you can do it before you die, then you get to be a soul right here on earth. For one thing, it gives you a better appetite. And you can keep on working, but now with ancient mischief and the wild energy of many worlds. What a deal! And think how good the Mexican food will taste!"

Renato looked at Chiara. "If I was a teacher that's what I would teach: the journey of the soul coming round on earth to hot food with good chile sauce."

And the painter walked straight over to the house on the truck, got in, and slammed the door behind him. His kitten was still there. Someone had to look after him.

"A bit plain, a bit short, I would say," commented Iz.

"We're new at this," said her mother. "What did you expect, *War and Peace*?"

Jeb burst out: "I think I get it! This thing about the soul! It's in there the whole time, just like the worm in a jumping bean." He was proud.

Chiara came over and stood before Jeb, looking him straight in the eyes—a first for Jeb, in his dealings with women. And since it was the woman he and Mike had chased across a whole continent, he thought some manly act was called for.

"Look, we're at your service. Don't rub it in."

Chiara looked closely at him, and then at Mike, and gave them a smile as big as the Mediterranean.

"Welcome to the trip, you two. You're the brutes we love."

And she turned and with the others began walking back toward the truck and wagon.

"Let's all go make some honey at Honey Lake," she suggested.

"It's lucky you're a professor," said Izzy. "It's made you decorous."

"It's lucky you're my daughter," shot back Chiara. "Over most of the world by now you'd have been hanged from a tree."

"Nah. On the way to the hanging they'd be struck by my prowess mathematical and sexual, they'd take a rowdy vote and make me queen. I'd make a helluva queen."

Chiara shook her head at Ananda.

"I tried so hard. I baked her cupcakes. I taught her to waltz. She wore white gloves. She was so prim."

"When was it that you and your daughter fell into the habit of lying?" asked Ananda.

"Just after she was conceived," remembered Chiara.

"It becomes you both," said her lover.

"And about that honey—" inquired Juha.

But Cookie was looking around. "Husband! We're headed toward the mountains, and leaving everything behind."

"Except one thing," said her worthy beau.

"Let me guess—you stashed a flour tortilla."

"No, it's that damned harmonica we got from the angels in Fallon. We used the trumpet, and the bell. But that slimy harmonica is still rattling around. What's the use of it?"

"I'll ask the coyote," said Cookie, as they piled in.

The Great Basin was sorry they were leaving.

Beulah turned up in Gerlach. She sent Bolt off to melt rocks in the Calico Mountains to the north. Antelope on the Moon was there in the bar picking his teeth with a nail. Before long the junk truck pulled up in front of the Jalisco, and out of the cab swaggered the angels Peggy-Sue and June and Bret. Everybody went out to look at the junk: rakes and shovels, saddles and bayonets and uniforms from the army of Napoleon, couches, comic books, tins of tobacco, pancake batter and branding irons and crown jewels, fishing rods and lost Vermeers, tape measures, contraceptive jellies and parchments bearing the secrets of the Illuminati: and among these things, a big fridge stuffed with tequila, gin, and beer.

Hansel and Gertie showed up, and the Paiutes of Pyramid. The desert wind and its light came round, and all in all it was one more wingding of a meal that was set brewing in the kitchen of the Jalisco Club by the twelve moon-eyed sisters.

With a terrific confluence of spirits they packed in. Lava flowed in the Calicos. Antelope on the Moon called into the room from the House of the Winds a bucking azure stream with the cool of deep space; the angels draped the beams of the Jalisco with rainbows and then unfolded through the middle of the room like a soul of the sky—the aurora borealis. The *salsa picante* roared on the stove, Peggy-Sue stood up and proposed a toast to our innocent travelers:

"Lovers that you are, here's to your strange work! Here's to you and your travels, you dear ones. And to the day when we see you again, not so many months from now!

And they all took a hearty slug.

14

ROLLING DOWN the road in the house on the truck, Ananda, Chiara, and Renato sat with all the animals.

"I feel like I never even got to decide," said Ananda. "That old point of no return, where you can say yea or nay, just zipped by."

"Me neither," said Chiara, grinning. "It's like a cartoon. I've been kidnapped by a blond securities attorney."

"But I keep thinking we have to do something," said Ananda.

"We do," said Renato dully. "We don't have any of us anything left. It's like a big blank canvas. I can't think of a thing." The kitten stared with amusement at him.

"Well, we're not back in civilization yet. But we're headed in that direction. In the next few weeks, we'll just see if we can come up with a life."

"Someone was going to ask the coyote—" began Renato dully.

And the animal went wild, scampering everywhere. In the tiny space of the ornate house she mimed a scrambling up hillsides, and being stock-still on the rimrock in the morning; she darted under covers and came out of a cupboard, leaped over the couch as though after rabbit and rousted the squawking peacock out of her deep blue nap, she batted around the house a jar from the counter and broke it cleanly, putting her tongue on the honey; she snarled, with her paws she boxed Renato's ears, somersaulted in the middle of them and lifted her head in a long howl, and then looked long at them all with her golden eyes.

Chiara and Ananda stood up at once and went over to her, sat on the floor next to her.

"She's telling us we need to improvise for a living," ventured Ananda.

"Of course! We'll go on stage! A traveling theater troupe!" exclaimed Chiara. What could have been more obvious? What a bunch of numbskulls!

When they hit Honey Lake, everyone tumbled out, propositions were exchanged, names were thrown around, winks were shot here and there, and within two minutes they had done an old-fashioned fateful thing: they had formed the **Hat Tricks and Hot-Pillows Lowlife Storytelling Dirty-Angel Plain-Folks Improvisational Hurricane Theater Troupe.**

The coyote bolted off into the basin and was gone.

"She looked a little impatient. Guess it took us a long time to get the message," said Chiara.

"What do we put on first?" asked Musco.

"How about *King Lear?*" suggested Izzy.

"A stage rendering of *Gone With the Wind?*"

"*Oedipus in Las Vegas?*" offered Ananda.

"A good idea!" threw in Chiara. "We need to write our own. Bring in some ancient figures. How about *Socrates on the Slide Guitar?*"

"*Alexander the Great in His Life as a Male Model.*"

"Nah, you're all just being university jackasses. We need something romantic: how about *A Can of Pop, a Fatty Salami, and Thee?*" Cookie wanted to play the lead.

"Myself, now, I was thinking more of plays that would have them pulp-newspaper titles," mused Juha. "You know—*God Turned My Son into a Chile Relleno.*"

"Jesus Comes to Surf City," confirmed Cookie. "Or maybe *The First Orgasm in Flatbush*—it'll be a whodunit."

"Something more ethereal, hinting at the supernatural, say, *The Astronaut and the Unicorn,*" said Renato—even he wanted in on this game. "Or maybe *Chips n' Dip at the Last Supper.*"

"Maybe we should do a whole play about searching for a title for a play we want to write," suggested Chiara.

"How about *The Talking Peacock?*" suggested the peacock.

And, as they talked, the Sierra, still painted with snow on the peaks, moved like a colt in the sunlight. By their side, Honey Lake held slashes of light, here and there nicks and kindlings of light. There was a little breeze, enough to waft Muscovado's savor of allspice straight to Izzy.

"Musco," she said, "all right already."

"I can't help it," he pleaded.

"Then tell us a story," said the flashing Iz. And the peacock came over and stood expectantly in front of Muscovado. Tupelo the cat climbed up Ananda's leg and onto her shoulders, where she sat, gazing at the swarthy Jamaican with her green eyes.

"OK, OK," surrendered Musco. And so commenced

THE STORY OF THE FISHERMAN AND HIS LOVE-GIFTS; OR, THE MAKING OF MUSCOVADO TAINE; OR, THE HUMDRUM MYSTERIES OF LIFE #3, A SERIES WHICH WILL GO ON AND ON UNLESS THIS BUNCH STOPS SWERVING AROUND, GETS INTO PERSONAL GROOMING, DOES SOME RESPONSIBLE FINANCIAL PLANNING, AND JUST PIPES DOWN

"When I was a boy," Musco began, "I met a young man out fishing in the bay near Port Maria, near my house in the southwest of Jamaica. I went out with him in his boat, and he threw his line in; instead of catching a fish, he caught a pair of new sneakers. Now, I needed some sneakers at the time, so I didn't pay no mind to his cursing and moaning. The shoes were a little big, but he did some pushing on them, and they fit me fine. After that he brought in seven fish, one right after another, until our whole boat was shiny and heavy, and he rowed into shore and said to me, 'I'm taking these home to my love.'

"Every week I fished with him. He would hum and sing, and he never failed to catch a boatful of fish, and he always said he was taking them home to his love. And so finally I asked him about this woman, and why he worked all day and every day for her. And he said, 'Well, I met her a hundred million years ago, when I gave her my first love-gift; and now she and I are visiting here for old times' sake.'

"Now that was the strangest thing I ever heard, and I thought he was crazy as a cuttlefish, and I stayed away from him. But I couldn't forget him. And so one day there I was in his boat again, and he said, 'I knew you would come back.' "

" 'A hundred million years ago? You crazy?'

" 'When you get to be a little older, you'll start learning love-tricks,' he said. 'And if you're a real lover, if you get really good at them—well, these love-tricks mean that you start living in a stranger, happier, wider world. You can dip into time anywhere you want, turn up here and there, if you got things to do. And here I am, 'cause I had some things to do.'

" 'What do you have to do?' I asked.

" 'Fish,' he said.

"Now, I had to decide whether to jump from the boat right then, just from being scared of that wild creature. But he spoke so quietly, with such assurance and care, that I couldn't jump, though the water was blue and clear as a promise. And so he went on:

" 'Now I will tell you the story of my love, from the time we first met. It was very long ago, there was nothing here, nothing at all, just the quiet and the smooth blue sea. I had just met her, and I wanted to give her a love-gift. Now, I loved kissing her neck, so I thought I'd get her a necklace. But it had to be just the right necklace; this was going to take some thinking. And if I was going to do some thinking, I had to go fishing, because I'm one of those people who can only think if he's fishing. And so I built a little boat.'

" 'I built a boat and I went fishing, right in this big sea where in those times there was not a single island. And I thought, How in this blue world could I find the necklace I knew belonged to my love, had always belonged to her? And I thought and thought of her.'

" 'Just then I felt something enormous on my line, and I reeled and reeled, for days and days, licked by moonlight and by sunlight. The world was new. Everything in this world was new—the water of the sea was still married to the light of the heavens. I reeled and reeled. Panthers walked by me on the water, you can still see their pawprints. Day and night I reeled.

" '—Until at the end of my line out of the sea rose the island of Jamaica.'

" 'The island of Jamaica!' I exclaimed.

" 'That's right, I had caught an island. It stumped me. Here I was fishing for my love, fishing for her gift, and I caught an island.'

" 'What to do? I kept fishing. And along the length of what was to become the Caribbean Sea I caught island after island, in a long crescent down along the song lines of sunlight. And then I understood—with my fishing I was making my love a necklace of islands.'

" 'And that is why, little boy, there are islands in the Caribbean Sea. I brought them up, each a different jewel, each one something made new in a world that moved for her alone.'

" 'It is so with every thing beautiful in this world: once it was a love-gift. This is why what a thing is, is different from what it means. This is why the world turns to stories.'

"And he was quiet, looking at me, looking into the sea.

"Now what? I thought.

"Just then, after that strange telling, right there as I sat with this strange man out there in the bay in the south of Jamaica, there was an enormous tug on the fisherman's line."

Chiara looked over at her daughter. "Does he always talk like this?"

"Usually it's more whispery and outlandish," said Izzy.

"So what was on the fisherman's line?" Cookie wanted to know.

"Well, now I've told about all a story a man can in one day," said Musco. "Especially without any rum in hand."

"Why don't we do some building together, Musco?" suggested Juha. "I'll take you on if you tell stories as we work."

Tupelo the cat leaped down from Ananda's shoulders and flopped over on her back, just under the end of the peacock's tail; the cat clawed and nipped, rolled into and embraced the fluffy arcs of feathers. The bird squawked. Tupelo buried her paws into his tail for a happy feline rummaging. The bird tried to swing round and peck at Tupelo.

"Will no one stop this brute animal?" inquired the peacock.

"I like this," said Cookie, "cats and birds roughing each other up."

"Let's go rough up the whole town of Doyle," said Chiara, her eyes moving from the moving Sierra, to the animals, to the light caterwauling with the lake.

It was just then that a shiny blue pickup shot down the road past them, roaring by and covering the lot of them with dust. They watched it skid to a stop about a hundred yards away and a man got out, slamming the door, and going around to the passenger side he pulled open that door and reached in and yanked out a little boy, slapped him five times and threw him to the ground. Across the playa came his shout: "Now walk home, shithead! Idiot!" And he got back in the truck and roared away.

Ananda and Chiara jumped in the wagon and sped off toward the kid.

"Back to civilization," sighed Izzy.

Tabby and Grimes drove east, going day and night. The closer they got to the Sierra the better they felt. The beautiful pale blue of the morning sky, all the stars at night, they had never seen them. After they had gotten to northern California, the first night they looked up it seemed to them like a show from some other world.

But now they were getting used to it; they waited all day for nightfall. They counted out stars as they drove along. As the stars appeared they would sing out—another one! look over there, a red one! a light blue one!—and as the sky filled in they felt happier and happier. It was clear and constant and it looked like a future.

"We were meant to be here," said Tabby, who felt weathered and tough. And he was sure he looked it, even in his spotless clothes. Something had started for him, since the pistol-whipping in San Jose. Right when the pistol had smacked his father's face the first time, it was as though he was able to watch himself. He could see what he did from outside. And all through San Francisco and up the coast together, whenever they stopped by the side of the sea, he could remember it all so clearly—he could just imagine how he looked, his poses. It was like he didn't need the mirrors anymore. He had something better, a way of watching. It was like he had a seat at the movie of himself. He had the part he wanted; and he watched and watched, all through the giveaways in Arcata, the driving, the stupid cop. That cop should have known he was in someone else's show. He got what he deserved, not being able to follow the story.

"I knew we could make it together," said Grimes, as he handled one after another the five pistols he kept in the front seat.

Grimes was still smarting from the beating. Sometimes you can't tell Monsters right away. They're in disguise. But the two of them couldn't be fooled for long. No way.

"We need a stronghold."

"In the woods."

"A hideout."

"Beautiful."

"A hideout to practice in."

"Deep in the woods."

"No one will find us."

"Some good people. A good man could find us," theorized Tabby. "A brave one."

Tabby had never felt so good. He watched the road, but it was as though he saw the car from the side of the road, as a lonely girl would see them: two young titans, with their strong arms, Tabby's powerful hands on the wheel. Exciting.

Grimes sounded off: "Maybe we can get Angelica to come up. I miss her. I wish she could have seen us with the cop. He got so mad. I always hate it when people get mad. Why get red in the face and look ugly? There are no ugly heroes. When heroes get mad, they're beautiful."

Grimes was looking into the big sky—

"We got to find some pretty bitches," he said.

"They'll be some pretty ones up here. Polite ones. Innocent ones. I like those ones with the dark hair and wet lips."

In the middle of the night they got past Highway 5 and headed toward Chico. Beyond that they saw on the map a town called Paradise. And beyond that, the Feather River canyon, Sierra Valley, and the Yuba Pass.

In front of the bar in Doyle the Improvisational Hurricane Theater Troupe had their first show. The troupe would have many a day of performance in the next months, in the North Sierras and then afterward in the central valley and all along the coast, all the way to the Lost Coast. But today they were ready to kick it off. Ananda and Chiara had taken care of the little boy a few hours, then met secretly and at length with the boy's grandfather, who lived in town. The father, a cowboy named Somerset Markley, had run off his wife and kept the child, just to have someone to hit.

Ananda had been to the courthouse and with the help of a colleague in Los Angeles had prepared all the necessary documents. They had talked to people throughout the little town of Doyle, and everybody just wanted to be rid of the asshole. Chiara had gotten together the exhibits. Musco and Izzy had worked on the props and did most of the writing; and they were designated directors of a little play that, for a first shot, was pretty damned elaborate; it was

THE VISIT OF THE COSMIC DOCTORS TO SOLVE A LITTLE PROBLEM IN THE TOWN OF DOYLE, CALIFORNIA; OR, A COWBOY AND HIS TESTES

It was in the afternoon late in the week of the visit to Doyle. Cookie sat on a bench on the old wooden sidewalk in front of the bar. A cowhand near her leaned on a post and, fishing from his vest a tin of tobacco, took a fingerful for his lip. Out in the street stood a shiny blue pickup.

"I shore do have a kinda empty feeling in my lower lip—I mean real empty," said Cookie immediately.

The cowhand turned around.

"Yep, it's like a big empty space that makes me think life will be a useless thing all the damned day."

He held out a tin. "Mebbe a gal like you takes a plug now n' then?" he said courteously.

"Well, thank you, don't mind if I do," said Cookie. " 'Bout time you got your lazy ass in gear and showed some hospitality."

The cowboy moved closer to her. He could see she'd be a challenge, but he was drawn to her. He liked challenges. He had the feeling that this was his lucky day. Cookie could see the violent stew of his soul.

Somerset was just on the way back out to the house. He meant to check on the boy. The things the little dipshit made him do! He hit the boy out of love: he loved anger: anger was his sidekick, confidant, security: in anger he felt himself rise up into a fullness in the world.

At least once a week he rode home to the mood he cherished.

In other words, a theatrical personality.

Cookie had slowly taken some tobacco from the tin he held out, and she watched him watch her tuck it away. Standing up, she brushed him, and then took a few steps away, looked back and smiled at him.

"Now, you do have some tasty stuff," she said.

Somerset was thinking, yep, this is my lucky day; and indeed it was. Ananda, wearing a suit and carrying a briefcase, had emerged from the bar. She walked right up to Somerset, shook his hand, gave him an appraising and interested look.

"And you, sir, is your name Somerset Markley?"

"That's right, ma'am," he answered politely, wowed by the shining hair of the attorney.

"I have been searching for you all over the town, sir. I was told at the courthouse that you often come into town at this hour, and so I was hoping to catch you. I have some welcome news for you."

"You're kiddin'! That kind o' news don't come round too often, now, ma'am, and so I would dearly like to know what it is you are sayin'," said Somerset in his best hat-in-hand manner.

"I am an attorney with the firm of Vladimir, Estragon, Pozzo, and Lucky, and I represent a gold mining firm that has been conducting surveys in the area, looking for those geological formations associated with mineral deposits. Some of these formations exist on deeded land of a cattle ranch, that, according to county records, is owned by you."

"I own the ranch 'bout three mile on the east side of the lake, and my land curls around the base of the northern ridge; that the one you mean?"

Somerset gave a long wink to Cookie. He thought maybe she might like to see him win something.

"That's the one," went on Ananda, "and I have come prepared to make you a very attractive offer for the rights to explore for gold and silver, as well as other minerals, on your land. This offer would provide for a one-hundred-thousand-dollar cash bonus to you, upon execution of the documents; and a substantial royalty if the occurrence of precious metals is confirmed. Does this sound like something of interest?"

Cookie shook her head at Ananda. This gal is an *operator*, she thought.

Somerset nodded toward Cookie and said to her, "Well now, this is my lucky day, meeting a cowgirl like you and making some money right out of the sky, pretty thing, now watch me do this business," and, turning back to Ananda, he furrowed up his brow some and said, "You know I jes' might have to think about this, I knowed that there was some companies pokin' around here. I'll jes' kinda bide my time." And he winked at Cookie.

"Mr. Markley, you may certainly do that. But I must inform you that my offer to you expires at close of business today. My company is a large one that has many prospects, and if they cannot close on yours, they will move on to others."

Ananda set her briefcase down on the table, crossed her arms, and looked straight at him.

"Where do I sign?" he asked.

And Ananda popped her briefcase and shepherded him through the documents. She leaned close to him so that he could smell midsummer in her hair, she pointed out this and that, she put her arm on his shoulder, she smelled like sunlight on wildflowers. Cookie was looking admiringly at him, she looked like she'd do anything for him; Ananda was shaking his hand, taking a long time at it, too, and he was thinking that this was the best day of his life when he noticed that the check she gave him was made out to his son, with the boy's grandfather named as guardian.

He rose up. "What the fuck is this? Do you want to tell me, bitch?"

"That's your check. You can tell—it feels like a check. It's shaped like a check. It has numbers and dates, like a check. You know, it must *be* a check."

"What's my goddam son and his goddam grandfather doing here?"

"The documents you signed vested title to the ranch in the name of the two of them. Therefore, the check by law must be made payable to them."

"Well then, maybe by my law I'll just change things," and he advanced on Ananda, drew back and backhanded her across the face with such force that she dropped to the floor.

Now, there are some things that, however improvisatory, our Hurricane Troupe was not wholly prepared for. Cookie, for instance, thought immediately of galloping a horse over Somerset's face. Muscovado Taine thought of taking away the cowboy and frying him like a fish. But it was Ananda who, just like she was supposed to, carried on the show.

"Sir," said Ananda as she rose to her feet, "I will have to refer you to our fisticuffs department," and with a wave of her hand she gestured to the door of the bar, as Cookie rose up and showed a rope and dropped a loop around Somerset's shoulders, binding his arms. Thus bound, Somerset was further surprised when Mike and Jeb stepped out and handcuffed him to the railing at the front of the wooden sidewalk. The two detectives, happy to be able to use their skills in an entirely new venue, then stepped back and regarded him with virile grimaces.

"What the shit? Who are you? Am I under arrest?"

Cookie and Ananda were standing very near to him, which redoubled his fury, since he could not smash them.

"No, you're not under arrest," said Ananda. "But you *do* have to take a test. We'll even remove the cuffs. If you pass, you can have the ranch back."

"I'll take a sonofabitching test. Let me go, bitch!"

"This is the test: you have to tell a story that would make a child laugh."

Somerset's eyes bugged out at that one.

"That's right. And you have to tell it now. If you can do it, I have high hopes we will finish this day as the very best of friends. Let me introduce you to our story judge, a learned and capable man."

And the two detectives stepped aside as from the door came the enormous Juha, who was all decked out in natty slacks and a tweed coat. He wore wire-rimmed glasses and had about him a studious air. He gazed critically about him. He carried a notebook and a big professional leather case; finding a chair Juha sat down, unlocked the case, and revealed to all an array of scholarly books on folklore and the modern novel; and as well, secured with straps, a dozen gleaming and razor-sharp blades.

Ananda stepped back up to Somerset. "However, there is one more thing, before we set you free. You should know what happens if you cannot tell a witty story, and so fail the test."

"Let me go, you cunt!" shouted Somerset.

"What happens is this: our judge Juha will regretfully be compelled to use his tools, as it were, on your tool. Here to explain this in more detail is a university authority who has followed the tests we have given across the nation."

And out walked Chiara with a pointer. She whisked away a drapery that had covered some heavy shelves on which sat huge jars of formaldehyde. Suspended there in the liquid were various irregular pouches of flesh.

Chiara whacked her pointer on the first jar:

"The testes of a steelworker—too proud to tell even one little story—excised by Juha on the streets of Chicago. Next, these sizable bags that belonged to an Olympic karate champion who could spin a tale, but alas, a dull one—he who once grunted in his workouts, now warbles. Next"—and here the professor indicated some small, peach-pit-sized organs—"are the glands of a famous castrato—no sense of plot, serves him right—who happens to be World Leader of an Industrialized Nation, followed by"—and she tapped with the pointer on the jar containing the tiniest pair anyone had ever seen, no bigger than olives—"the gonads of a professor of comparative literature, no sense of closure, just chattered on like a magpie; followed in the next jar by these enormous numbers, just for general interest, big as tires: the balls of a rogue elephant our Juha slaughtered in hand-to-hand combat."

"You may now tell your story, dear Somerset," said Ananda.

Jeb and Mike were biting their tongues.

Juha looked thoughtfully at the captive. He stroked his chin. He got up and approached him, getting very close. His glasses at the end of his nose, he examined slowly and appraisingly the body of the cowboy. Then he returned to his chair, leaned back and looked really rather judgmental. Cookie undid the rope from Somerset's arms. Jeb took the cuffs off.

Funny stories suitable for children did not, shall we say, flood the mind of the cowboy. In fact, Somerset did not feel wholly in possession of his usual carefree nature. He dove into the dust of the street and rolled away, and got to this feet and started to run and he ran straight up into the mountains and into the Sierra forest, running through the sunlight and then through the moonlight and the sunrise, keeping right on going. From over the tops of the peaks he descended through the red fir and yellow pines, through the black oak and mountain alder into the central valley of California, for days and days he ran all through the hundreds of miles of fields of alfalfa and spinach, carrots and onions, peppers and tomatoes. He ran all the way through the highway towns and clean across the Coast Range through the redwoods, for days and more days until at last he ran into the sea.

By a beachcomber in the town of Arcata he was fished out and taken to a doctor. Later, he found work as a track coach.

Back in Doyle, Izzy walked out among the Hurricane Troupe.

"Good job," she said.

"You look *great* all gussied up. Though it was tough keeping a straight face," Cookie told Juha.

Juha's first foray into the world of theater had been such a gas that he had to be persuaded to change clothes and return to the world.

"Why should I?" he asked. "I've got my glasses and briefcase at the ready. Let's go hit the universities."

"No one ever said that a play couldn't have animals in it," said the peacock with petulance.

"At least I wouldn't have to paint you," said Renato.

"Ananda and I are going to celebrate. We hoped we'd find some work to do on this trip, and now we have," said Chiara.

The town of Doyle had throughly enjoyed the show, and was so glad to be done with Somerset that it gave the troupe a farewell banquet of pork and beans, followed by a local pie known as Lumpy Apple.

Ananda gave the grandfather some lessons in investment management, so that the earnings off the hundred grand would be enough to support the ranch.

The members of the Hurricane Troupe spent a week at the ranch. Juha and Cookie repaired the tools and machinery, Muscovado and Izzy cleaned the whole ranch house, every inch of every room, and put clean sheets on the beds. Chiara and Ananda roamed around with the boy and the granddad, talking about schoolwork and legal arrangements. And Renato, yanked once more out of his funk, painted the barn.

And then they hit the road. As they pulled out of the ranch, the little boy and his grandfather stood waving and waving.

In the wagon and in the truck with their house, the troupe headed from Doyle south to the big green testament of Sierra Valley. The valley, set off by itself high in the mountains, was a world unto itself. There were rumors about a strange town where the people lived with wild animals—a place of pleasure, spirits, and metamorphosis.

The turnoff into the valley was called Hallelujah Junction.

"Now, that could be our motto, Iz, heaven's sake, I couldn't have said it better myself," said Musco, elbowing his young lover as he guided the truck through the junction, west toward the valley.

And Izzy tossed off a few hallelujahs; it set the peacock squawking in the back.

In their four-wheel drive at the back of the caravan, Mike said, "Well, it worked. But kind of a queer idea of fun, I say."

"But it *was* fun," rejoined Jeb. "Did you see that Somerset run! Hooweee! That was some flimflam! We've got to stick around! This group is going to do some stunts!"

Mike looked over at his friend.

"I'm tellin' you I *like* this," Jeb went on breezily. "The whole story. I didn't even mind gettin' bombed. It was worth it."

* * *

As they came into the valley, Cookie piped up, "Juha, I see green. I smell water. So what about that cabin you promised, husband?"

"I'll see about it. I'm looking. But it'll have to fit into my acting career, which has really taken off lately," said Juha with a swagger.

Cookie sighed. "Juha, you're just a Nevada kid; how did you get so weird?"

Juha looked out into the green and soaring valley. "Ever since I could remember I jes' liked things, Cookie, even as a kid I was a big bruiser, but most of time I jes' felt so good, you know. Even when I was sick, it was a good sick. It was as if with everything I did I was lookin' for someone to . . . to thank. I don't know for what exactly; jes' being able to work, to have a chance to do anything. Jes' to put on a tool belt. The biggest problem I had, was I still couldn't figure out *who* to thank. I mean who to thank for the whole show, the . . ."—Juha motioned to the valley—"the way we've got all this without doin' a damn thing, even one damn thing ourselves." Juha went silent for a minute. "But I've solved that one," he said.

Cookie looked a question at him.

"I'll be thankin' you."

Cookie, cowgirl, fry cook, hard drinker from Eureka, Nevada, even after all the stories and the wandering, thought she'd never heard anything so wacky.

And they went over the Beckworth Pass into the valley. All of them went silent, because of heaven. There are just some places heaven feels at home.

"I got to say I never expected it would just keep on being open country. I mean, it's never going to be like downtown Philadelphia," said Jeb.

"Jeb, you know, I been thinkin'. We're just a couple of big fumblers. We got to hang on tight. I mean, this is a weird bunch. But

I got to say that I don't want nothing to go wrong for them. I want to look out for 'em. It's what we got to do. At first I thought when we joined up with them that they got everything and we got nothing. But it ain't true. We know something."

"We do? Us?"

"We know most stories don't have no happy ending."

Jeb thought this over. "You telling me you think we still got a job?"

"Not only that. It's a job that might take some guts, after all."

The caravan turned off of Highway 70 onto a country road that led over a bridge. Beneath them were the headwaters of the Feather River, pooling up in the innocent way of headwaters everywhere. There were herons in the grass, hawks in the sky, foals in the pastures, and in the blessing of the heat the promised bounty of summer.

They were headed south, and straight ahead they looked down the line of the Sierra Nevada. The snow-covered peaks tossed the light among themselves, and pines stood full of the months of spring: hives of pollen and resin.

It was a valley where time didn't just run on: it stopped in and talked things over.

They pulled into Sattley at the far south end of the valley and swung around to the right, headed for the Yuba Pass.

THROUGH THE YELLOW pines and Douglas firs they made a way, up to the pass and over, with Juha and Cookie leading the whole troupe down slowly into the North Yuba Canyon.

Juha, used to the desert, had never seen anything so green. It was green that held a peace, but pulled at him. A riptide of green, but one he could give himself to, without fear.

Cookie, used to the desert, had never seen so much water. Rivulets let go spokes of silver through the trees, big creeks ran under the bridges, late-spring patches of snow soaked the ground, there was a feathery rushing in the air. As they headed down the canyon, off to the left of them the North Yuba River took form. First there were little pools, like beads of mercury; then the mingling and a movement with cut-loose clarity down stony slopes. Then, as they watched, other streams fell into the canyon, there was a crisscrossing of waters, the streambed broadened out, and the Sierra stood up high over a lustrous green river.

"Sure, I'd stay a while," said Cookie.

"Looks like a stage to me, Ananda," said Chiara. "A big one. We're going to have to settle in, learn some things, just be patient and wait for the world to come round to the Hurricane Troupe."

Ananda came over and kissed her on the corners of her eyes.

They moved down past Sierra Buttes—sharp granite drawn with a dark pen onto the sky—and hit Sierra City and the Buckhorn Bar: wooden sidewalk in front, stone walls around; long bar, jukebox, and big fireplace within.

"Celebration. Someone has to," suggested Chiara.

And the whole caravan pulled off the road.

Izzy strode into the bar and, as was her custom, displaced the bartender, who was thinking anyway that it was a good hour for a dip in the river. Izzy served up a round, and the bar settled down. All around the miners and lumberjacks watched her and watched Muscovado by her side; even the sheriff was there, but he could not bring himself to bust Izzy for being underage because his respect for the law was overcome by his weakness for female bartenders. And so the girl leaned against the back wall of the bar and the Hurricane Troupe chatted it up once again.

"Are we sure it's time to settle down?" asked the angular, incorrigible Izzy.

"At least it's something we haven't tried," said her mother.

"Me and Cookie got our plans," said the towering, beloved Juha.

"You're a teenager, Iz," pointed out Muscovado Taine. "You should have a summer job."

"I guess you're right. But we have to keep improvising. This is theater, after all."

"I think we've got momentum—some stories taking flesh," ventured Ananda.

"I'd like to stick around here for a while," said Iz, "to spread around a secret."

"Secret, what secret?" boomed Juha.

"Not any of *our* secrets, I hope," said Musco impishly.

Izzy was leaning with her arms crossed. Some miners and lumberjacks were ordering drinks; she served them up and kept talking; they couldn't help but listen, and she delivered a kind of warmup improvisation, just to set things off.

"It's the best-kept secret in the world: and how?" The opal shadows started to mill around our Iz. The whole bar went quiet.

"If you really want to keep a secret, you have to be sure that no one ever talks about it, no one ever writes it down. More than that: you have to make sure that even if the secret is spoken out loud, no one would believe you. It's as though there was no east on a compass: no one would know how to look toward the sunrise—even though the light was all around them.

"And lies are told to protect the secret, and everything goes wrong: If your family tells you that you are a dog, you will want to get the best training you can, so that you will be a good dog. For everyone wants to be good.

"And it has mostly worked. It has worked."

Izzy paused and looked around the room, looked each man in the eye, winked at some. But otherwise just let the opals run.

"But no longer," she announced. "The secret is out. We know the truth."

This news stirred up the crowd in the Buckhorn. There was agitation at the pool table and along the bar and by the fireplace. A couple of guys even came out of the restroom. A few lit up cigs and leaned back to listen.

"So what the hell is it? What is it?" one shouted.

"It ain't no use keepin' back from us," said another.

The peacock roistered around, opening his tail, then passing along with a strut and squawk.

Chiara rolled her eyes. "Somehow I always knew that she would be a performer in bars," she whispered to Ananda.

Izzy tossed it out. "The secret is this: the world belongs to girls. When everyone found out the earth turned around the sun, what a big deal that was. But nothing compared to this—now every girl knows the world is turning in her. This world is ours. We have learned."

There was silence in the Buckhorn. They had been expecting something like, say, the location of the Ark of the Covenant. Or at least maybe a lost recipe for pot roast.

"Girls?" said a miner.

And Izzy strode out from behind the bar and over to the pool table; she grabbed a cue and rocketed in a few shots, chalked up and pocketed a double ricochet; she walked a close and smiling circle around Muscovado Taine, bussed the peacock on top of its blue head, spun her way through the men and with a twist and sidestep took up once again her post behind the bar.

The room was quiet. And her story might have been forgotten in the taking up once again of the habits of the day; there was a movement of the men back into themselves. But her story was not over:

The coyote bolted strong and tawny through the door and dashed through the barroom, snarling and darting at limbs, the men yelled and kicked and dodged, knocking over chairs and falling into each other, the animal barked and lunged, men flattened against the walls, the coyote streaked across the room and leaped onto the bar, she pivoted around and sat in the quickened midday air, just by the side of Izzy she sat and looked out at all of them with her golden eyes.

"What's she going to be like at twenty?" Musco asked.

"Even funnier, I'll bet," said Chiara.

"I see a jazz musician," ventured Ananda. "I could teach her—"

"I think she *is* the jazz. I think the world is playing her, making a music of this girl," said Chiara.

Tabby saw it: the whole of the northern Sierra: a stronghold.

Riding up the Feather River Canyon, along the North Fork, sweet mountain air billowing around them, it looked to them like another planet.

"Amazing!" exclaimed Grimes. He couldn't even smell any shit.

"We need to get ourselves a place. This is it. This country. I knew this was somewhere. I knew if we just kept on going—"

"We made it, Tabby."

Grimes was thinking—this was better than whores in the gun shop, even.

"Mountain men," said Tabby.

"Brave like them."

"We really need some new outfits," mused Tabby.

"They'll talk about us," Grimes went on. "Tell stories! We weren't afraid to judge!"

"You know, we'll have to find a gym."

"Up here, people will understand. They know about the festering down below. I'll bet they don't put up with any Chumps. I'll bet they've already taken care of the Maggot problem up here."

"We'll just see about that!" said Tabby.

"I think we need some ski pants and stuff like that—"

"And a camera!" added Tabby. "So much happens . . . And you've got to take some notes. You know, the things we say sometimes . . ."

"I kind of miss the gun shop."

"Let's get a place, you can get back in touch with some of your cop friends, tell them to come up and join us. We need force. Once they see it up here, they're not going to want to go back down to pukeville. Except to do a rescue."

"I'd like to do rescues. Of course, when we got one of the Innocents up here, we could put them in quarantine or something, just to make sure they weren't contaminated."

Tabby liked that. It showed Grimes was still thinking.

When they pulled into Quincy it was like two new arrivals wanting to make the best possible impression. They went into stores and bought candies and comic books. They bought more clothes, this time some good work boots and down coats and khaki pants. They needed clothes they could work in, that were clean.

They were both full of yes ma'am and no ma'am, yessir and nosir, they made their way through town, taking a look at things.

Everyone, they noticed, moved kind of slow. Everything looked so good. Just like they thought.

Tabby and Grimes could see right away that none of these folks really knew what was going on down in San Jose.

"There are so many good people here!" exclaimed Tabby. "We have to help them!"

They spent a couple of hours reading the comics in the car, just sitting by the side of the road, listening to music and talking about heroes. Then they walked around for a while. Tabby spent an hour with the old man that ran the hardware store in town, for thirty-five years stocking everything. He had his whole life in the store. He carried a lot of extra things—children's toys, cleansers, suspenders—that the little community needed. He was the kind of guy that had always given credit to the locals during the down times. But now he was having a tough time making it, the big stores down in the cities sold things so cheap, and mail order cut into his business. He felt tired.

He was so decent! Tabby went away in tears, and went back to the car and counted out two thousand in hundreds, put it in an envelope and slipped it through the mail slot of the hardware store.

"There's just no one to love them," he told Grimes.

"They need protection," agreed Grimes.

Tabby leaned against a brick wall and crossed his arms, staring out at the little town they had chosen.

"Let's hit the road," he said grimly, like a man who feels his responsibilities weighing in all at once.

And they strolled back along the main street. Nothing is better in the world than to be young with a car full of weapons, to be in clean country where you don't have to carry the whole world around like a bag of vomit.

Nothing is better than to be making the movie of yourself.

Cookie and Juha, who had taken over from Izzy after her stint in the Buckhorn, had gotten to know the stunned locals. Sitting that night close by the fireplace in the barroom, Juha summed it up: "If the road follows the river, we need to find a bend. Something that would set us off in the trees a little. A quiet spot for a house, woman."

"One of the lumberjacks was sayin' that you can still get good lodgepole pines for buildin'. We might as well get to it. We're newlyweds, ain't we?" asked Cookie.

Our travelers set about finding habitations for the summer. Izzy and Muscovado found a cabin on the outskirts of Sierra City, a town that did not have a wide experience with miscegenation. The sheriff resolved loudly to bust Musco for statutory, and was sure he could get him thrown in a hole for ten or twenty years. Juha, however, heard the sheriff boasting about his plan, and he found the man and plucked his badge off his chest. Juha then, using only thumb and forefinger, bent the badge in half, then in fours, and politely handed it back.

"Muscovado and Izzy are in a play," he explained. "It's an act."

And for emphasis, he picked up the sheriff in one hand and shook him like a puppy. The officer decided that the law should, in some cases, be interpreted more leniently, so that his community might satisfy their longing for theater.

Chiara and Ananda found themselves a room right in town in a bed-and-breakfast, with brass bed and a down comforter for the cool mountain nights. Walking around town together that summer, they traded war stories from the years in the professional trenches, shared cigarettes, braided each other's hair, dined out eloquently in old lodges set up high by the side of the glacial lakes of the Sierra; and having dressed the day in love, undressed in the same mood.

As for Renato, he was press-ganged into working on the poster that soon festooned the walls of the Buckhorn and many another bar in the little towns of the mountains, and the walls of community halls and the bulletin boards of grocery stores. It always made people stop for a look-see—

The Hat Tricks and Hot-Pillows Lowlife
Storytelling Dirty-Angel Plain-Folks
Improvisational Hurricane Theater Troupe

PRESENTS

A Summer of Theater in Bars, In the Streets, In Your House Stories! Skits! Wine-Bibbing! Suspense! Last-Minute Rescues! Smart-Assed Guys! God!

When: Now and Then
Where: There
Admission: Free

The Hurricane Troupe is carrying on an ancient tradition of improvisation. From antiquity, and all over the world, little bands of crazies have settled into towns to join them in their own theaters, the ones they put on all day and night.

We can't help ourselves. Neither can you.

Thrills! Slow Romances! Jokes of Real Tastiness! Angels! Amorous Women Who Will Answer Once and for All the Question—

Is this love, or some kinda firecrackers going off all day in our hearts?

• • •

There was some clustering around the poster at first.

"Does this mean I have to start lockin' the goddam doors?" someone asked.

"Don't 'spect so," replied his neighbor, "it ain't the kind of thing someone would write if they're after your toaster."

And so, following Izzy's lead, each of the troupe went out and kicked off their individual shows—

Old Ben McCrae was walking down the street in Sierra City, and just by the side of the big grassy acreage on the west side of town he ran smack into a makeshift booth. The wood still had the hammer marks of Juha's pounding, the sign at the top read PHILOSOPHY SHOP, and inside sat Chiara.

"What lizard's gizzard did you jump out of?" asked Ben, who wasn't having his best morning.

"I used to teach in a university back east. Deep in the lizard, let me tell you. One day I thought, Why stand up and do this yammering? I could sit down and do it. So I decided to come out here and go into the business."

This entrepreneurial approach appealed to Ben. He sat right down himself.

"Mebbe you could help me with my grandchild Boone. Now, Boone, he thinks he's a bear. Scratches hisself on trees, eats a lot of honey. Keeps biting me."

Chiara mulled that one over.

"Maybe he *is* a bear," she suggested.

Ben lit up. "That's got to be it!" he cried, and he laid five bucks on Chiara and went off home feeling much better.

A local high-school teacher, Candy Rollins, came and sat down at the Philosophy Shop.

"I can tell you are a teacher," Chiara said.

"How did you know?"

"You have the roughed-up look of someone who does an impossible thing."

Chiara looked admiringly at the woman.

"So help me," Candy said directly.

"You need, I take it, some method of directing your students toward their work?"

"They're good kids," Candy answered, "but they're thinking of the woods or the river or getting laid or married or rich. They're thinking, thinking, but of the wrong thing. What do I do?"

Chiara drew on her own method of teaching. "You have to get their attention before you use their attention," she said.

"Well," said Candy, "they love stories. That's when they give themselves to me. But what story could I tell them to teach them?"

"We can't be too direct. There's nothing more degenerate than the didactic story."

Chiara came round the side of the booth and sat by Candy, and the two teachers, close there in the sunlight, slung ideas back and forth for an hour.

"It comes down to this," Candy said finally. "School is where nothing happens."

"Headed through Nevada, the stories came to us. They *were* what happened," mused Chiara.

"I've got it," cried Candy. "The Gut-eating Giant Hyena!"

"That sounds like it to me—"

"In the time of the gold rush there was some folklore about a giant hyena, with a big pig-snout, a mountain creature that would rush out and stomp the throats of the miners and eat their guts out. Now, what I need to do is tell some hyena stories and then have one turn right up in class! A few snorts, a bloody snout!"

"And then?"

"Forevermore they'd be good students—knowing that what I say, the world means."

"It'll work," confirmed Chiara. She felt like signing up at the high school herself. "Maybe we could do some team-teaching?" she said.

"Love to! But one more thing!" Candy said.

"Shoot!"

"Where am I going to find someone to play the hyena? It would have to be a big man—I mean, a *big* man—strong; he has to be able to make animal noises, lots of animal noises, and have some recent acting experience, so he could scare the bejesus out of my high schoolers. Anybody come to mind?"

Chiara gave a big smile.

So prospered the Philosophy Shop.

*   *   *

Muscovado Taine, ever faithful to the dignified profession of journalism, with its draconian standards of accuracy and momentous social responsibilities, signed up for work at the *Mountain Messenger*, the local newspaper just a spell along the road in Downieville. Within hours he posted his first story:

HOMER SEEN IN DOWNIEVILLE

The blind man begging in front of the bar last week, who baffled so many of us with his booming voice, has turned out to be from Asia Minor. It's not Asia, and it's not Minor; but it's not Europe, either. You know how confused they are in the Old World.

Today, it is known to us as Turkey. It's one of those countries always squabbling.

The blind man says his name is Homer, and that he is over three thousand years old. He looks it. But that voice! At first some of us in town mistook him for the noonday siren. And what was all that about chariots and spears and breakers of horses? Rivers and leaves and shields? And who is this gal that everybody is so hepped up about?

There was a near fight when this Homer, who keeps asking for something to play, got hold of Elmer Hawkins's guitar, and after feeling around with it for a few minutes smashed it to bits against the wall, calling it the "lyre from hell." A picky guy.

A strong guy, too. When Elmer tried to club him with a length of rebar, Homer snatched it from his hands, and instead of thrashing Elmer, took the rebar in both hands and tied it into a knot.

Maybe this blind man has hefted a few swords himself. Who knows?

Anyway, for now he has piped down. Some say he has been taken up by the theater troupe that has been running amuck here this summer. Some say that whenever they stoke up a big fire in the barroom hearth, he comes in and sits down and starts booming away.

I know for sure that he's been spending some time with Helena Jacobs, who raises quarterhorses up in the big meadow. Helena says he likes the pounding of the hooves.

Muscovado also did some research for the historical section of the newspaper, finding, as usual, that the past in one place may well contain the future in another:

40 YEARS AGO TODAY

It was just 40 years ago that Sierra City had the famous deep-dish-pie rumpus still talked about on the streets of our fair town. For on that date was born one of our finest traditions: Animosity Day.

To celebrate the Summer solstice the town every year had sponsored its side-armed pastry-throwing contest, the Pie Fling. And the fine year of 1955 was no different. Mariah's Bakery stepped forward with its concoctions. Five young stalwarts were chosen from the town to fling deep-dish pies in the meadow; the pie had to land right side up, and skid along the grass, not breaking up or turning over. Mere brute strength would never do. It took finesse.

This happy event always brought out the townsfolk, ready to sing the virtues of the pie champion. And whichever of the young bucks had just that right combination of power and delicacy was awarded free sweets all summer long.

It was on Midsummer's Eve, the young men were ready, and Mariah's pies smelled so good that whole families of bear peeped out of the woods.

It was young Mortimer Thomas that started the trouble, when his side-arm throw went awry and he caught the crotchety old miner Ezekiel Dinkus flush in the face with a lemon meringue. A quiet went over the crowd. Ezekiel went over to the bakery and returned with a five-gallon can of pastry cream, into which he ducked Mortimer's head several times.

Things might have settled down after that, but the next contestant, Rick Feister, whether he meant to or not, spun his deep-dish chocolate creamer through the air and blasted Ezekiel a second time. A small explosion was heard, as with a hydrogen bomb. But it was not a hydrogen bomb; it was Ezekiel.

Rick and Mort raided the bakery and started passing sweets around. Old grudges popped into everyone's head. Petty animosities went off like pinwheels in the air. Past marital spats rose to mind with great freshness. And the general crankiness in everyone came to the fore.

It was the dueling pastries. A visiting priest was given an angel food cake for a collar. A bride-to-be clobbered her fiancé with their wedding cake, one layer at a time. Several cars had their gas tanks filled with chocolate éclairs. Trays of glazed doughnuts were fed to the hogs that came out to root around in the mess. The bear families trotted out of the woods, stalking around and lapping things up. Squeals, yells, grunts, and snarls vied for supremacy.

The fun finally ended when Ezekiel demolished the bakery with his tractor, in the effort severing a gas main that was ignited by a spark from the crushed oven. The explosion wiped clean the faces of everyone in town.

And that's how our most famous tradition began: Animosity Day.

Don't miss Animosity Day this summer. Sock a friend! Hurl an epithet! Spin a pie! Root with the hogs!

Let's blow it all to Kingdom Come this year!

Muscovado loved small-town reporting. For it was in the small towns of the mountains that the press was able to remember what was so often forgotten in the big cities—that the events of a day are never fully real. But what the day means by what it does— now that may be something.

Musco would dig all morning through old issues of the *Messenger,* then go out and wander the streets. In Sierra City and Downieville a lot of folks just sat out on porches or on the benches along the wooden sidewalks. Everyone talked to him, even Homer.

The days were hot. He felt good. He felt outrageous.

"The day will come when they'll understand they've been picked out. All of them, this whole part of the mountains. We know what's coming. They don't," insisted Tabby.

"The first time we save somebody, they'll know."

"They won't be able to find us."

"But they won't feel alone."

"They'll leave us pretty bitches," laughed Tabby.

"It's so important to be respectful," said Grimes. "We've got to buy one of those books of etiquette."

"You know, I've been thinking," mused Tabby, "about the kids we saw in Quincy, so innocent. They're so beautiful. I want a family. This is where I want to settle down, have little Tabbys. Sweet little boys. Someone to take care of. I'd tell my wife all about us, all the stories."

Grimes loved this. So proper. "We'll have to be on the look-out," he said smiling.

"—For some pretty ones. They have to be healthy. We can all work out together."

It was so moving. Tabby felt so happy.

All around Izzy: bone-white and cloud-gray granite, close azure sky, verdant pine, oak, cedar; and the river, ancestor and future of green—this was country for a girl with opal eyes.

Izzy landed a job with a Forest Service summer crew, building trails, hauling brush, counting owls, and roaming around boisterously in pickup trucks. It was a crew of mostly teenagers, with some thirty-year-olds, thought to be old as Methuselah, in supervision.

No one much knew what to do about this supple newcomer, who in the morning smelled like her skin had been dusted with allspice. No one knew what to do, that is, until the other girls on the crew came to understand that the world belonged to them. With Izzy they made a ferocious band, pounding stakes, wielding brush cutters, firing up chain saws, stalking around in big boots and practicing their hack-and-spit. The spitting increased in volume when the boys, like so many oversize rodents, came round to gaze stupidly at the female laborers.

Iz and her newfound compatriots worked three months that summer, and the mountains fell in love with them. They were young, their muscles full of nectar; their strength grew, and just to live in the mountain air and have work to do, to have responsibilities put in their hands like ripe blackberries: this was a crew of girls that did not need to think of the future, because the future was in them like a song.

Juha knew it when he saw it: just at a bend of the Yuba below Downieville, a meadow; four apple trees and a plum tree, wild rose, a sweet tussle of raspberry bushes; fir and yellow pine spiraling up the surrounding hillsides, and the whole of it easy in the mountain air, light in the light hours, the land listening day and night to the green declarations of the river.

Juha headed straight for Sierra City and found Cookie, and, not saying a word, took her there. They walked around hand in hand, and camped there a few nights.

There are times when a man and woman are entrusted to a place.

They headed for a lumberyard, hoping to find some uncut logs.

"Stone foundation, lodgepole pine for the walls," said Cookie.

"Fir planking on the floor and ceiling, cedar shake roof," finished Juha.

No two lovers ever took as long to choose the lodgepoles for their little cabin. Each one at the yard they studied, touched, sniffed; they stood each one on end and studied its knots and cracks, they set each one down and rolled it to gauge its camber; they compared diameters and grain; and by the end of the day they had a selection of raw logs that were just what they wanted: transcendent with imperfections.

To their meadow the lodgepoles were delivered. Cookie scouted around for some local stone, and soon had a truckful of beauties.

Juha brought over the truck with its house and parked it near the river. He had all his tools. And it was still early in the summer when the two of them slung on carpenter's belts and set to work.

Stone, wood, a river; their labor of embraces; the watching summer: Cookie would remember it as the happiest work ever done—the summer when they lived together in the middle of the whole handmade world.

Ananda brought to the local community a new system of law, with its own court. It is important, she thought, for court to be accessible. So she set up in the bar, accompanied by the peacock and her cat Tupelo.

Her sign read: BLOND JUSTICE.

Within days, all disputes in town were referred to her. The police started dropping off suspects, and the community was so relieved not to have to administer justice itself that the months fell into a new and zany order. As downriver Cookie and Juha were starting their cabin, Ananda was taking up

THE CASE OF THE FIGHTING MEN AND THE BABY BOY

The two miners could not stop fighting. They had been friends a long time, went to the same high school, worked in the same diggings, hunted and fished together. They were both still in their midtwenties, and every week it seemed as if an argument would start, then the temper, the yelling, the punches. The town was so small, they couldn't stop running into each other, even if they tried. The sheriff was disgusted; there was a lot of head shaking around town; the bartender at the Buckhorn had to keep gauze pads and disinfectant at the ready, and was considering seriously the purchase of a tranquilizer gun.

Now they stood before her, disheveled, bruised, haggard. The peacock rustled around their feet. Tupelo rubbed her cheeks on their boots.

Ananda looked at the two: mountain men; there couldn't be that much excitement in pounding on each other. What was going on?

It was clear, she thought, that up here in this little town they would never be able to admit why they were so often in contact: they were in love.

She swung her gavel, startling Tupelo.

"This is my decision!" she said. "Today I will phone Los Angeles; I know of a baby boy there, an orphan, two years old, whose parents were shot to death in a revenge killing. For his own protection, the boy must soon be placed in a home outside of the area. The Northern Sierra would be perfect."

"This baby the two of you will jointly adopt, each of you becoming its legal father. Since you are such busy young men, you will have to share responsibility for raising the child. This court has noted that in your pretended conflict was a real devotion to each other. That same devotion will now be offered to the child. To damage each other, will damage this little boy. Yet in caring for him, you will care for each other."

The two rough men looked at her with astonishment. But such was her authority and wild certainty that they couldn't help thinking how much they wanted the child. Besides, they both trusted blonds.

THE CASE OF THE BOY WHO IN A LIBERATED BEER TRUCK WOULD CLIMB THE HIGHEST PEAK

Ananda's second case that day was a thief: Buddy, a young smart-ass and ne'er-do-well. In his sophomore year in high school he had read all the books for the rest of what he called his "sentence"—the time until graduation. He corrected his teachers, wisecracked his way through his classes, and in team sports consistently scored for his school's opponents. Then he turned into a truant, spending a lot of time in the forest trying to tame a black bear he had named Fuzzle. Fuzzle he thought he understood: kind of a brooder, kind of baffled, like him.

Buddy, one afternoon after a grunting and burbling conversation with the wild animal, had walked into town to find a big beautiful beer delivery truck. What's more, it was a hot afternoon. He took fourteen cases of beer out of the back; to give himself extra time, he locked the driver in the bathroom at the gas station. Amused by the pounding on the door and the cussing of the driver, who threatened to rope him to the truck and drag him "by his stupid little dick straight over the pass," Buddy had put back the fourteen cases and driven off with the whole truck.

To be the sole owner of two hundred fifty-five cases of beer, climbing up a beautiful road in the Sierras, the diesel pounding under his feet—he felt close to God. Maybe he could pick up Fuzzle?

All in all, his best day, until the police cars swirled around like so much white water. If Ananda couldn't think of something, he was looking at a felony conviction.

But Ananda could think of something.

"Look, Buddy, you're in trouble. Big time."

"I know. But it was such a nice truck. Solid. My teachers always told me to be adventurous in learning. So hey, I was just trying to be a good boy."

"Did you want the beer or the truck?"

"First the beer. Then the truck. Then neither, really. I wanted to make a mark on the day, you know? A place to start again. Do it right. Have more fun."

Ananda considered. "There's only one way out."

"You're the judge. Best-looking goddam judge in the county. Would you like to meet my bear?"

"First, you have to attend an eighteen-month diesel school in Cleveland. While there, you will learn Spanish. I had as a client in my law practice an international company with a Latin American trucking subsidiary. Through them, I can arrange for you a job repairing engines in Costa Rica, which has forests of its own, believe me.

"Besides, there trucks are used to do everything. They need mechanics. And the country has lots of animals. You can get to know the sloths. They're already tame. You'll be at home."

"I'm not leaving the mountains. I grew up here. This *is* my home," replied Buddy.

"Then go to San Quentin and get fucked in the ass every day. The system dotes on nice young cheeks like yours."

"Let's talk this over: do I take a bus to Cleveland?"

"I have your ticket right here."

"Why do you think this is justice?"

"It's a form coming back. You send people into exile, and they work."

Ananda pounded the gavel, Tupelo went over to Buddy and gave him a winsome look, and the peacock cackled at him.

"And don't feel bad. All of us are exiled, in one way or another—for however long it takes."

And the judge stalked out the door in a candent passage that left blond ripples in the light; she went to meet another worker, who ran a Philosophy Shop in town.

The weeks passed, summer was upon them. For Renato it was the green of the North Yuba that finally did it. With the rest of the troupe having to attend sympathetically to him, assign him work, check on him, and in general haul him around like a sack of grain, he was still in his derelict mood when one afternoon the green of the river got to him.

—Not the deep green of the conifers, nor the green of the alders in the spring; neither the chalky green of Great Basin sagebrush, nor the swirling mint green of Sierra Valley; nor yet the pale tropical green of a Jamaican bay, or the band of green above the yellow on a desert horizon at sunset . . .

It was the beginning of green: birth of a color in a Sierra canyon.

Renato, the beginning of a man, picked up his brushes and began to paint for Maria-Elena, with no line, pattern, design, arrangement of figure, no perspective or placement set forth, except to make the world where he wanted to live with her.

He understood the moment he put brush to canvas.

The voice of Maria-Elena had been present, but hidden: as moonlight is hidden in sunlight—

"Sweet Renato, paint for me and for your little one—

"Little one?"

"The baby girl that now I carry."

"Baby girl?"

"Are you not Renato?"

"Maria-Elena!"

"Are you not Renato, the father of one of the Daughters of the Moon?"

"Maria-Elena!"

"The thirteenth moon-eyed daughter, the one we have been waiting for—"

"Maria-Elena!"

And Renato stood stock-still by the side of the Yuba.

He would paint; she would come.

Colors swirled around him.

Warm days followed.

Renato brushed slowly, slowly—

It was a wonder to him all through that summer. Painting in Eureka all those years, he had never thought to be a father.

Now he wanted someday to talk long and low with his daughter on some porch over the sea where they could watch moonlight coming for them across the water.

Renato, high in the Sierra in midsummer, on mountainsides and by rivers, in the little towns and in his tiny cabin, worked. The sunny months were in his brushes.

Everyone around him was in love.

HOW DOES LOVE work in the world?

Ananda wondered at a love that had led her far out in the Great Basin to play the trumpet of the angels and bring a pelican to life and send it back again, bearing messages to the land of the dead; to venture into a wilderness of stories that like so many lovers sought them out wherever they went; to learn axheaving; to bed down with a dark-eyed professor in a motel at the edge of an endless desert playa; to be in a little Sierra town the judge in a theater of her own making.

Was this to be expected of an acclaimed, austere, conservative securities attorney?

In Sierra City Ananda sat waiting for Chiara to return from the Philosophy Shop. There is no waiting like that for a lover you know will come. It had come to this, all her strategies and calculations, the arcana and finesse of her years: this waiting, a certainty at the midmost of things.

It seemed centuries ago she had put her Tupelo in the car and headed out across California and into the Basin, coasting along the Nevada roads into Eureka.

Ananda in her bright languors sat waiting in Sierra City, and black-haired Chiara came around the corner, and in their embrace was an easy ascendant affection; in their hands the cool of the mountain twilight.

Muscovado Taine, after his exertions as a small-town reporter, never could walk the last half mile to the cabin where he and Izzy had set up house. As soon as it came into sight at the far end of a dirt road, he would start to run and in the house go to the covers, the pillow; he would press to his face anything she had touched, just for the smell of her.

This was his hour; he knew that in the twilight Izzy would be walking down the long road. He would wait; he would watch her.

It was a watching that made the summer itself.

He watched her walk up the whole road of his life.

She came along with the coyote, who trotted ahead, then doubled back; dashed into the pines, then circled around and ran up behind her; kept with her. Muscovado could see within that quickness only the golden eyes.

Izzy never did walk in a straight line. She sauntered, she meandered, she strolled; she stopped for the coyote, she gazed off into the woods. And it seemed to Musco that the forest was following her. Her black hair gathered the violet out of the sky; swinging easy steps marked out the motion of her lover's hopes; she brought home hillsides of fragrant pine and the sight of brilliant rivers bearing their light through big canyons.

She was near him now, her skin darkened by the day in the sun; the dusk gathered close, the trees arched round to hide the cabin, the coyote bolted in the door, she stepped into Muscovado's arms.

The original sin was not disobedience; the original sin was clothes. And from that burden they stripped each other, they found their way to each other's skin, his perfect ebony and her pale olive.

The cabin offered to them the most inviting trysting places— tucked-away cushioned crannies, deftly positioned tables, the swinging chair outside on the porch in the cool mountain air, an old brass-frame bed with a cotton quilt worn soft by pressure of delectations . . .

Midevening, after licking the sweat from her, Muscovado carried Izzy to a big old bathtub and by candlelight, in the hot water, he soaped her slowly; steam rose around her beauties.

They made a simple dinner. The small-town reporter and forest worker swapped tales, they ticked glasses in their little kitchen; afterward they built a fire and lay around with some books. Musco every now and then would go to her and silently kiss her hands; they read into the night; each of them now and then would get up and in the sweet resinous evening of the mountains tend the fire.

Izzy thought this was the perfect time to study St. Augustine. After polishing off the *City of God* she cast about for some truly earnest text; and in what she saw as a colorful move, she took up *Paradise Lost,* intoning aloud to Muscovado sundry passages in that clattering hysterical work. Then, in the interests of truly exciting the Jamaican, she read *Prolegomena to Any Future Metaphysics,* and, with their supple amorous logic, they found the text to have many delicious concepts.

As the hours passed Muscovado and Izzy would move closer until they were reading together on the couch, legs entwined, laughing; until night, seeing them and wanting to come closer, swept through the window and put the lights out. And our two cherishers, looking long at each other, would rise and in front of the fire strip each other again—because firelight was in love with them; because they were the lovers with summer in their hands.

Juha and Cookie had few belongings: a set of tools, Cookie's bow and arrows, some rumpled blankets, the harmonica given them by the angels, and now, bought with the money left from the work Juha did for Hansel and Gertie in Eureka, two new things: a used pickup for hauling, and an acre at the bend of the North Yuba River, near Downieville.

It does not take many days for a pair as strong as Juha and Cookie to lay a foundation. They leveled their site, dug out the perimeter, mixed the mortar for their stones. With granite they built up the outlines of one big room, an adjoining kitchen, a little bedroom facing the river. Upon the stone they secured the lodgepoles, each one different, with its own tilt, whorl, bend; with its own strangeness of proportion, standing side by side, formed by the storytelling of the mountains.

They didn't need to talk much; it was more of a studying together the stone and pine; of a lifting and placing, of the arrangement of things, of their calling home the future with their hands. Work of rough-and-ready precisions; the simple construction of a life.

They would hammer for hours in their T-shirts and denims out in the middle of the clear Sierra days, and then take their midday sweatiness down to the bank and throw off their clothes for a dive into the pale green water of the North Yuba. The coolness of the wild river ran so deep in the flesh, it washed their ragged and muscular souls.

Out of the deep pools they would pull up onto the rocks, and bask in the sun like big seals until the coolness called them back.

Walking back up to the cabin one afternoon, they appraised their work: the walls in place, seven big lodgepoles aloft as beams, and two sets of rafters of whole pines set slanting to a peak. They were ready to form the roof by laying fir planks crosswise over those rafters, and then finish it off on top with cedar shingles.

"I think I've got it figured," Cookie said.

Juha looked at his stocky wife.

"As long as we've got work to finish, we can't die."

"I kinda always figured the same myself," said Juha.

"I want us always to work together. Always," followed up Cookie. "We know what we're doing."

"You can count on Juha," he said with one of his bear hugs. "What are husbands for?"

Around them, the yellow pine and black oak and red cedar and fir stepped up the sides of the river canyon, and their cabin, so unlikely, stood there like some outpost of innocence. It stood, roofless, taking the light into itself—as though the shining of the whole Sierra inhabited the space they had made, and readied it for their lives.

They stayed out at night among the stars in their meadow, listening to the swirl and murmur of the Yuba; though after they had set down oak plank flooring, they spread big soft blankets in the cabin and spent a whole day and night carousing and roughhousing, so that the both of them were pleasured, even to their very calluses; and so that the wood would have always the proper muskiness, as required by the building code.

Like clear water the days ran with satisfactions. Juha and Cookie were the lovers with a river in their hands.

Our wanderers had found their stage, made their plays. All the summer months Muscovado did his reporting on the Sierras. Before, he was used to sniffing out stories, to following up leads, to interviewing here and there. But now he just walked around the streets and waited until events sought him out. He was like a hive filled up day after day by the honey of news.

The Philosophy Shop dispensed its wily commentary; in increasing numbers people stopped by and got a say-so on the nettling troubles of the day. This gave Chiara hope that philosophy might return to its illustrious origins and be a way of life, something with some day-to-day spitfire and gusto, rather than a collection of verminous university squeakings.

Ananda continued all summer her judicial activities. It had brought her attention around to the art of judgment. She settled on this: to begin to judge, you first have to deliver the right punchline to your own life.

Renato slept by his canvas. He ate by the side of his easel. At midmorning and at midafternoon, he took a walk. And during the course of the summer, he watched the Sierra light with such longing that the light was beginning to watch him.

*   *   *

It was on a midsummer afternoon: Ananda and Chiara were walking together along the street in Sierra City, when they saw the low-riding Chevy, howling to cut speed after a screaming descent down from the Yuba Pass along Highway 49.

Grimes was at the wheel when they saw the two women.

"Fantastic!"

"Who gets the blond?"

Renato, at the same end of town, was just going out for his walk. He headed for the river. All he did, when he went there, was listen. But just before he turned off the main road, he saw the Chevy coming to a stop near Chiara and Ananda; and he heard Tabby's confident voice, saw the thick neck, the white shirt rolled up at the sleeves, the muscular arm.

"Two of you and two of us. How 'bout that? What does that make? And a loving cool afternoon like this—I mean, don't even stop for lipstick. We'll take you, pretty bitches."

Grimes was uneasy because of their being in the middle of town, and he was upset at Tabby.

"Don't call them bitches! Be polite! And don't show the gun!" he hissed at Tabby, who with this hand was stroking the barrel. But Tabby was on a roll.

"Why wait? How many chances are there to go off with a legend? And just at the beginning of things? We've got a story we want you in? A movie. Exciting! Now pretty bitches—"

"Don't call them fucking bitches, dammit!"

"—you got men around that say this and they say that, but we been there. We got a different kind of stories. Because they're true. Real stories. Not a lot of sitting around like shitheads and making up things, wimps and cowards make up things. We *live*. So what about it, pretty things?" Even Chiara was astonished by the grit and oil in his voice.

Ananda, though, recognized the type, which is common in the securities industry. As Renato came up to stand by Chiara, Ananda stepped over and called into the open door of the Buckhorn. With all the authority of renowned blond justice she said,

248

"OK! It's time to come on out and stare. Don't say anything. Don't make a move toward the punks in the car. Just stare at them."

And all the miners and lumberjacks shuffled out and lined up along the wooden railing outside the bar. No one spoke.

Tabby and Grimes watched them, unbelieving. Grimes hissed, "It's like fucking Appalachia. It looks like a pigpen. They'll hold us down and fuck us. It's no use!"

Tabby was sad. "Look at the two of them. So sweet! Don't they know the chance they have? This is hurting my feelings. Really hurting my feelings. This was exciting!"

Tabby could see them there idling in the street, the car, the people around, what a scene! Everything was critical, everyone was waiting, waiting to see what they would do. They were in the center of the whole world, just like he knew they'd be.

"I'll let you fuck the gas tank for a while, OK?" suggested Grimes.

And Grimes slowly eased the car along the street.

Some of the forest service crew that worked with Izzy always dropped the coyote and her off near town. She would head along the main road for a while and then she and the animal would turn in at the road that led up into the woods to their cabin and to Muscovado. And it was just as she was dropped off that the Chevy came round a bend and they saw her.

"It's fate!" exclaimed Tabby. "A thrill! Our story! My girl and our story!"

"What are you talkin' about?"

Tabby was confident.

"You see her up ahead? My bride. Look how young. She coulda seen us comin'! Look at her!"

Grimes did. Maybe Tabby was right this time, she did kind of have the look and walk of a girl in love.

"And besides, I know what we did wrong back in town! We left something out!" Tabby went on.

"What is it?"

"Our music! We didn't have our music on. The scene wasn't right, we weren't men. We need beautiful music. Then we can set the scene the way we want."

Tabby slipped in a tape and the cello roared in the car and he looked at Izzy and was quiet for a minute and he said, "Where is she going to find something better than us? A bride, I tell ya!"

"Is she a bride?"

"A bride!"

Grimes saw the coyote, and everything fell into place. A wild girl, a wild animal. They get their place in the woods. It *was* perfect. He cruised up next to her and stopped.

"You're in luck!" Tabby called out.

"You're too late, kids!" sang back Izzy very melodiously, not even breaking her stride.

"You got to stop and hear our story," suggested Grimes, saying the only thing in the world that might make our Iz even slow down.

"Well, I'm walking on about fifty yards before I turn off the road. You just cruise along beside me and tell me a story. But that's it."

"What do you mean, that's it?"

"I mean my family likes me home for supper. A long supper. I'm a family kind of girl, you know what I mean?"

Grimes *loved* this. A proper girl. Very sweet. Class.

Tabby and Grimes both thought they wouldn't need more than fifty yards. And it was a reasonable inference. For none of our dear traveling band, not even Iz, had the ability to spot men of lethal virtue. Even though cultivating this ability should be a basic part of American education, like knowing how to read. But as reading has been neglected, so people don't know sophistication when it's right in front of them.

Izzy walked. The Chevy rolled slowly beside her.

Tabby started his patter:

"Nothin's gettin' any better. You're the age to know. For everybody else it's too late. It seemed like nothin' could be done but pound Maggots. But we were in the gun shop, we talked, it was up to us. We both had Angelica that night, guns gleamin' on the walls, this is a woman goin' to be famous. She knew us at the start. You should talk to her. Kinda like a reference. But we need to start all over—all over again. A family doesn't work out, you make a new one. You don't whine. We were *fated* to meet, goddamit, fated. You're so beautiful. We'll be family, hide out, clean things, do raids, start with the Suits, they want to be judged. We'll hit the cities with their vomit and shit and get some cops and clean. We'll freshen it up. Do what's right. And wherever I am, I'll be thinkin' of you. Thinkin' of comin' home with my story."

It sounded so good. Tabby, full of desire, looked hopefully at Izzy.

Iz had been half listening, and the low light slanted into her eyes so that Tabby and Grimes could see the glittering, and they saw her black hair with its rippling of silver.

Grimes threw in, "He's tellin' you the truth. Everyone else is just goin' along. They're afraid. We're not afraid. We were ready. Come and be brave. You're part of our luck. Join us. You want to be lucky, don't you?"

Izzy hurried along. "Thanks anyway. I'm already lucky."

Tabby held five hundred-dollar bills out the window.

"Are you this lucky, little bitch? Do you want the real thing, or do you want to go home to your godforsaken supper?"

Izzy was going up the road; scared now, she turned abruptly and walked away from the main road, the coyote behind her, keeping between her and the Chevy.

Tabby glared after her. "Goddammit!"

Grimes wheeled the car around, spitting dirt, and shot up the side road after Izzy, catching her, grinding and sliding to a stop. Clouds of dust rose around them. Tabby folded his big hand around his favorite pistol, the little snubbie.

"I'm just going to whack her once, just once. She has to play her part."

And he jumped out. The coyote was growling, he kicked at it, Izzy was watching him. Upright and strong Tabby advanced on Iz—

"The best chance is the second chance, pretty thing. I'll

explain everything, you love me, I can see that, come along now . . ." he said as he squeezed the pistol in his hand, and he was thinking how the contours of the steel he knew so well were going to fit into the side of Izzy's face when he belted her one— how much of a bruise did he want? Exactly how much? And how did he want it to look? Like an hourglass? Like a dog?

—Like a dog, he thought.

But his ruminations were interrupted by a hand on his collar and the pressure of a gun barrel against his temple.

"Nope. I don't think she loves you," said Jeb.

Mike called from the car: "I got the other one covered."

Mike and Jeb had always known that sixteen-year-old girls should not be out walking alone; and every evening without her knowing they had shadowed her along the main road.

"March back to the car," said Jeb.

Tabby looked at Iz. "I'll be seeing you around, sweetheart."

And he moved toward the car.

Just then along the main road a school bus turned up and disembarked a whole crowd of children. They had been on a field trip up to the mine museum, and now they came up the road in a group, headed for their houses up on the next street. Tabby smiled.

"You're not going to be spraying bullets around these kids, are you? You don't have the guts to shoot me in front of these kids, do you?"

And he walked away from Jeb's gun.

"Goddam punk!"

Tabby whirled around. He could hear the music from the car.

"So the little cunt is safe now and what are you going to do, you scum of the earth? You Chump? Shoot a hero? Shoot me for talking to a girl? Well, you better start sprayin' slugs, take out a few little ones while you're at it, because I don't give a shit, I don't give a living shit. And you know why? I'm too good to live, I know too much, you know I do. If I spill my guts on your face, it'll be the luckiest thing that ever happened to you, you poor bastard, you poor slob, shit-eating fool. Take my guts home and eat them, it's the best thing you'll ever taste, fuckface."

The dust rose around the car and all of them, the children milled around. Tabby smiled and turned toward the Chevy, got in and slammed the door.

Mike stood at the driver-side window. Grimes looked out at him. He and Tabby hadn't been courteous; it wasn't right.

"Very pleased to have made your acquaintance; and I wish you the very best luck in all your endeavors," he said as he started up.

Mike and Jeb walked Izzy up the road to the cabin; when they turned into the dirt road, it was not ten heartbeats before Iz saw another girl coming toward her.

"Peggy-Sue!" she cried.

The wild girls ran to answering embraces.

The twilight was filling up the canyon.

"Why have you come now?" asked Iz.

"For the playing of the harmonica," said Peggy-Sue. And even though she loved Izzy and even though they would together make more mischief on the way to the ocean, Peggy-Sue the angel did not smile.

They went down the road together, to the cabin. Peggy-Sue had already talked with Muscovado Taine, and he gave Izzy a desperate hug.

Juha and Cookie finished the flooring in the cabin. They needed to move inside to do the finish work, now that the structure was done. In the meadow, all that remained was to lay some pipe and set up some water valves for the garden they meant to plant.

"I'll take the truck in," said Juha that day, "and leave it at the station to get the gauges fixed. Meet me with the pickup. Be about ten minutes."

Cookie liked this: no standing around savoring the end of the job. They stored up their savoring.

"I always loved pickin' you up," she said.

As Juha was walking away, he saw Cookie turn back to finish some work on the garden beds, and stopped to watch as she moved there in the meadow full of mountain light; and if ever there was a love that might lead us to think that love was enough, it is the love of Cookie and Juha.

When he drove out the road to Highway 49, a great blue heron flew over high above the river, and if ever there was a beauty that might lead us to think that beauty was enough, it is the beauty of midsummer days deep in the green and flowering North Yuba canyon.

And if ever there were an improbable journey of an honest man with newfound friends into a land of stories, so that we might be led to think that stories were enough, it was the journey of Juha from Eureka all through the Great Basin, into Sierra Valley, up into the mountains and down from the passes to the little meadow he found for his wife.

But love is not enough, nor beauty, nor their cherished stories—

Juha drove up to 49, turned, and headed toward Downieville.

The road from Sierra City to Downieville runs along the river, following the cutaways made in the canyon walls; a swerving narrow road through the rocks and trees. Grimes jetted along it, tires singing, the mountain air whistling around them and the car jerking to the side when he hit the soft shoulders.

Tabby was upset: "Perfect! A perfect lady! We'll go back and get her, once we have our place. She'll be waiting for us, she's thinking about us just now, wondering where we went and when we'll be back, where can she go to find men like us? she's thinking right now. Running around with Chumps like that, what the fuck does she think she's doing? She just needs some education. Some time and education. There is no one but us to show her. We came all this way to find her. We'll rescue her. It'll make such a good story! My wife. She'll be so happy."

Tabby mused on: "How 'bout if we get ourselves another car? We need something with some class. We need something roomy. I'm going to need room to stretch her out and show her I love her and stuff her with babies."

"Right-O, Tabby. One new car, coming up." And he took a corner wide, just missing an oncoming car that contained Homer, booming away, headed up the road to find another fire to sit by, and proving that blind men can drive. Echolocation, maybe?

They went through Downieville slow. The sheriff paid them no mind even though he had gotten the call from Mike complaining about kids trying to pick up teenage girls on the street. This Mike had said he thought the kids had some guns in their car. The sheriff thought, Now there's a big-city detective for you. If I arrested every catcalling boy there'd be no jail to hold them all. And the guns? There's no boy here without a gun. And taught to use them right.

So there was nothing to stop Tabby and Grimes from getting to the pulloff just beyond Downieville, the one with the old cannon and the historical marker. And they saw parked there a splendid house perched on the bed of a truck, and beside it a big man who had stopped because he was curious about the marker, about the river; and he had looked around some.

The two boys spun off the road, turned off their engine, and sat in wonderment, looking at the beautiful house.

"A place to have my queen!" said Tabby.

Juha noticed the two boys, and they didn't look like anyone he'd ever seen. He liked the Chevy, though.

Juha, in the euphoria of their cabinbuilding, had lost track of the world, except for the green of the Yuba, Cookie's rough hugs, their stone and wood cabin, and by the side of the river, their future clear as the mountain morning.

Tabby spoke to him: "And who do you think you are, riding around in our house? And after all we've done! That belongs to us. It's what we need. It's class. It's perfect for my girl. What she'd expect. Thanks."

Juha couldn't quite hear them; he walked toward them, he wanted to show them the house. He was proud of it, it had taken them all down the road in style. He loved taking people through it. Maybe he'd take these kids into town and then out to the meadow. They could see the cabin too.

Tabby looked at Grimes. "Scum shine?"

"Let me look at him." And Grimes got out of the car and studied Juha. What a big piece of meat! Horrible!

"Tell me, tell me!" insisted Tabby.

Grimes looked some more. Who knows how many people this huge ape had hurt? Did he think that there was no judgment? "I can see it!" he said.

"Scum shine?" asked Tabby. He wanted to be sure they got it right. So exciting! "A big one then! A big Monster!"

"*Definitely* a Monster," agreed Grimes. It was so obvious. They were really getting good at this.

Tabby aimed a rifle at Juha, a carbine with a thirty-shot magazine. When the first bullet hit, Juha didn't believe it, because Juha was so gentle that the gentleness went right to sinew and bone. An outrage of steel was not something his body could report—the piercing of a bullet made no sense. And so he stopped, puzzled. Didn't they want to see the house?

The next twenty-nine bullets made no sense, either.

But he didn't need to make sense of the boys and their guns, for he was watching the land gather around him; he was a big man but the arms of a canyon are big. He watched the canyon get ready an embrace of stone to carry him away because that is what canyons do. Where were his tools? He needed his tools. There would be work to do. He reached his hand out to Cookie. He could smell her.

Tabby and Grimes had gone in the truck when Cookie drove up. She came along the road and saw the mountains, and then in the dirt at the back of the pulloff she saw Juha. And Cookie, who had seen a lot of animals die, knew right away he was dead.

The mountains were moving.

But Juha was dearer to her than mountains. Across the rocking ground she went to him and she thought right away that dying was a work they could do together. They worked so well together. They still had a lot to do, she had to help him.

Maybe it wasn't Juha.

Maybe if she went back to the meadow by the cabin and started cooking, he'd come to the door, hungry.

If she went to the little beach at the curve of the river where late afternoon light streamed up the canyon he would be there coming up from a dive in the green water.

In town at the bar she would find him with the locals, whistling and joking and ready to bust out with the whole zoo of his animal calls.

But it was Juha; he looked so surprised.

The mountains moved, she was at his side.

Cookie whispered to him. A truck pulled off the road, and suddenly near her were two Paiutes from Pyramid Lake, and without saying anything they sat her down and took up positions by her side.

Peggy-Sue and Izzy and Muscovado Taine were the next to arrive. The two girls came quietly up and stood over Cookie, just brushing her, their hands lightly upon her. And then the Shoshone called Antelope on the Moon walked up from nowhere; he stood on the other side of Juha and looked intently at him; he looked at Cookie for a long time and then he watched the movement of the mountains to see where they went. Then Chiara and Ananda, holding hands, came to sit down by the side of Juha, and Bret and June, the angels, were there, Renato and by his side Maria-Elena, his lover, and next to them like an arc of our nights stood all of the Daughters of the Moon. Off the road came a big pickup and from it swung Beulah, who stalked over and stood massive by the side of the massive frame of Juha. Then came Hansel and Gertie, quiet as they had ever been in their lives—all of them silently near Cookie who sat with both her hands around one of the big callused hands of her husband.

They were there for hours.

Finally Muscovado and Izzy because of their love; and Beulah, because of her strength, went to the side of Cookie, who was rooted to the ground. They lifted her up, only the three of them could have done it, and Cookie passed into the hands of angels and Daughters of the Moon, of Paiutes who had come to tell her about the Land of the Dead, and the Shoshone who would tell her how to get there, and what to do there. Cookie passed into the hands of her friends.

*　*　*

Juha was buried in the Downieville Cemetery alongside miners and ranchers and roustabouts and travelers and ne'er-do-wells; but everyone in town said he was the biggest man they had ever seen and they gave him two gravesites.

Over the grave Cookie stood and played him a death song; she played it on the harmonica they had brought with them from the house of the angels. It had never been meant for anything else.

Hansel came up afterward, hat in hand.

"Now I know mebbe you don't feel much like comin' on back to Eureka, but we sure could use a good hand like you out at the ranch. Now mebbe you never want to come back but we've got a job for you if you do and just in case we'll keep a horse in the corral for you, it'll be your horse for all time and nobody else's ever, OK? OK, bye."

And he walked stiffly away.

Beulah took Cookie in hand.

"My boy, he knows. He wants to help, always wants to help."

She went to the other women.

They walked together up in the mountains for the night, all of them: Peggy-Sue and her mother June, Izzy and Chiara and Ananda, Maria-Elena and her sisters.

There was a new moon.

Around the campfire, Chiara said, "We can leave tomorrow for the Lost Coast. I've mapped out the roads on the way."

"I'm ready to go," Cookie said, looking at her steadily.

"Do you know how to get to the Land of the Dead?" asked Peggy-Sue. She had seen Cookie with the Indians.

"The Paiutes and Antelope on the Moon—they promised me."

The campfire blazed up, and glittered in the eyes of the moon-eyed sisters.

Not a one of the women said anything more. Beulah led them along a ridge above a big valley, through the woods to an enormous mineshaft. The opening of the shaft was a clamor and seethe of light.

The citizens of Downieville remember that night for the biggest lightning storm any of them had ever seen, the bright strokes exploding high on the rock of the Sierras, dropping again and again, as if coiled in the sky and taking aim; as if at play.

Even Cookie, watching the show from so close, felt a little better.

In the morning, she went to Chiara. "We have to go on to the Lost Coast, but we can't leave today."

Chiara looked at her, waiting.

"I'm going to finish our cabin."

And she did, by herself, there by the river, in the clear autumn. When she was finished she left inside a love that would take over the man and woman who one day would find that cabin, and with wonderment make it their home.

The North Yuba ran toward the sea. And beside that green current they readied themselves to head down out of the Sierras into the central valley, to move along the Sacramento River toward San Francisco Bay, this traveling theater, this band of lovers, the peacock and the coyote still in their company—

Ahead of them were long-simmered stories, the lucent watching Pacific, the divine riddles still to be spoken by the peacock, and the night when Ananda would be called once more to the jazz trumpet; and would the community of angels rise around them when most needed?

Ahead of them was the delivery of a moon-eyed daughter into the arms of Renato, all their plays in the Berkeley Hills, the skits on the streets of San Francisco and up on the buttes along the beautiful coast; the ocean currents they would learn to ride; and would Muscovado Taine find in storms coming dark off the sea the love-gifts he wants for his Izzy?

Ahead of them was the fog rolling in to protect a strange new chance; slow love in warm rooms, one more marriage, redwoods moving in their old dance, the visit of Cookie to the Land of the Dead, and on the Lost Coast the wild light of God.